Cracked

Louise McCreesh is a freelance journalist working in London. She is an alumnus of the Curtis Brown Creative Writing Course, where she was offered a scholarship to continue work on this novel. *Cracked* is her debut novel.

Cracked

Louise McCreesh

HODDER

First published in Great Britain in 2020 by Hodder & Stoughton
An Hachette UK company

This paperback edition published in 2020

1

From *The Handmaid's Tale* by Margaret Atwood
Published by Vintage
Reprinted by permission of The Random House Group Limited. © 2014

A CIP catalogue record for this title is
available from the British Library

Paperback ISBN 978 1 473 69936 6

Typeset in Plantin Light by Palimpsest Book Production Limited,
Falkirk, Stirlingshire

Printed and bound in Great Britain by Clays Ltd, Elcograf S.p.A.

Hodder & Stoughton policy is to use papers that are
natural, renewable and recyclable products and made from
wood grown in sustainable forests. The logging and manufacturing processes
are expected to conform to the environmental
regulations of the country of origin.

Hodder & Stoughton Ltd
Carmelite House
50 Victoria Embankment
London EC4Y 0DZ

www.hodder.co.uk

For Ger

Nobody's heart is perfect

Margaret Atwood, *The Handmaid's Tale*

Before

They load the body bag into the ambulance waiting outside. It doesn't look like a body; it's hard to believe there's a formerly living, breathing person inside that rough navy canvas, but I know there is. I saw it get zipped into the bag myself and am now watching the paramedics struggle under the weight as they throw it carelessly into the back, not giving any thought to the condition of the person inside. I guess that makes sense. The person inside is no longer alive. No more harm can come to them.

It feels like too much to handle. A lot of things do and I often find that gets me into trouble, although this is the most trouble it's got me in yet. *Fragile*, people call me, when I know deep down that isn't the case and I'm nowhere near as delicate as they'd like to imagine.

The truth – all of it – paints me differently. Really, I am the breaker of fragile things. Things that slip through my fingers and smash on the ground at my feet, quite simply because I can't keep them in my grip and have a tendency to destruct if not myself then something. Take the person in the body bag. The person no longer living. The person only dead because I broke them, and no one thought I could.

I

PART ONE

Chapter 1

After

7 January 2016
7.28 a.m.

James is gone. By this time, he normally is but today he shouldn't be. I'm not worried. He's been working a lot of overtime on the Bleecher case and that's probably where he is now; asleep on his desk with drool wedged between his cheek and the table, having mistakenly thought he could get the whole thing filed away before what was supposed to be his day off. One thing you can say about James is that his intentions are always good. Better than mine have ever been.

The Bleecher case. One of the worst in Sutton police's history and certainly the worst I can remember. Rosie Bleecher. Nineteen years old and a fully popped six months pregnant; raped, beaten and left to die in a skip behind the flat she'd been renting with her fiancé, Carl. Nasty business all round but particularly for the family, who were left devastated and scratching their heads as to what prompted so grisly an execution. Everyone else had a theory of course. None of them were right.

Carl's older cousin Mark was arrested ten days in. The motive: wanting from Rosie what she had made very clear he would never have, leaving him no option but to take it by force and clean up the mess thereafter.

It was an ugly outcome. Ugly that the killer's own mother turned him in, found a bag of bloodied clothes beneath his bed and thought it odd enough to bring to the police's attention. Uglier still that Mark uploaded several lengthy video messages to his Facebook page just hours before his arrest vowing to avenge his slain cousin-in-law and his own cousin's unborn child.

A paper shredder, Simon called it. One of the few major murders to slow down the national news cycle, people hurrying past the newspaper section with their eyes averted rather than stopping to read the stomach-churning headlines. *'And right before Christmas, too.'*

It's the kind of ugly that makes the scars on my wrists tingle, though they rarely do these days. The kind that disgusts and relieves me in equal measure because, on a good day, I can convince myself it's one worse than my own.

Shuddering for Rosie, I reach for my phone to see if James has at least bothered to call me but he hasn't. I have no call. No text. No clue as to where my husband is or why he's there, hours after finishing what was supposed to be a twelve-hour shift.

Nothing, bar my favourite picture of us and an alarm clock in the top right-hand corner, reminding me I have 31 minutes left of sleeping. Not that I feel like sleeping. Not anymore.

Aggravated by my concern I sit up and call him, the dial tone of my own phone ringing through the room for a few hopeful moments. I know after the first couple of bleeps he won't answer. That it will ring out to voicemail, which it does – and I get out of bed and open the blinds at our bedroom window to find his car also gone.

It's too early to be worried but it's definitely weird, and I think about trying his phone one more time before I spot Car Thief a few houses over and grow distracted.

Watching Car Thief is a relatively new pastime of mine. I first saw him a few months ago, jogging from drive to drive. Not thinking much of it until I saw what he was really doing; which was checking all the cars on the street to see if any of my neighbours had been stupid or naïve enough to leave their vehicles unlocked. Punishing them, if they had.

Car Thief doesn't steal any cars, just whatever valuables are left inside them and only ever enough to fill his crappy brown satchel, so maybe the name Car Thief is misleading. He probably has a normal name – something like Brian or David – but I wouldn't know it. I don't know anything about Car Thief, other than the fact he likes to steal things out of cars and I like to watch while he does.

I'm still staring out of the window when my phone buzzes violently in my hands. I take a deep breath and answer it.

'Jenny, I'm sorry.'

It's James's voice. Croaky. Apologetic.

I leave Car Thief to it and retreat to the bed, folding my toes beneath my thighs to thaw them from the cool of the floor. I feel a cooling at my centre too. A relief that James is safe (so perhaps I was more worried than I thought) but also a frostiness. A shard-like iceberg bobbing through the cavern of my chest at his lack of consideration.

'You could have called,' I say, my voice an unusual shade of plum. 'Texted me, even.'

'I know. I was going to text you but . . .'

James starts talking to someone whose voice I don't recognise while I wait on the other end of the line.

'*Thanks, mate,*' he murmurs, before breathing back into

7

the receiver. 'Jen, I'm so sorry. Nightmare morning. Are you still there?'

'Yes,' I say curiously. 'What's going on? Where are you?'

'I'm at work.'

I hear more people in the background. 'So you're at the station?'

'No,' he says slowly, apologetically, and I immediately know what it means.

'Another one?' I ask. 'But you're already working the Bleecher case.'

'We wrapped Bleecher last night,' he says apologetic yet again. 'Keith and I had just finished the paperwork and were heading home when this call came in and it all spiralled from there.'

Unsure of how to respond, I don't.

James sighs. 'Come on, Jen. You know what Keith is like when he gets his teeth into something. He thinks the Bleecher solve fell into our laps. He wants the credit for this one.'

Again, I say nothing because I refuse to be the nagging wife. The asshole wife. Sometimes, I think James would prefer it.

I'm four years younger than he is, a collegiate twenty-eight to his grey-around-the-sides thirty-two, and I think he worries I'll eventually grow tired of waiting around for him: That I'll figure I have my best years left ahead of me and bugger off, though he'd never admit it to me. James and I have a good marriage. We have fun, but in any relationship we both know it's dangerous to be the one who cares more.

I squint at the clock on my phone, which tells me I now have twenty-five minutes left before I have to get ready for work. It's twenty-five minutes more than the amount of sleep James had all night, and I wonder what about this case in particular made Keith want to work it.

I press the phone back to my ear.

'So, what's the job?' I ask. 'Is it as bad as Bleecher?'

'Nothing's as bad as Bleecher Jen,' James replies, darkly. 'Certainly not this. It's just one victim. White male. Over fifty years old. I'm pretty sure over sixty, which is actually a bit unusual . . .'

'Definitely murder?'

'No question.'

I hear static down the line and can imagine James clear as day, tucking his phone beneath his chin and reaching for his pen or little black book to make it look like he's doing something useful in front of his colleagues. The thought thaws the iciness and makes me smile but I quickly scold myself for being callous. A person had died today and I know the kind of hole that can leave. More than anyone, I know how many lives can be changed by the death of a single person.

'Where did it happen?' I ask, soberly now. 'Where are you?'

'That's the weird part. Do you know the psychiatric hospital on Mondsey Road? Hillside?'

The name hits me like a slap I'm not expecting, ringing through my ears and stiffening my neck.

Hillside. It'd been a while since I'd heard the name, though I'd thought of it often. It's even more of a shock to hear it from James.

'Kind of,' I say, discomfited. 'Why? What happened? Who died?'

James clears his throat. 'One of the psychiatrists or doctors or whatever you call them. It looks like he was murdered while clearing out his office. He'd only just retired as well, poor guy.'

Each word is a falling domino. The displacement of a sense of self, years in the making – and I pull the duvet up to my knees, the frost steadily returning.

'What was his name?'

'Phillip Walton,' James says, and I feel a lot of things. Fear. Disbelief. Oddly, nostalgia, and the instinctual relief of a hunch just proven, because it is who I thought it would be. The name that's haunted me for almost a decade, alongside a few others.

I'd heard of Phil's retirement a few months back, but only by chance. A local news bulletin on my phone and a blessing, I thought, once the shame and every other bad feeling I associated with Phil had subsided. A relief, in knowing our shared and terrible Hillside memories would finally leave there with him, although I never wanted it to happen like this.

That he's dead is hard to believe and I drop my phone but it doesn't go far. It falls on to the duvet covering my knees and I pick it back up, a tremor to my grip that wasn't there before.

'Jen, you there?'

'Yes,' I say, my tongue like cotton wool. 'Do you know who killed him? Do you know why?'

'No.' James replies. 'We don't know anything yet.'

My stomach flutters gratefully although I don't know why it should. It's been years since I'd seen or spoken to Phil and I certainly didn't kill him. But there are things I knew about Phil, things he knew about me, and I know I'm too close to this. That James can't work the case.

'James, listen . . .'

I hear a door open and voices, laughter in the background. James calls out to someone nearby.

'Babe, I can't talk now,' he says, to me this time. 'I'll call back when I can . . .'

'No, wait.'

James must hear the anxiety in my voice. He moves away from the laughter to somewhere much quieter.

'What is it? Are you OK?'

'I'm fine,' I garble, shakily. 'I just don't think you should work this case. I think you should hand it to someone else.'

James laughs. 'What? Honestly, I'm not that tired. I can catch a few hours' sleep back at the office while the forensic guys do a sweep.'

'It's not that. Please, just don't work it.'

There's a brief pause. 'Jenny, I don't have time for this. Why not?'

There's an awkward pause and I seriously think about telling him. Not everything, but at least that I had gone to Hillside and was Phil's patient while there, though I soon dismiss the idea. I can't tell James anything now. It would only invite more questions.

'Because . . . you're tired.' I say lamely, 'You need a break.'

James doesn't reply for a few moments, and I imagine his fingers at the back of his neck. The anguish on his face; the effort of trying to please not only me but Keith as well – because I know James but he doesn't know me. Not as well as he thinks he does.

'Jen, I'll be fine.' Through the phone, I hear footsteps and once again he's back with the noise.

'No, James—'

'I have to go. I'm sorry. I love you.'

He hangs up like nothing much has happened. I know everything has changed.

9.39 a.m.

I'm still in bed. Lost in thought, my fingers locked around the stress ball Simon gave me for Christmas. Well, it's more of a stress square, shaped like a fire alarm and emblazoned with the phrase '*squeeze in case of an emergency*'. Whatever shape it is, it's not working and I launch it across the room. I waste a few more minutes worrying and call the office, letting them know I'll be late but not the reason why. Simon will want more of an explanation when I turn up. He won't get one.

My mind wanders and I think of the investigation. About how right this minute, James and Keith and their police colleagues will be looking for a motive; a reason why someone would want Phil dead. Possibly, something bad from Phil's past. A secret.

We had one. Phil and I, and a few others I haven't spoken to in an equally long while. Technically, it was more my secret than Phil's or any of theirs. One they'd all kept for me.

It's unlikely anyone else knows this secret. Unlikelier, it's related to Phil's death for too many reasons to count. What happened was a long time ago. Keeping it quiet, in all of our interests. It wasn't Phil's fault, it was mine – and yet, the idea gnaws persistently at my stomach, prolonging my sense of unease.

It's why my heart curdled when James first told me he was at Hillside, and it makes me anxious to think of him there now. Inside Phil's office. Mere metres away from the worst thing I've ever done; this secret, inching closer with every second he spends there – although, maybe this was supposed to happen. Things had been good for a while. Trouble feels like the logical next step.

Perturbed by the thought, I get out of bed and move towards the window. Car Thief is still out there and I recall the time I left my own car unlocked for two weeks; my iPod tucked into a brand-new brown satchel on the passenger seat for him to take, which he did. I think about how James would never understand my reasons for doing so or why I sometimes walk out of the house with my earphones in just to keep up the pretence that I hadn't empathised with this man, whatever his name, and lost my iPod to him – because James has no clue who I can be at my worst, but there are others who do. People, who have as much to lose as I do if our secret is exposed and who may, irrationally or otherwise, worry that it might be once news of Phil's murder reaches them but there's only one I trust and I should let him know about Phil. Tell him, before the internet or his television does.

I grab my phone and scroll through my contacts, glad I'd saved his number and hoping it hasn't changed in the many years since he'd left it with me. Trembling slightly, I hit dial, almost hoping it will ring out to voicemail. It doesn't.

'Hello.'

'Tony?'

'Yes, who is this?'

'It's Jenny . . . Parker,' I say, careful to use my maiden name. There's a stunned silence.

'Jenny, I can't believe it. Are you OK?'

'I'm fine.'

He laughs, sounding relieved. 'I'm sorry, I just didn't expect to hear from you . . .'

'Phil died,' I say brusquely. 'That's why I'm calling.'

'How?'

'He was murdered. Someone killed him.'

There's another stunned silence.

'Are you free to meet today?'

My throat thickens. 'No. I'm working.'

'Well, how about lunch?'

'Sure. Lunch is fine.'

Someone yells for Tony in the background. A woman, I think.

'Jenny, I've got to go. Text me the address and time and I'll be there.'

My phone abruptly emits a dial tone and I realise I've been hung up on for the second time this morning. I decide on a time and place and text it to Tony and almost immediately, regret doing so.

Reluctantly, I get ready for work. There's no longer enough time to shower so I grab the dry shampoo from my dresser and spray it through my roots, flipping my head up just in time to see Car Thief scurrying away from our street, wearing the satchel I bought him.

10.47 a.m.

I read the headlines on the train. Not ours but all of the nationals. There are multiple articles about the forthcoming trial in the Bleecher case and one particularly tragic tale about a pair of twins, one of them killed by a drunk driver. It's too soon, obviously, for any coverage of Phil's murder but it's only a matter of time. A psychiatric institution. A slaughter. As Simon would call it, *a hell of a story*, but not on patch so, thankfully, none of our concern.

The *Ealing Gazette* comes out once a week, has a circulation of a couple of thousand and a readership of even less. There are four reporters in total (three of whom work from home) and an even scarcer sales and advertising department.

I've had the job for over three years now, though I didn't think I had a chance in hell of even getting it after bombing the interview; my inexperience clouding the room like a bad smell. Simon hired me anyway, forgoing much more experienced reporters for a trainee still in need of her journalism diploma. A diploma he ended up paying for, alongside my various newspaper subscriptions.

It's not an easy commute from Sutton – a twenty-minute drive followed by an hour-and-a-half train journey – but one I do happily if it means I don't have to work closer to home. I live in Sutton, yes, but Hillside is in Sutton too and I had just about escaped Hillside with my life. As of this morning, Phil hadn't.

I get to work, stopping by one of the catering vans for coffee before and buzzing myself into the office with my key card, which has always seemed an unnecessary precaution. The *Ealing Gazette* is exactly what you'd expect a z-list local newspaper office to look like: a cheap, rented space in some converted garages just off the industrial estate. There's nothing much of value inside it.

Everything's grubby, even though I bump into the cleaning ladies most mornings, like that's how it was built; finished with a coat of vanilla grime and furnished with boxy, poly-plastic cubicles and red wheelie chairs that itch the skin of your back if your shirt isn't long enough.

There's not much in the way of amenities apart from a dusty old vending machine and a dishwasher that's been under maintenance since 2012, but then most things at the *Gazette* are under maintenance. *Shabby*, that's what the office is; an environment that, despite my best intentions, I've never had much trouble fitting into.

I sit down at my desk, push my coffee to one side and load up my laptop-connected-to-a-screen, scrolling through my emails until something makes sense but nothing does. My mind is scrambled by the worry I'm trying my best to ignore and the words on the screen might as well be gibberish. Frustrated, I close my email browser and unwrap the Snickers bar next to my keyboard, shoving the end into my mouth. I take a couple more merciless chews and lean back in my chair, pondering what James is doing right now.

'Some bloody health correspondent you are.'

I jump slightly in my chair, turning to see Simon leaning against the empty desk beside me and pointing to the chocolate bar on my desk with an unimpressed grimace.

Simon. Big belly. Heavy breather. Heavier drinker. Tie ever loosened, smells like Amaretto and Listerine. Simon, who kept me on despite the mass staff exodus two years ago because I cared about the person not just the story, a quality he deemed more important than years spent in the trenches. Simon, whose first wife killed herself if you believe the rumours and I'd seen him drink – really drink – so I do.

Sometimes, I wonder if Simon only gave me the job because he could smell the damage on me during our first meeting. The same way I could smell his.

I wipe chocolate from the corner of my mouth and swallow hard.

'I'm not your health correspondent, Simon,' I say diplomatically. 'You don't have one.'

'But if I did, they'd show up on time,' he says with a subtle wink. 'So? Where were ya?'

'I slept in. I'm sorry.'

I shuffle back on my chair. Simon nudges the paper coffee cup on my desk with the tip of his pen.

'Slept in – but still time for a coffee run.' He tuts loudly. 'This from Maggie's van?'

I nod.

'Where's mine?'

'I didn't have the change. Left my bank card at home,' I say, which is a lie. He and I both know it.

It's no secret that Simon puts alcohol in his morning coffee, nor that his second wife Yvonne is desperate to get him to stop; so much so that she'd sought help from the Ealing Industrial Estate caterers. That's why I don't have a coffee for Simon. Maggie from Maggie's food van wouldn't let me take one.

Simon sighs and grabs a warm bottle of Diet Coke that's at the end of my desk, opening it with a heavy-handed crack.

'So, what'd ya have for me story-wise kid? Something good, I hope?'

I rack my brain trying to come up with something, though it's no use. There's only one thing on my mind currently – and it'd be unwise for me to tell Simon anything about it.

'I've got a meeting after lunch, actually. A potential scoop, but I don't want to jinx anything.'

I tense in my seat, burdened by the lie. Simon takes a sip from the bottle in his hand and nods approvingly. 'Excellent. I knew you wouldn't let us down. That's why you're my favourite.'

I don't say it but Simon's my favourite too, common as muck with a Classics degree from Cambridge. Potential: that's what Simon has. More potential than the converted garages of the *Ealing Gazette*, but then life gets in the way of potential. Death, even more so.

He doesn't know it but Simon and I have that in common. As did Phil and I.

2.06 p.m.

The Pig's Head is a crummy pub a few roads over from the *Gazette* which never draws much of a crowd. The kind with pale ales no one has heard of and billiards where the pool table should be. I arrive first and buy two pints from the moody barman, grabbing a booth in the back because it's where I told Tony I'd be sitting. Now here, I'm nervous and I sip at my beer, which is a few degrees below room temperature but tastes better than expected. Tony turns the corner soon after.

He's older and thicker but it's definitely him. Same lofty brown hair. Same good-natured expression. He walks towards me, ducking his head to avoid bumping it against the low ceiling and I notice he still has a limp, which surprises me all these years later.

Finally, Tony reaches me. Nervously I stand to greet him.

'Jenny?' he asks, squinting slightly. 'I can't believe . . . I'm so glad you called.'

Tony rounds his arms as if to hug me, before apparently changing his mind and taking a seat at the table. I drop down on the chair opposite his and push a beer towards him. He nods gratefully but fails to take a sip. I consider for the first time that his stomach might be in as many knots as mine.

'Sorry I'm late,' he says, his fingers still clenching the glass. 'This is a bit further from Sutton than I was expecting. I just assumed because we both lived there . . . but this is fine too.'

'How do you know I still live in Sutton?' My voice is more suspicious than I intend it. Tony blushes.

'I saw your wedding announcement in the *Sutton Orient* a few years back,' he says. 'Congratulations, by the way. If you missed the announcement, I can give you my copy. I kept it . . . well, in case you ever called.'

His words bruise more than I thought they would, not that they're undeserved; a throb of shame in knowing I was the one who tore our friendship apart. Not Tony, who visited me at Hillside after he left and insisted we stay in touch. Who gave me his phone number and told me to call whenever I got out. It was me, who could

18

barely meet his eye during those visits. Nor see him without remembering all the bad stuff that sat parallel to our friendship, like trying to enjoy a cheeseburger outside an abattoir.

I struggle to come up with a response and we fall into an uncomfortable silence. Politely, Tony sips at his beer though I can tell he doesn't like it.

'You don't have to drink that . . .'

'It's great,' he says. 'Thank you. Awful news about Phil.'

'It is,' I reply, ashamed that in my own self-serving interests I'd forgotten to be sad.

'How was he killed?' Tony asks, foam now enshrouding his top lip.

It's an obvious question and yet I stammer.

'I – I don't know. My husband said—'

'*Detective Sergeant James Nilson,*' Tony interrupts, no doubt another recall from the *Sutton Orient*. 'I'm surprised they'd let him be involved in the investigation given . . . your history and everything. I mean, that you were a patient of Phil's.'

Guilt sloshes heavily in my stomach. I take another sip of beer, hoping to wash it down.

'Tony, James – my husband – he doesn't know about Hillside, I never told him I went there.'

Tony looks stunned. 'You didn't? Why not?'

'I don't know.' Tony's brow furrows. I lower my pint back to the table.

'Jenny, I think you should. If his colleagues find out, he could get into trouble.'

'Do you think they will?'

'I don't know, but they might.'

It's not the answer I'm looking for. I used to like how Tony always told me the truth but I guess I don't care for it much any more. I feel a tension in the air where awkwardness had been previously, but try to ignore it. There are more pressing issues Tony and I still need to discuss.

'It's too late,' I reply, shaking my head. 'If I tell James now, he'll want to know why I didn't tell him sooner. He'll start digging things up.'

Confusion fills Tony's eyes before, slowly, it clears.

He looks around the pub uneasily and hunches closer to the table before speaking next.

'Wait. You don't think this has anything to do with what happened to—'

'Don't say her name.'

Tony blinks harshly. 'I'm sorry but, do you? Is that why you called me?'

I nod. Then, shake my head.

'I'm not sure.' I say uncertainly. 'Either way, it's not a good thing the police are at Hillside asking questions. That they're in that office.'

Tony's hand spasms, reaching to grab mine before once again thinking better of it. 'No, Jenny. Whatever happened to Phil has nothing to do with what happened . . . back then. It doesn't mean anyone else has found out. That anyone else will.'

'Doesn't it?'

'No.' Tony replies fiercely. 'Think of all the patients Phil had over the years. He knew thousands of secrets . . .'

'It's a pretty big secret.'

'From years ago. Almost ten years ago now.'

I know he's probably right. What happened was so long ago that the chances of it being connected to Phil's murder are almost impossible. Still, it nags at me: the sense that Phil's murder will somehow bring up what happened then. That my secret will soon be exposed.

'I don't know. What if the others told someone?'

Tony shakes his head. 'They didn't.' Tony replies. 'They have no reason to.'

I can't think of a response so we sit in silence for a few moments. Finished with my beer, I pick at the edge of the coaster it's sitting on, black residue getting caught beneath my nails.

'Are you OK, Jenny?'

Tony's eyes pierce my own with a familiarity I find comfortable.

I look down, away from him. 'Yes. That isn't what this is about . . .'

'I'm not saying it is,' he says gently, 'but you're reading too much into this. Phil's death is terrible, of course it is, but no one else knows what happened . . . that night. It's not the reason he was killed. There's no way the police or anyone else, is going to find out about it.'

Again, I have no riposte. It's easier to believe, more comforting than to keep arguing against him.

The conversation from there moves on. Tony tells me about his wife and his job cleaning aeroplanes at Gatwick airport, though I soon tell him I have to get back to work and make a quick escape, promising to stay in touch but unsure I mean it. As expected, seeing Tony again, while nice, had brought back old memories. Most of which, I was much happier forgetting.

I head back to the office, trying to forget about Tony. Hillside. My past. While walking, my phone buzzes and I take it out of my bag, hoping it isn't Tony and it's not. It's a text from James, which I open with much more trepidation than usual.

Going for a nap in 20. Don't worry. J. xx

A comforting gesture, not that it comforts me much. James, trying to appease my worries while my lie of omission will do nothing but exacerbate his if he were ever to find out about it.

Hopefully he won't. As Tony said, Phil's death was probably about something else. A confused patient in a psychotic state. A disgruntled Hillside employee with an axe to grind. A case James will solve quickly without even finding out what I did. What Phil protected me from.

Still in hand, my phone buzzes again. This time, it's a work email with the subject line *Urgent* and because I'm still struggling for story suggestions to pitch to Simon later, I open it.

Don't say anything.

I blink at the message, convinced it's not really there but it is. It really is, and I feel a ripple from my neck to the base of my spine.

I look around and then back to my phone, tapping on the sender icon though it takes a few attempts, such is the shaking of my hands. It doesn't help: the Gmail address is nothing but a random assortment of letters and numbers, and that's when I really start to panic because I may not know who sent the email but I know exactly what it's about – and Tony's wrong. We should be very worried indeed.

Chapter 2

Before

7 January 2007
10.02 a.m.

I sit cross-legged on the ground, my ankles rubbing uncomfortably against the matted carpet, which I imagine was once red but is now an undeniable shade of pink. Faded, from the stamping and desecrating of people making a mess and the hoovering and shampooing of those tasked with cleaning it up. My ankles are pink now too. Speckled, from the pattern of the carpet which is no longer visible apart from its imprint on my skin; small, red hexagons that line my fibula and pinch my leg hair. I haven't shaved since the incident.

It was my second failed attempt at ending my life. The first, three dozen painkillers and an ambulance ride straight to the stomach pump, the side effects of which – mainly severe nausea and constipation for weeks on end – were just about grisly enough to make me try something else. So, I did. A bathroom. A razor. Red, open smiles curved at my wrists. Mum home early from work because she wasn't feeling well that day, another ambulance and then another. That last one brought me here.

It was almost a month ago now but I still have the scars. I'll have them forever, the doctor said.

I rub at my ankles some more. Until the red hexagons match the pink of the carpet and Sally turns breathlessly into the corridor, her cobalt-blue uniform covered in green paint.

I like Sally. I've only been here three weeks but I already know she's my favourite nurse; beautiful and blonde and American, with enough sincerity to make me feel bad about not being the same.

I wish I could be that kind of person. A salt-of-the-earth, would-do-anything-for-anybody type person. The type of person whose name is preceded by a list of anecdotal good deeds they've done for other people – but I just don't have it in me. *Some people are radiators and the rest are drains*, Mum used to say. A morality tale to try and fix my bent-out-of-shape personality, though it hasn't worked yet.

'Sorry I'm late,' Sally says now. 'We had some trouble with Irene this morning.'

I shrug and stand up, wiping the butt of my jeans. Sally grabs the electronic key swinging from the lanyard around her neck – though it doesn't look like any key I've ever seen: a small cylinder of black plastic.

'You ready?'

I nod and Sally holds her key to the electronic lock on the door a few yards from where I'd been sitting. There's a red light on the door, it turns to green with a soft bleep and Sally grabs my arm and ferries me through it, which I'm expecting. This door leads to the basement. I'm not allowed to walk through the basement alone.

Phillip Walton's office is in the basement. That's where Sally is taking me. He's a doctor here. A real one, I'm told.

Walton's a big deal at Hillside. *The Fixer*, Sally and the other nurses call him. He's renowned for only taking on six patients at a time, for which he's equally resented; the first

Hillside therapist I had – Lisa – rolling her eyes at the mere mention of his name. His methods are unusual I've heard but he fixes people. He wouldn't have that nickname if he didn't.

Sally leads me through the door and out on to the basement's landing. It's colder here. Quieter, too; the landing decked out in the same ugly red as the carpet I'd just been sitting on. The stairs and the floor below however, boast the same hard linoleum as the canteen.

It's a long staircase and it takes Sally and I a while to descend it, Sally not loosening her grip on me once. It's not hard to see why.

From the landing to the bottom of the stairs is at least a forty-foot drop, guarded by only a waist-high wooden banister an overzealous toddler could jump if they put in the effort; a fall you might survive but certainly not unscathed, which is more than enough to put me off trying. Sally doesn't know that, to be fair.

We reach the bottom of the staircase. Ahead of me now is another door: the door to Dr Walton's office. Sally opens it with the same key she used before and pushes me gently inside. Moments later, I hear her climbing the stairs and venture further in.

It's nice, the office. Nicer than I was expecting. Tartan tones and plush leather seating. A blue carpet floor not yet faded; each table a different shade of mahogany, and fluorescent lights in the absence of windows. There's a filing cabinet on each wall and still, enough room to rival the shared spaces above us. It looks like the office of someone important.

Dr Walton does not look like that someone.

He looks like any old man. Auburn-framed glasses and a shabby haircut; a cable-knit jumper a few sizes too big and mismatched khaki trousers, two inches too short exposing his mustard socks. Stray eyebrow hairs peek over the top of his glasses in a maddening fashion, while his hair – which is neither blonde nor brown, but something much less definite – sticks up in tufts.

'Jennifer Parker?'

His voice is soft. More nervous than I'd imagined it.

'Jenny's fine,' I reply. My voice sounds nervous too.

'It's nice to meet you, Jenny. I'm Dr Phillip Walton. Phil is also fine.'

He smiles warmly, and gestures towards the tan leather sofa across from him. I take the cue and sit down, quick to notice he's holding a pen and a few sheets of paper which rest in a file on his lap.

'OK, Jenny,' he says. 'What seems to be the problem?'

'Excuse me?'

'Well, why are you here?'

I feel inexplicably pricked by the question. 'I don't know.'

He stares at me with what appears to be genuine concern and folds one khaki-panted leg over the other. Then, he nods slow.

'OK,' he says. 'I want you to come back next week, and tell me what is wrong with you in five simple words. Can you do that?'

I blink at him. 'But I'm not—'

'I don't want to know what you're not. Five words. Next week. Can you do it?'

'I guess.'

He smiles. 'Good. This is going to be good.'

I don't agree but say nothing. Of all the people I'd met at Hillside, Phillip Walton seems by far the maddest.

10.35 a.m.

I walk out of the office to find Tony leaning against a wall, swinging a lanyard around his finger. I soon recognise it as Sally's. At the end of it, the same electronic key she'd used earlier.

Some of Dr Walton's patients are allowed to borrow keys from nurses and walk down to the basement alone and on his good days, Tony's one of them. He's been an inpatient at Hillside frequently enough now for the nurses to recognise when those are, which I find troubling. Tony isn't much older than I am.

'How did it go with Phil?' he asks, the lanyard falling to his side.

'With Dr Walton? It was weird.'

Tony smiles. 'It gets weirder – and call him Phil. He prefers it.'

I nod and think some more about Phil. The Fixer. The name seems like even more of a joke now I've actually met him, and if he does fix people, I can already tell I won't be one of them. I don't know if there's anyone who feels as bad as I do.

I've wanted to die for a long time. For as long as I can remember. If that's an illness, I have it, though I don't know what you'd call it. Depression seems too mild. Too temporary. Self-harm, because of the cuts, but the cuts only really give form to something more sinister. Something I can't quite name.

Tony has a different problem. He has trouble distinguishing fact from fiction; reality swirling in his mind like letters on the page of a dyslexic reader, although I haven't seen him have a bad day thus far. I only know he has them at all because of what people have told me, the word salad and – obviously – because of the limp.

No one knows for sure how it happened. There are rumours, but whatever the reason, it caused Tony to amputate his own big toe with a rusty floor scraper, so frenetically that the doctors were unable to re-attach it afterwards.

Three months ago that happened, so Tony's limp is still bad and I know it hurts: the place where his toe used to be. Sometimes, I imagine my mind as a grey cloud with black at its centre. I imagine Tony's as transparent but translucent in a certain light, some things refracted wrongly along its ridges.

We begin climbing up the stairs, Tony limping nobly and me pretending not to notice.

'You know, you missed a lot of Irene drama this morning,' he tells me.

'Sally told me the same thing,' I reply. 'What happened?'

Tony shrugs. 'The usual stuff. She found out she was being released from Hillside and kicked off. Tried to hide in the art room by painting herself into the mural. Quite the mess . . . but they got her out eventually.'

The story isn't a surprising one. Irene never wants to leave Hillside. 'The Garage', she calls it, because it's where she comes 'after a breakdown'. Her favourite joke and funny, the first time I heard it. It wasn't so funny by the fifth, once I realised it's the only joke Irene knows.

She claimed to have come up with it herself until Gina – my most recent roommate, a kleptomaniac and compulsive liar who moved out two days ago – found it in Irene's favourite book, underlined so many times that black ink obscured the rest of the page. Irene sobbed for hours after Gina's discovery but came back and told the same joke the next day like nothing had happened at all, her eyes still red and puffy.

Irene is the biggest drain I know.

Finally, we reach the top of the staircase. Tony holds Sally's key to the lock and once the light turns green prods me through it. We're a few yards further down the main corridor when he speaks again.

'With Irene gone, Phil only has five patients now,' he says, sticking out all his fingers on one hand to demonstrate. 'Tony, Alicia, Nick, Tom, Jenny. Five.'

I nod because it's true. 'Who's going to be number six?'

'Nobody knows.'

We fall silent again and continue through the corridors uninterrupted. Unlike the doors to the basement and Phil's office, those on the main ward are controlled by the same four-digit code and always left on latch to make it easier, I think, for the nurses. Tony accidentally knocks into me a few more times and leaves me just outside the women's dorm area, where no men – other than the male nurses – are allowed.

I approach my bedroom door and I am alarmed to see a zebra-printed suitcase propping it open. *Number six*, I think to myself before walking past the suitcase and entering my room.

The first person I see is Margaret – another nurse but not a kind one, the antithesis to Sally in every possible way – but there's also someone else. A girl.

She has to be at least eighteen, because this is the adult unit, but she looks younger. She's maybe five feet tall and stood next to Gina's old bed, dressed solely in black and eyeing the room with the kind of dull-eyed scepticism that tells me she's used to much nicer accommodation.

'Jenny,' Margaret says now, and I'm surprised she knows my name. 'This is Heidi Allman.'

I nod towards Heidi but don't get a response. She continues to glare around the room, her eyes framed by dark pencil.

'Can you help her unpack and take her to lunch in a few hours?' Margaret asks me. 'You should have a lot in common. Heidi's eighteen years old as well.'

'I'm nineteen,' I say mindlessly.

'I'm twenty,' Heidi says straight after and Margaret turns a luminous red.

'Well, you're both young women,' she declares, shaking her head as if to say we're too young for this place. Like we've wasted our lives, certainly our youths, by ending up in here. 'Just take her to lunch.'

Margaret pushes Heidi's suitcase inside and leaves. Heidi starts to unpack her things, dumping clothes out of the suitcase and on to the floor. Once the case is empty, she stands up and shakes it a few times, smoothing out the black nylon lining though I'm not sure why. I'm about to ask, when there's a click and the sound of Velcro ripping and I watch astonished as Heidi pulls the whole bottom section of her suitcase away to reveal a bunch of stuff hidden below it.

She looks up at me. 'Don't tell anyone about this.'

'I won't,' I say quietly, but feel uneasy all the same.

Heidi tosses the fake bottom of the suitcase on to the floor and starts emptying the contents of the secret compartment; multiple black lighters and even more packets of cigarettes. A pair of earphones, with a wire. Once finished, she grabs the discarded lining and fashions a makeshift bag, filling it with her quarry and tying its remaining loose ends into a bow before dumping that on the floor as well.

Next, she then approaches her bed, attempting to lift the mattress from its frame.

'That won't work,' I say, unusually self-conscious. 'The mattress is welded down.'

Sighing, Heidi abandons the mattress, and picks up the stuffed teddy bear she brought with her.

It's a cute thing. Chocolate brown and wearing a yellow chequered dress, a felt flower clutched between its paws. It's an unlikely choice for Heidi – so I'm not surprised when she lifts up the chequered dress and pushes her makeshift bag into the bear's now unzipped back, manipulating it until it fits inside, although not perfectly. A sharp, square corner still protrudes from the bear's left hip.

'What are you waiting for?' she asks me, smoothing down the yellow dress and placing the teddy bear on the window-sill nearest my bed.

I swallow nervously.

'To help you unpack. To take you to lunch.'

She snorts dismissively. 'I can take myself to lunch. I'm not a child. You can leave.'

'Are you sure?'

'I said get out,' she says more impatiently this time, leaving me no option but to do just that.

I leave the room, feeling humiliated. Gina had her faults but I already know Heidi will be worse. That she's another drain, just like Irene.

A little way along the corridor, I remember that I need a tampon. Reluctantly, I turn back around to get one.

I get to the room and open the door, though it takes a few moments for me to understand what I'm seeing. Heidi, not exactly where I left her but standing in the middle of the room, just a few yards in front of my wall mirror. She's halfway through changing. Her arms raised above her head and a T-shirt tangled between them, leaving her milky white torso exposed. Instinctively, I avert my eyes but something pulls them back because Heidi's torso isn't milky white at all. It's covered in little red circles.

They're everywhere, these circles. Dotted across her lower back; crescent moons disappearing beneath the black of her bra, with enough consistency to look like chicken pox, only bigger. Some red. Some purple. Some yellow. They're burns, I realise. Cigarette burns. And, through the mirror, I see the same circles covering her stomach.

T-shirt now untangled, Heidi's eyes meet mine; each of our shocked expressions reflected in the face of the other person. Quickly, she grabs for the jumper closest to her feet and tugs it down, covering herself before pushing past me and out through the door.

I don't know what to do. I feel light-headed. A little sick, and grab the tampon I came back for. Then, I follow Heidi from the room because I know I can't stay here either; trying to push the image of her burned torso from the grey cloud of my mind.

Chapter 3

After

14 January 2016
9.32 a.m.

Tony isn't answering my calls. I rang him as soon as I saw the email. Left voicemails and texts (the elusive kind, in case anyone else were to read them), but he's been dodging all my attempts to contact him since we met up last week. He's read the messages. He just isn't replying to them, which makes me think he received the same email I did. That he's freaked out, and I get it. I am too.

An icy gust whips the side of my face and I shiver. I know I shouldn't be here – especially after the email – but I couldn't stay away; the press blockade down so I can finally see it up close.

It looks different from the outside. Different from how I remember. Smaller and harmless, the steel bars of the windows painted white. Flower bouquets for Phil line the building in such numbers you can't see where the brick meets the ground, most of them dead and frozen over. A bunch of yellow lilies that have survived against the odds catch my eye and I bend down to read the heart-shaped card clipped to them: *Thanks for helping me. You will be missed xxx.*

I lay down my own flowers – an £8.99 bouquet of trashy

orange carnations, the most expensive I could find in the petrol garage down the road – as my own personal tribute. An apology of sorts, because the email may help the police track down Phil's killer and still, I won't hand it over. I have my own reasons for that.

My phone buzzes and I jump. Not an email, thank God, but a text from photographer Mike asking me to *hurry the fuck up* because he's waiting for me on location. I feel bad. I wouldn't want to be waiting around in this weather – but I stay a little longer nonetheless, staring up at Hillside until the frost dampens my toes.

3.12 p.m.

I get back to the office, my toes damp and mood worsened, having left Hillside and walked straight into a muddy fun run. I've had it in my diary for weeks, the event held by a local primary school that lost one of its students to leukaemia just before Christmas. A nice idea, until you consider the logistics of a muddy fun run in January. A field of mud and water. The rest of it turned to ice.

I didn't want to go. Normally, I'd just do a phoner with a few attendees; save the paper a few quid in expenses and myself the trouble, but Simon insisted. He was practically in tears while making his own donation to the late girl's parents over the phone, promising to do everything he could to get our readers to follow suit.

'*What readers?*' I'd shouted when Simon came out of his office and I smile at the memory of his expletive-filled response, without really feeling it inside. It's been like that since the email arrived. Every smile hard-won and at surface level – because I think I know what the email is alluding to; what whoever sent it doesn't want me to say anything about.

What I don't understand is who would send me that message, and why now? After all this time? Did he or she murder Phil over something I did? If so, why would they want me to stay quiet? Why would they kill Phil first?

I sit down at my desk and fire up my laptop, filling the page Simon gave me for the story with my fun run notes. It's more work than I've done all week but I soon lose concentration and end up online, searching Phil's name on Google. Clicking into the first article I can find.

MEMORIAL HELD FOR MURDERED PSYCHIATRIST

A memorial will be held on Thursday to celebrate the life of a Sutton psychiatrist who was brutally murdered.

Phillip Walton was found dead in his former office at the Hillside Psychiatric Unit in the early hours of 7 January with multiple stab wounds. The celebrated doctor and academic, who recently announced his retirement, will be memorialised at St Augustine's Christian Church, Queen's Way, Surbiton, with proceedings starting at 2 p.m.

The memorial comes as police continue to investigate the incident and appeal for witnesses to come forward.

In a statement, Detective Sergeant James Nilson of Sutton police said: 'The team investigating the murder of Phillip Walton are working day and night to find out what happened and hold those responsible to account.

'We firmly believe there are people out there who know something and are asking anyone who has any information – anyone who is maybe wrestling with their conscience – to come forward and allow us to bring justice for Dr Walton, a well-loved and cherished member of the community.'

Anyone with information is urged to contact Sutton police immediately or call Crimestoppers on 0800 555 111.

The article doesn't tell me anything new. James already told me Phil's memorial is being held this afternoon and that he and Keith are both attending, seeing it as an opportunity to scout out potential suspects. '*Wrestling with their conscience*' is an interesting phrase though. It wouldn't roll naturally off James's tongue and I wonder why he used it. If he knows, possibly, that I'm wrestling with my own – although that can't be true.

James talks to me about the case. Tells me things he never would if he thought, or even suspected, Phil's murder had anything to do with me and every time he tells me something, I make a note of it, looking for that one clue that will confirm my worst fear.

Phil was stabbed seventeen times in the chest and stomach. The last phone call he received was from a PPI company more than a week before his death, and the last call he made was to a taxi company, asking for a ride to Hillside that night. His email provided no cause for suspicion either.

There's no CCTV at Hillside because local government had never gotten around to funding it, and no written log of Phil or anyone else entering the building after dark that night though there should have been, because every Hillside visitor is required to sign themselves in and out. As James tells it, there's not much evidence in Phil's murder inquiry besides a body and a bloodied floor. Then again, he doesn't know about the email I'd received. That I suspect Tony had as well.

'Working hard, I see.'

I turn to see Simon standing behind my chair, reading my screen over my shoulder.

'That's the Walton murder, right?' he asks, with a frown. 'Hillside?'

I scramble for the mouse to close the tab but he slaps my back lightly, dismissing the action.

'Relax,' he says. 'It's an interesting story, no denying it. You'd think there'd be CCTV. Prints everywhere . . .' Simon reaches over my shoulder to scroll through the article himself. 'Yep. No leads and . . . James Nilson. Wait; is he working this?'

I nod, wishing I could do something different. Simon looks surprised and winces, the glare from my screen reflecting unflatteringly against the dark skin of his eye bags.

'Hell of a case after Bleecher.'

'I know.'

'Well, let's just hope your man James does,' he adds, sighing and and restoring himself to an upright position. For the first time, I notice the sheets of paper between his fingers. 'You got the quotes and photos for that fun run?'

'Yes.'

He looks impressed. 'Surprised it went ahead. Freeze your toes off, did ya?'

'Just a little.'

'Well, at least it was for a good cause. Raise a few quid for that kiddie's charity.'

Simon's eyes blur. On a better day, I'd tease him for it.

'By the way, I'm giving this back to you,' he adds, tossing the paper in his hand on to my desk.

Vaguely, I recognise it as a story I'd written about the new X-ray machines at the Royal Ealing Hospital a few days ago, large chunks of it now underlined in red.

Simon clears his throat. 'A lot of errors, kid. Don't sweat it too much. It happens to the best of us – although not usually you, I must admit. Is everything OK?'

I swallow thickly. 'Yes.'

Feeling awkward, I stare at the screen while Simon watches me. Carefully. Studiously. Eventually though, he lets out an exaggerated breath.

'All right,' he says. 'Get those done before you go tonight; I've got a paper to print.'

'Will do.'

Simon leaves and I sink further into my chair, knowing I'll be here for hours but my mind will be completely elsewhere.

9.13 p.m.

I'm still in the office trying to finish my article, not that it's an issue. There's not much point in me going home.

James is sleeping at the station tonight. He called earlier. Said he and Keith have a big meeting with the chief tomorrow morning to prepare for, and that I shouldn't wait up. He also told me Keith wanted to discuss something with him and we talked briefly about Phil's memorial. James said they didn't learn anything new while there. That it was a normal service, if a little overcrowded.

His meeting with the chief is a concern. James said he didn't know what it was about but, after pressing him, he said he might have an idea. That idea brought goosebumps to my skin.

James told me about a negligence claim filed against Phil on behalf of one of his patients. A claim filed years ago. James doesn't yet know who made it. He said something about the chief submitting a request for information warrant to Phil's lawyers so they could find out, and that the meeting tomorrow could be the chief's way of revealing that person to him.

It's the first time I'd heard of any such claim. Besides

38

what he did for me, I didn't think Phil had put a toe out of line, and I felt a glimmer of optimism because a negligence claim gives someone else a motive. A reason to kill Phil, quite apart from what he helped me cover up.

It's certainly a better lead than my other theories thus far. The flattering posthumous news coverage of Phil put to bed my suspicion that he could have fatally riled up a Hillside staff member, while the lack of at-scene evidence suggests that whoever murdered Phil is clever, skewering my deranged patient guess.

It was a lazy guess, anyway. One I'm ashamed to have come up with because I'd been at Hillside myself. I know what the patients inside are really like. As for the email, well, I'm unsure now as to whether Phil's killer and its sender are even the same person. Whoever sent me the email clearly knows what I did, but how would Phil's killer have found out about it?

I sit at my desk, thinking about the claim, and consider ringing Tony to ask if he knows anything about it but quickly remember he's avoiding my calls. I'm wondering about trying him anyway just as a little flag appears at the bottom of my screen. Another email. An *Urgent* one.

I mean it. Keep quiet.

I jump out of my chair and search the office for someone – anyone – but I'm completely alone. Unnerved, I try to get into Simon's office but it's locked and I return to my seat, my renewed hope wilting like the dead flowers I'd seen outside Hillside hours ago.

I know what it means. One email is bad luck but two is confirmation that whoever killed Phil, is behind this. That someone knows that night didn't pan out exactly as we said it did. It's also clear from the nature of the messages that they don't want me to tell anyone about it, but why would I ever do that?

My phone vibrates in my hand yet again. This time it's a text message and I do know the sender. After days of giving me the silent treatment, Tony has finally replied.

U were right. Wat do we do?

I feel a flicker of relief, I'm not in this alone, but it can't just be Tony and me. The others must be receiving the emails too, because there were five of us who saw what really happened that night. Four of us, excluding Phil.

Shaken, I type out my reply to Tony and delete this email, just like I deleted the first. It won't be enough though – and I know what I need to do. I need to find the others, to see if they know who's doing this. If they told anyone the truth about what I did.

Chapter 4

Before

14 January 2007
10.02 a.m.

I don't tell anyone about Heidi's burns, nor her secret lighters and cigarettes. She has it in for me anyway. We haven't spoken since I saw her burns last week but she does other things to show her disdain, like spilling coffee over my favourite jumper and leaving wet towels on my bed. They're petty things, I guess, but pettiness gets to you in here.

There's also something else. Something I'm convinced Heidi is behind, though I'm too embarrassed to ask her or tell anyone else what it is.

I'm in Phil's office now, his puke-yellow cardigan offensive to my overtired eyelids, like the glare of the sun through a gap in a pair of curtains, not that there are any curtains in here. My eyes feel heavy and I drop them from Phil's torso to see a file in his lap yet again. One about me, presumably. It's pretty small and I imagine Heidi's is much larger. That she has an entire cabinet to herself.

'Is everything all right?' Phil asks, concern etched at his brow. 'You look anxious.'

I don't know how to reply so I don't say anything. Phil frowns and scribbles something I can't make out.

'So, did you do what I asked? The five words?'

At first, I don't know what he's talking about. Then I remember. The five words. What's wrong with me. Impossible, I think, to sum that up in less than a sentence, even if I had tried.

'No.'

Phil looks surprised. 'No?'

'I couldn't, and then I forgot.'

He blinks at me disapprovingly over the top of his glasses. 'OK. I'll see you next week, Jenny.'

His abruptness hits me like whiplash. 'What? Why?'

'Because I can't help you. Not if I don't know what's wrong.'

I'm stunned and sit in silence while Phil phones up to the buzz room; the one place in Hillside patients can always find a nurse if they need one. Minutes later, Sally arrives to escort me back upstairs.

12.52 p.m.

The rest of the morning passes slowly. I worry about Heidi, what she might do with what I think she's found – my own personal contraband – and at lunchtime, drag myself to the canteen. I look out for Tony but can't find him, so head to the serving area alone. There's no decent food left: an egg sandwich stale at its crusts, and a burned end slice of chicken pie. I opt for the sandwich only to regret that decision and quickly abandon it once seated.

I rub at my eyes. When I open them, Alicia is standing a few yards ahead of me. She's been in quarantine for the past few days, so I haven't seen her in a while. Beside her stands Margaret, holding a tray of food that looks a lot more substantial than my own – lasagne, a few bread rolls, a yoghurt and a bottle of Ensure – and my mouth waters.

42

'Here's fine.'

Alicia drops into the seat opposite mine. I hear her bones clatter against the plastic bench while Margaret places the tray of food on the table in front of her.

'Every bite,' Margaret says warningly and Alicia waves her away, the vein in her hand inky blue and overexposed enough to clench my jaw.

Alicia is twenty-nine years old but she looks much younger and acts even younger than she looks. She's been at Hillside for a while. Eleven months, I think, which is a long time for someone to stay so consecutively. She's Phil's patient too but he hasn't fixed her yet, unless she was skinnier before I got here. It's a troubling thought. I've never seen anyone as thin as Alicia.

Margaret walks away from our table. Once her back is turned, Alicia thrusts one of the buttered rolls down her trousers, snaking it beneath the belt she'd fashioned from Gina's old headband a few weeks ago.

'Bitch,' Alicia says, tearing her eyes away from a retreating Margaret towards me. 'Jenny? They haven't got rid of you yet?'

'Not yet,' I say with a friendly grimace.

Tony's my best friend at Hillside. Alicia, a close second. We shouldn't be friends. Her presence puts me on edge most of the time and we don't have much in common except the fact that we both want to die while other girls have more pleasant goals. In truth, I don't know if dying is what Alicia wants, but she is killing herself. Whether or not she knows it.

Alicia picks up her spork and twirls it around her fingers.

'I saw Tony getting his meds this morning,' she says. 'He told me you've got a new roommate; Phil's latest patient. What's she like?'

43

'A nightmare,' I reply.

Talk of Heidi immediately sours my mood, the grimace transforming to a frown.

Alicia looks interested and presses the handle of her spork into her temple. 'Why? What's wrong with her?'

'She's got a bad personality.'

'Ha. Doesn't everyone?'

Alicia shows her teeth, which are wafer-thin in the harsh light of the canteen. She then lowers her spork and picks up her spoon, arching around her yoghurt as if arching around a newborn.

A lot of people think Alicia hates food. It's the most logical conclusion to draw when you look at her – at the bald patches peppering her hairline, and her clavicle, sharp as a razor blade – but I know something they don't. Alicia doesn't hate food at all. She loves it too much. At least, in her head.

'What?'

I must have been staring without realising it. Alicia is glaring at me now.

'Nothing.'

Her eyes stay on me, lingering over my coffee-stained jumper and the knots at the end of my hair.

'You look like shit today,' she says finally and I laugh.

'I feel it.'

'Feel what?'

A different voice. The bench shifts beneath me and Heidi sits down at our table. Her question, the first thing she's said to me all week.

Alicia glares at her – an unwelcome interruption on her part as well, because Alicia hates people interrupting her mealtimes – but she doesn't say anything. Because of what Heidi possibly has over me, neither do I.

Heidi shuffles closer, lowering the chicken pie I rejected

44

on to the table alongside a cup of decaffeinated coffee; the only kind Hillside serves.

'Are you really going to eat that?' she asks.

I shake my head and push the egg sandwich away from me. 'No, it's—'

'Not you,' she says, nodding towards Alicia. 'Are *you* going to eat that?'

Alicia doesn't respond. Heidi leans closer to her.

'It is Alicia, isn't it? You're the girl with the eating disorder, aren't you?'

'It's none of your business.'

Alicia's voice sounds disaffected, bored, but the flicker in her eyes conveys she's hating this, because Alicia is a private person. She doesn't like people asking questions about herself or her food or her treatment. Her fingers, still holding the yoghurt spoon, start to tremble.

Heidi smiles. 'That's fine. You don't have to tell me.'

'Great.'

'I only ask because . . .'

'Because what?' Defiantly, Alicia drops her spoon.

Heidi's smile widens, and I know I should stand up for Alicia and stop this before it escalates – but I can't. I'm too scared of what Heidi may do to me in retaliation.

'Oh,' Heidi says a few seconds later, 'because you don't look that skinny to me.'

A stunned silence follows. I watch Alicia for any reaction but her eyes seem impenetrable now. I see no emotion on her face at all. Then, she smiles. In fact, she grins.

'You're right. Thank you.'

'You're welcome,' Heidi replies and horrified, I shake my head.

'Alicia, don't—' But I'm too late.

Alicia tips her plate over the edge of the table; the yoghurt

45

and lasagne landing in a messy pile at her feet, while the Ensure milkshake spills all over, splashing my ankles and flooding my trainers. Heidi acts faster, tucking her feet on to the bench before she gets hit by the strawberry-scented puddle, laughing at Alicia's total loss of control.

I don't know what to do. I can only watch as Margaret marches over and drags Alicia from the canteen, imagining what the consequences will be for her. Heidi watches too. For a while. She then grabs her tray from the table, swings her legs past the puddle still forming at my feet and walks off – and I realise I underestimated her. I didn't take seriously before just how cruel Heidi could be.

2.43 p.m.

I'm in the lounge, trying to come up with my five words for Phil next week but all I can think about is Alicia. About Heidi. About what Heidi did to Alicia when Alicia had done nothing at all to her, and I fear what she may have in store for me, since I've seen her burns. Her contraband. And I'm almost positive she's seen mine.

'Jenny.'

Tony walks into the lounge and sits next to me.

'What's wrong?' he asks, looking worried.

'Nothing,' I murmur distractedly. 'Have you seen Alicia?'

He shakes his head. 'Tom said he saw Margaret dragging her somewhere after lunch and that she was in a bad way. I don't know what happened. I saw her this morning and she seemed in a better mood than usual.'

I don't reply but I feel a stirring at my centre. A queasy, hot, irrational hate that can only be described as fury.

I leave the lounge and get back to my room, greeted by the overwhelming stench of coffee. No need to ponder the source: half-drunk mugs of it line the desk on Heidi's side of the room and have done ever since she arrived, some fresh but others with puckered skin thick enough to turn my stomach. Heidi says she forgets to take them back to the kitchen when the nurses question her about it, but I know that isn't why. It's because our room otherwise smells of cigarettes and Heidi hasn't once asked a nurse for a lighter.

She's asleep on top of her covers when I walk in, earphones plugged in, and I can hear their buzz from this distance. Asleep, Heidi looks almost peaceful but I pull them out because she doesn't deserve any peace. Not a second of it.

Her eyes open, squinting in confusion. 'What the . . .'

'Why did you do that to Alicia? She hasn't done anything to you.'

Heidi sits up, eyeliner smudged down one cheek, looking irritated. 'Well, I could have told her she looks like a skeleton wrapped in cling-film – but hasn't everyone said that already? Has it worked?'

I pause, not expecting that response. Heidi picks up one of her fallen earphones and puts it back in but I snatch it out yet again.

'No,' I say angrily. 'It's not right what you did, Heidi. You can't do that to other people. No matter how badly you treat yourself.'

I'm referring to her burns and she knows it. A malicious look settles on Heidi's face and she stands up, pocketing her earphones as she does.

'You're right,' she replies flatly. 'I shouldn't have said that to Alicia. I . . . it was out of line. I'm sorry.'

The U-turn isn't what I'm expecting, I'm once again uncertain what to say next.

In my silence, the corners of Heidi's mouth twitch.

47

'I don't know *why* I did it.' She digs her fingernails into her scalp. 'I guess I'm just not very good with boundaries. I'm no *doctor*, that's for sure.'

Red consumes me. Horror fills my stomach, because what Heidi said is confirmation she took it: the thing I hoped no one else would find.

My contraband is a page from a dirty magazine. A picture of a naked woman bent over and a man standing behind her, wearing a lab coat and nothing else. *Doctors without boundaries*, is the caption.

Technically, it's not mine. I didn't bring it into Hillside and I don't know who did. I found it in the reading room one day, nestled between some untouched books and decided to take it. I don't know why. Curiosity made me pick it up more than anything because the image itself makes me feel nothing but inadequate, and I've looked at it a few times since taking it.

I don't know how Heidi found it. I'd hidden the page inside the stem of my hairbrush – the bottom is removable, so you can fit something small inside its handle – which I thought was a good hiding place until I came back to the room a few days ago and found it gone.

Knowing Heidi has the page now is horrifying. Any minute, she could hand it over to Phil or the nurses and tell them it's mine. Even worse, she could show Tony and Alicia and the other patients and they'd all think I was a freak or a pervert and that I'd brought it in here with me – but I didn't.

Heidi laughs and steps past me, leaving the room; and I know I need to get rid of her. That, also, I might know how.

Chapter 5

After

20 January 2016
3.34 p.m.

I tell Tony to do nothing; comply with the emails and keep his head down, although secretly I've been trying to find the others. I just don't want to tell him that. Not yet.

So far, my search has been unsuccessful. I can't find any Heidi Allman's online and there's a lot of Tom Naughton's to sift through. There's no chance I can go to the one place where I may find their details because that place is Phil's Hillside office, which is still under police guard. I just want to know if they received the same emails Tony and I did; if they told anyone what happened that night; if they think it's possible someone else could have found out our secret that for many years had been kept. Finding the others, however, is far from my only concern.

James has been off with me since his meeting with the chief last week. At first, I told myself I was just imagining it but after a few days of him failing to meet my eye and leaving for work without waking me, I know it's something more than paranoia. He stopped telling me about Phil's murder case around the same time. It doesn't take a genius to connect them.

I haven't really seen him since. He's been working longer hours than usual the past few days, and his hours were long enough already, so he must have found out something. I'm too scared to ask what.

I hear a faint buzz. Anxiety grips my stomach and I lean away from my desktop screen and paw through my bag for my phone, surprised to find a text message from James.

Just got off. Can I ring?

The lack of kisses on the end is suspicious but the timing even more so. It's too early for his shift to end and James would never clock off early, especially not while working a major case. Tentatively, I press my finger to the phone icon next to his name. He picks up almost immediately.

'Hey—'

'You need to come home.'

I tense in my chair. 'Why?'

'I can't explain over the phone, Jen, but you need to get here now.'

I steel myself, bristled by his bossy demeanour and equally terrified by whatever he knows that's causing him to act this way. 'I can't.'

'You have to.'

'Not until you tell me why.'

James huffs angrily into the receiver, and I can tell he's mad. Really mad but trying to control it.

'The chief called me in today,' he says eventually. 'They're taking me off the case. Keith, as well.'

'What? Why?'

There's a brief pause.

'Jenny, you know why.'

His words sink in my gut like an anchor. As does the

knowledge that James must know at the very least that I went to Hillside, and he's probably now in trouble because of it.

'I'll leave now,' I say, hoping he doesn't know anything else.

5.52 p.m.

I leave work in a hurry, telling Simon I have a migraine, and all too soon pull on to the drive. James's black Mercedes is parked in my usual spot and another car is parked behind it in his. A blue Insignia I haven't seen before.

Shakily, I reverse and park on the roadside and when I open the front door, I hear the voices. Deep, solemn tones of people who have never been here before.

'Keith will come round, mate,' says one of them. 'Don't worry about it.'

I swallow and keep walking towards the voices with an idea, now, of who it may be. Next, I step into the kitchen, praying I'm wrong.

The first person I see is James, who's standing at the sink opposite the door, clutching a coffee. He looks handsome as always – a tan, slightly freckled complexion; with stubble I'd encouraged him to keep – but also tired. Pensive, though it takes me a while to read his expression. Embarrassment, I gather, with a hint of pissed off; his temples reddened and shoulders hunched.

Next to him are two men. The first is thin and very tall, and looks to be my age. Definitely, he's younger than James, which is an opinion I rarely have about his work colleagues.

He's leaning lankily against our marble worktop; brown skin and curled hair which looks a few weeks longer than it should be, I'm guessing, from the way its edges frizz. He has a nice face. The kind of face I could stare at without much time passing, though he doesn't look directly at me. He looks between me and the floor, his eyelids fluttering as if struggling to focus. As if he's sorry for being here.

The second man appears less apologetic. He's older than James – white and in his mid-fifties, I'd guess – but of similar height and hair colour, with the kind of no-nonsense face that makes him the last person you want visiting on a winter evening. He stands stiffly against the radiator and unlike his shyer colleague, stares straight at me.

I'm unnerved by their presence but try to appear otherwise. James walks over and kisses me frostily on the cheek.

'Jen,' he says, stepping back. 'These are detectives Craig Lancey and Paul Roberts. Nancy and Paul for short.'

My eyes dart to the two men. The taller one, Lancey, nods shyly and steps forward.

'We have a few questions about the death of Phillip Walton, if that's all right?' he says, 'We'll be leading the investigation from here.'

I look towards James but he fails to meet my eye.

'Can I stay?' James asks, staring at Lancey instead.

He nods. 'As long as that's OK with you, Mrs Nilson?'

'That's fine,' I say, lowering myself on to one of the dining chairs while dread trickles through me, ominous and hazard yellow.

I imagine James is furious with me. At the very least, I've humiliated him, if not cost him his career – but I take him wanting to stay as a good sign. It suggests he's still trying to protect me. I don't yet know from what. The detectives' presence indicates the police know something connecting me to Phil or Hillside, but I'm comforted slightly by the fact they can't know everything. I'd already be in handcuffs if that were the case.

Lancey sits down next to me, while James and Roberts

stay standing. From his trouser pocket, Lancey produces a Dictaphone and a little black book, like the one I've so often seen on James's bedside table.

'You don't mind, do you?' he asks. 'We're just following procedure.'

'It's fine. No problem at all.'

He smiles reassuringly. 'OK, Mrs Nilson . . .'

'Please, call me Jenny.'

'OK, Jenny. Is it all right if we check a few details with you?'

'Sure.'

'Your name is Jennifer Katherine Nilson?' he asks. 'Parker, before that?'

'Yes.'

'And you've previously been an inpatient at the Hillside psychiatric facility on Mondsey Road? You were involuntarily sectioned and admitted in December 2006, is that correct?'

'Yes.'

My stomach flies into my chest. I look to James for reassurance but again he won't look at me, staring intently into his coffee cup.

It's understandable. He must have been so confused to discover this part of my life that I'd told him nothing about, so I don't blame him for not looking at me now. I just hope he hasn't learned anything else.

I look back towards Lancey who checks his little black book, his eyes still hovering nervously.

'What was the nature of your relationship with Phillip Walton, Jenny?' He asks.

It's a weird question but one I can answer honestly and my stomach falls down from my chest. 'I was his patient. He was my psychiatrist.'

Lancey nods. 'How old were you when you first met him?'

'Nineteen.'

'And when was the last time you saw Phillip Walton? Spoke to him, even?'

'October 2008.'

I know I should take longer to answer the question but again, I can answer it honestly so don't feel the need. I remember my last meeting with Phil. Quite well, in fact.

It was just after my twenty-first birthday. My last day at Hillside and I had spent the morning with Phil in tears. I was often in tears back then.

I know it doesn't look good and I can see James doing the maths in his head. 22 months is a long time to spend in a psychiatric hospital. *Only a truly insane person would need to stay for such a lengthy period*, he's probably thinking. From the disgusted expression that appears to be on the older man's – Roberts – face, he may be thinking it too.

Lancey, however, looks surprised. 'You're sure?'

'Yes.'

There's a momentary silence. Lancey closes his little black book and places it on the table in front of him. Roberts wipes the disgust from his face and raises his eyebrows, and I realise they don't believe me. That, for a reason they have yet to reveal, they think I'm lying about the last time I saw Phil.

My heart starts to beat a little harder. Lancey picks up the Dictaphone again.

'OK. Would you say you were close to Phillip Walton, Jenny?'

'Not particularly. I'm sad he died.'

The detectives exchange further looks. Lancey grabs his little black book from the table, checking something inside before laying it down yet again.

'I'm sorry to ask you this,' he says nervously, 'but would

you mind telling me where you were in the late hours of 6 January and the early hours of 7 January?'

'Here,' I say. 'At home.'

'You didn't leave at any point?'

'No.'

'Were you alone?'

'Yes.'

'And, as well as not seeing Phillip Walton since October 2008, you haven't been back to Hillside since then either?'

'Um, no.'

'You're sure, Jenny?'

'Yes.'

It's my first lie, but not a major one. I'd been at Hillside last week, yes, but I hadn't been inside the building and I know it'd be unwise to tell the detectives I'd been anywhere near it. Not without finding out what they know first.

James looks the most perturbed by my answer this time. I try not to let it worry me as Roberts finally steps forward.

'Do you remember your Hillside patient file, Jenny?' He asks, looking squarely at me. 'The one Phillip Walton kept in his office?'

'Sure.'

I nod because I do remember the files – my file – always on Phil's lap, sliding into the cabinets behind him at the end of each session.

Roberts folds his arms against his chest. James looks further away. I hear a quiet scraping sound as Lancey moves his chair away from mine, and I know whatever's coming is bad. That whatever Roberts says next is what the detectives came here to tell me.

'You're positive you haven't seen Phillip Walton or even visited Hillside since 2008?' he asks.

'Yes.' I swallow thickly. 'I haven't.'

'So, why is your file now missing?'

'I'm sorry, what?'

'Your Hillside patient file isn't in Hillside any more, Jenny.' Lancey adds. 'It's our belief it was stolen from Phillip Walton's office on the night he died.'

Horrified, I look to James. He meets my gaze this time, nodding to confirm it's true.

I start to feel unwell. My palms clam-up and the back of my shirt dampens.

Roberts, meanwhile, clears his throat. 'Why do you think that is, Jenny? Why would somebody – someone else – remove your file from Phillip Walton's Hillside office?'

The question is one I try to answer in my own head. Why me? I understand, but what I don't understand is why now? And who? Who would care after all this time?

'Any enemies at Hillside?' Roberts adds impatiently. 'Someone who might be looking to hurt you?'

'Not . . . not that I can think of.'

'Then why would your file, out of all the files in that office, be the only one taken?'

'I don't know.'

Roberts clearly doesn't believe me. A muscle in his face twitches.

'Alright. Here's what I don't understand, Jenny. You knew, presumably, that your husband was leading the investigation into Phillip Walton's murder. You must have also known this would be a huge conflict of interest violation for him and you stayed silent. Why?'

My leg trembles and I'm grateful for the dining table, which shields it from his view. I notice James is watching me curiously. This time, I can't look at him.

'I . . . it didn't seem relevant to mention,' I answer finally, thought it doesn't seem good enough for Roberts.

'I can think of another reason,' he adds bluntly. 'That maybe your relationship with Phillip Walton was a little more than just doctor and patient? That it was sexual in nature?'

I'm horrified by the insinuation.

'What? No. Of course not.'

'So, you weren't close to Phillip Walton?'

'No. Definitely not in that way.'

'In any way?'

'No.'

'Funny. That's not what Sally Edwards said.'

I jump at the mention of her name.

'You remember Sally Edwards, don't you, Jenny? Hillside nurse? Nice lady?'

'Yes.'

'She seems to think you and Mr Walton were very close indeed.' Roberts turns his head and looks at Lancey. 'What did she tell us, Nance? What was the expression she used?'

'She said you had a close bond,' Lancey replies, and Roberts snaps his fingers.

'*A close bond*, that was it. A bit confusing, given you just told us you and Walton weren't particularly close at all. Can you explain that, Jenny? Why Sally Edwards would say you had a close bond with Phillip Walton, if you weren't particularly close to him at all?'

Truthfully, I can't think of a reason why Sally would say that. I'm startled and a little confused she would suggest such a thing, because I liked Sally and up until now, I thought she liked me.

'No,' I say, quietly. 'I can't.'

Roberts sighs and I watch, confused, as he produces something from his pocket. Something long and red and snake-like, a rounded black nub hanging from its end. Immediately, I shiver.

'Recognise this?'

'Yes.'

'I thought you might.'

Roberts doesn't say anything else. He doesn't need to.

Lancey turns off the Dictaphone and leans towards me.

'It would help our investigation, Jenny, if you let us take a DNA sample,' he says. 'Maybe you could come down to the station one day next week and we could take your fingerprints? Do a mouth swab?'

'I'll take her in,' James says. 'Next week, first thing.'

Roberts clears his throat. 'Tomorrow would be preferable . . .'

'Tomorrow then.'

There's a hostile pause as James and Roberts exchange stern glances. Quickly, Lancey gets to his feet and slips a business card into my hand.

'In case you think of anything,' he says.

I nod and Lancey walks over to James, murmuring something I can't quite make out.

Roberts stares at me coldly but I look to the side, pretending not to realise the implications of what he'd just shown me.

7.07 p.m.

James sees Lancey and Roberts out while I remain seated. He returns to the kitchen a few minutes later with a furious look on his face.

'What the hell, Jen?'

'I'm sorry.'

'Why didn't you tell me about Hillside? That you were a patient there – for years, even?'

'There was never a good time . . . and I was scared.'

'Of what?'

'Of how you would react.'

58

He stares at me apoplectically. 'I could lose my job over this. We could lose the house . . .'

'I know,' I say, 'and I'm sorry. I panicked.'

James scrunches his eyebrows, as if he doesn't know how to reply. Probably because he doesn't.

James has seen my pills, my scars, and he's as supportive as any husband could be expected to be, but he also had a normal upbringing. No mental wobbles. No physical or emotional scars of his own. It's a fact I resent sometimes. One I begrudge, which makes me an awful person, I know, but it also gives me an advantage here because James doesn't understand what it's like to keep secrets. To have secrets burn inside you and still keep them concealed.

'Why was your file taken from Phillip Walton's office, Jen?' he asks now.

'I don't know.'

'That's all you have to say?'

'What do you want me to say? I don't know why it was taken.'

'You must have an idea . . .'

'I don't.'

James frowns, his eyes retaining the slightly crazed look I'm not used to seeing because James has his shit together. That was always part of his appeal, for me at least.

James must be thinking the same thing because he walks over to the kitchen cabinet, puts two thumbs of vodka in a glass and drinks them neat.

Glass still in hand, he turns back to face me, his expression now weary.

'Did you sleep with him? Walton?'

'No,' I say fast. 'How can you even ask me that?'

'Because you're lying.'

'I'm not lying . . .'

59

'Jenny, you are.'

There's a pause and I try to ignore it. The ominous feeling that more bad news is imminent.

James sighs and puts a hand to his forehead. 'Keith told me he saw you outside Hillside. On the day of Phillip Walton's memorial – and I just stood there and watched you lie about it.' He looks at me like a stranger and my gut turns, horrified Keith had seen me. 'Why were you even there?'

'I was just paying my respects,' I say, and James shakes his head, bewildered.

'Paying your respects? Can you imagine how that looked to Keith once he found out your file was missing?' His eyes bulge. 'I had to beg him not to tell the chief he saw you there – *beg him, Jenny* – and he only said yes because we've been partners for so long, and I convinced him you were innocent.'

'I am innocent.'

'Then why was your file taken?'

'How long have you known it was?'

It's a question I've been dying to ask and it just slipped out. James stares at me hard then pours another glass of vodka, downing that too.

'About a week,' he says, wiping his mouth with the knuckles of his hand. 'Keith interviewed Sally Edwards originally, before Craig and Paul did. She told him that Phillip Walton kept alluding to "making amends" about something in the months leading up to his retirement. "A failure", he'd described it as. Something he'd done wrong with a patient.

So, we looked at his patients. Walton had only been taking on a few a year since 1991; it didn't take us long to check them all. We'd find the records online and match them with the physical copies in Walton's office, and every single file was accounted for – except for yours, Jen.

'That's what the meeting with the chief was about. He wanted to tell me, personally, that the only lead the investigation had so far was . . . you.'

I swallow thickly. James drops his glass to the counter.

'Why would anyone want your file, Jenny? What's in it?'

I don't know how to respond so say nothing. James crosses the room and sits at the table, reaching to take my hand between his.

'If you know something, you have to tell me. Do you understand? This is serious. I don't care what it is. I love you and I can protect you.'

A part of me wants to cave and tell him everything, but I know I can't do that. Because of the emails. Because it was bad, what I did, and despite what James says, I know he wouldn't forgive me for it.

'No,' I say, finally. 'There's nothing.'

James lets go of my hand and sighs. 'That electronic door key Roberts had . . . Do you know anything about that?'

I wince though I try not to.

Sally's Hillside key was what Roberts had shown me. At least, a replica of it and I immediately understood the intended implication. It's been widely reported that nothing was stolen from Phil on the night he died – besides my file – his keys included. And, Roberts showing me the replica of Sally's old key – and it must be a replica because the real one, I knew, wouldn't be stored carelessly in Roberts' trouser pocket – means she must have told him that hers went missing. Years ago. Back when I was still a Hillside patient.

'Jenny?' James prompts and I scratch at the back of my neck.

'I know it existed. I've seen it before.'

61

'That's all?'

'Yes.'

The lie throbs in my throat like a pulse and I keep my hand at my neck. James's phone rings.

He digs a hand into his shirt pocket and answers it. 'Nilson.'

A conversation follows. I barely hear a word of it.

'I'll be there in ten,' James says a few minutes later, quitting the call and standing up. 'They want me at the station. I have to go.'

'You've been drinking . . .'

'I'll be fine.'

James leaves the room. The front door slams soon after and I get to my feet, circling the kitchen and trying to process everything he'd just told me. Everything Lancey and Roberts had as well. The file. The key. The knowledge that, before he died, Phil was looking to make amends about something he'd done wrong. About a patient he'd failed – was it her?

Is murdering Phil, taking my file, some kind of revenge for what I did that night? Did Phil tell someone what happened and if so, who?

I continue pacing, my thoughts chasing one another like a dog trying to catch its own tail. Worrying. Worrying. Worrying. And, slowly, I come to a halt.

James's briefcase is pressed up against the patio door. He must have left it here by mistake because he doesn't go anywhere without it. It's his prized possession: relatively slim and brown, made from high-quality leather with his initials embossed on the right-hand corner.

I wait a few minutes, thinking James will realise he's left it behind and rush back to retrieve it. He doesn't though, and it occurs to me that I should take a look inside it. That

62

the briefcase might contain a clue the police failed to see the relevance of. One that, to me, would make sense.

Trembling slightly, I approach the briefcase, punch in the numbers – *08/12*, the day we got married – and open it. There's paperwork. Plastic files. Legal pads, all of which I take out and spread across the dining table, keeping one ear tuned for the opening of the front door.

Next, I search through the materials though I don't find much: notes from the crime scene, a few photos of Phil's office, but mostly layout plans and DNA analysis that mean nothing to me whatsoever. I push them aside, rooting for something else – and finally find it. A yellow legal pad with James's handwriting at it's centre:

> *Hillside patients – Jenny's friends*
> *   (Sally Edwards interview)*
> *Tony Black*
> *Heidi Allman*
> *Alicia Davies*
> *Tom Naughton*
> *Nick Crewe*
> *Olivia Brennan*
> *See addresses overleaf.*

Immediately, I feel winded and lean over the dining table, trying to catch my breath.

There we all were in James's print handwriting. The seven of us, who, in varying degrees, knew about what happened back then. The four of us who witnessed it. The two who weren't there but played a small role in triggering how things played out, and the one of us who didn't survive.

My 'friends', Sally had called them, which doesn't make sense. We weren't all friends and Sally knew that. As much as anybody else.

With trepidation, I turn the page and see house numbers. Postcodes. The addresses of the people I'd been looking for; the ones still alive. It's clear James had been looking for them too, and he'd found them. Though not them all.

Nick's address isn't here, and the last I'd heard, he was alive. However, unfortunate I find it.

My phone buzzes and the legal pad slides from my fingers, landing on the floor with the sound of a collapsing Jenga tower. As, I bend to retrieve it, I notice something has fallen from its pages: a white piece of paper, which has been folded several times.

Slowly, I unfold it and see the hazed sprawl of printer ink: a news article from years ago.

I see the picture. The headline and, panicked, don't read beyond it. Instead, I gather everything I'd pulled from the briefcase and put it back the way I found it — with the exception of the article, which I tuck inside my trouser waistband. Because it's important to me, James doesn't have it.

My phone buzzes again and I walk to the table and grab it. I have a text waiting from Tony – *I'm worried, please call* – and, before that, another email. An *Urgent* one.

They don't know. Keep it that way.

I crush the phone between my fingers and delete the email, faster than I deleted the others. Then, I go back into the briefcase. In my panic about the news article, I'd forgotten all about James finding the others. How, I can now find them too; and I know exactly who to visit first. I just hope things will go better between us than the time I saw her last.

Chapter 6

Before

20 January 2007
9.11 a.m.

There's a knock at my bedroom door and I know Margaret is standing outside. It's my plan for her to be here. Albeit, not my original one.

I'm sat on my bed, holding a half-litre vodka bottle; the liquid sloshing with a density heavier than water as my hands tremor slightly. I'd thought about using vodka once before; chasing the pills with it the first time I tried to end my life, though I eventually dismissed the idea, fearing it would make me throw up. I've never been much of a drinker. It probably would have.

Heidi went off to breakfast half an hour ago, oblivious to what awaits her return. The plan may have changed but the outcome should be the same: Heidi will get thrown out of Hillside. And, even if she tells someone about the dirty magazine page before leaving, nobody after this will believe her.

'Come in.'

The door swings open and Margaret walks in, surveying the room with caution.

If patients want, we can request one-on-one time with

the nurses in an area of our choosing. When I told Margaret I wanted to see her, she looked suspicious and rightly so. But, I knew after the plan changed, Sally was never an option.

Margaret eyes me suspiciously, pointing to the vodka I'm holding. 'What are you doing with that?'

'It's not mine,' I say, passing it to her. 'I found it.'

'Where?'

'Inside the bear.'

'Inside the . . .' Margaret's eyes trail to the windowsill upon which Heidi's teddy bear is sitting. For convenience, I'd left its nose facing the window and its dress pulled up, the gaping hole in its back clearly visible.

Margaret frowns just as Heidi appears in the doorway and I smile. A smile that fades, once I see Sally is standing behind her.

They both enter the room and Heidi's eyes land on the bear immediately. It's facing a different direction to how she'd left it this morning and she must know she's in trouble. That only one person can be responsible. Nonetheless, she doesn't look concerned and her eyes soon find Margaret.

'What's going on?' she asks.

Margaret thrusts the vodka bottle towards her. Heidi's mouth gapes slightly but she folds her arms stubbornly across her chest.

'I'm twenty years old,' she says cooly. 'I like to party. Wasn't a crime, last time I checked.'

My heart thumps. I'd expected her to at least try and deny the vodka was hers. It concerns me that she hasn't – but what concerns me more is the cold look of fury Heidi shoots me now as Sally grabs her by the shoulder, making her flinch.

'How did it get here, darlin'?'

'I snuck it in the bottom of my suitcase,' Heidi replies, shrugging Sally off.

'That's all?' Margaret says.

'That's all,' she adds, her eyes still burning mine.

It's clear what Heidi's doing. Just as I knew the earphones wouldn't be enough – a slap on the wrist; the punishment, granular – Heidi knows the nurses finding the lighters and cigarettes in her possession would have been a lot worse than them finding the vodka. By confessing to sneaking in the vodka outright, she can continue to conceal them. The worst part is, I can't even contradict her because I don't know where she'd moved them to. I only know she removed them from the bear a few days ago, which is why my original plan changed.

I worry for a few seconds more. Until Margaret grabs Heidi's shoulder and steers her from the room. Sally follows closely behind them and I let out a sigh of relief, thinking I've got away with it. That the vodka alone will be enough and Heidi will soon be gone.

3.47 p.m.

Tony and I are sitting on one of the benches in the garden. It's cold out here. It's dark, too. The sun not yet set but certainly on its way, what's left of it nestled around the Hillside building like a halo. I sought Tony out before lunch because I feel safer in his presence and safe is not something I feel, knowing Heidi is still in the building.

They haven't kicked her out yet. After Margaret dragged her from our bedroom, I expected there to be a meeting of sorts to begin the process of removing her from Hillside, but they simply sent her down to quarantine, which meant letting Alicia out of it.

The thought makes me shiver. If Heidi is in quarantine, it means she's still in Hillside. That they could let her out any minute and we'd be back sharing a room, with more reason to hate each other than before.

Tony must be feeling cold, too. He lifts his bad foot off the ground and rubs it between his gloved fingers.

'It's weird about Heidi, isn't it?' he asks. 'Vodka? Here? Why? The purpose? Who knows?'

It's word salad and thankfully, easier to ignore because of it.

I let Tony ramble on and say nothing for a while. Not until he lowers his foot back to the ground and digs a hand into his trouser pocket, producing a pack of cigarettes.

'You need to get a nurse to light that for you,' I say absent-mindedly.

'Actually, I don't.'

'Tony . . .' I begin but stop talking as he reaches behind the back of the bench and pulls something from it. Again, I shiver; now, not even cold.

In Tony's hand sits a lighter. One I recognise. It's one of the lighters Heidi had smuggled into Hillside a few weeks ago. The lighters I'd been looking for just days ago.

Clearly, they're magnetic and at some point between the Alicia incident and our argument last week, Heidi removed the lighters from her teddy bear and stuck them to the metal scaffolding of this bench. I have to admit, it was smart of her to leave them here. At her convenience. In a place the nurses would never think to look.

Tony waves the lighter he's holding in my direction now, the hint of a triumphant smile broadening his face.

'These are Heidi's too,' he explains. 'She said I could use them as long as I didn't tell anyone else. So, don't tell anyone, Jenny.'

Tony chuckles to himself and puts a cigarette between his lips, readying the lighter. I sit on my hands and start to rock, a compacted ball of dread.

'Tony, it was me.'

'What was?'

'The vodka. I was the person who put it inside Heidi's bear.'

Tony finishes lighting his cigarette but looks shocked. Surprised I could be capable of doing such a thing. Worried too, a little bit, as the cigarette sits burning.

'You shouldn't have done that, Jenny.'

'But Alicia—'

'I'm not talking about Alicia,' he says darkly, all traces of word salad gone. 'You have to be careful around Heidi. She's clever.'

'I'm clever,' I reply childishly.

'Yes, but this is different. Heidi can do things. Bad things.'

'Like what?'

Tony shrugs. 'I don't know but she's devious. Cunning. Like, the last place she was sectioned? She broke into the main office and erased every observation the doctor there had made about her. No one knows how she did it but Heidi does and I wouldn't cross her, Jenny. She might start poking around in your secrets now.'

I think of the dirty magazine page and feel my jaw quiver. Tony takes a long draw on his cigarette, coughing slightly on exhale. I can sense he's annoyed at me and I don't like it. Heidi was in the wrong here. She started all this. Not me.

Tony breathes out yet more smoke. This time, it emerges from his nostrils and he stubs the cigarette out on the ground, smashing the butt into the path with the sole of his good foot. He goes to light another cigarette but then pauses, like there's something on his mind.

'The vodka,' he asks. 'Where did you get it from?'

'Nick,' I say quietly, hoping Tony won't hear but he does and winces.

It's not hard to see why.

Nick doesn't live on the normal ward. He lives in isolation, separately from the rest of us, because he's a criminal. He's supposed to be in jail but was sent here instead because what he did, whatever he did, was bad. So bad that Phil was the only Hillside psychiatrist willing to work with him – but he's good at sneaking things into Hillside. I'd never have gone to him otherwise.

I start to shake fiercely, the cold and worry about my failed plan too much to handle all at once. I stand up from the bench while Tony lights his second cigarette.

'I'm going inside,' I say.

'See you later,' he says frostily back and I slouch inside, blinking back tears. Not wanting Tony to be annoyed with me and sensitive, just the beginning.

Maybe they're the five words Phil is looking for: *sensitive is just the beginning*. I have my third meeting with him tomorrow morning and have yet to conjure anything better, not that I see the point. For me, I don't think it gets better; however much I want it to.

I wipe my face and head to the lounge. Tony doesn't follow me and I sink into an armchair, relieved to see the TV blaring loudly in the corner which means I can distract myself for an hour or two. I stare at the screen and try to concentrate and I don't even hear Heidi as she rushes up behind me.

All I hear is the crunch of my nose as my face flies into the ground. Feel, the small but furious hands hauling my body around so I'm facing upright and she's on top of me: glaring coldly at me with her hands around my throat.

The pressure sends alarm bells through my nervous system and my body fights for me, jostling to try to knock her off balance, but Heidi's stronger than she looks and I've never cared enough about my life to fight for it anyway.

The end doesn't come. Not like I'm expecting. I feel a weight lifted off me and the hands at my neck loosen. I then sit up, bleary-eyed but just about conscious enough, to watch Tony drag Heidi away, kicking and screaming.

Chapter 7

After

21 January 2016
12.12 p.m.

I'm standing outside a coffee shop in Uxbridge which looks abandoned. Broken sign. Boarded-up windows. The pavement slabs out front unsteady under my feet. It looks like the kind of business that should have shut down a long time ago, judging by the volume of cardboard used to patch up its exterior. It's the very last place I expected to find her.

I'm dressed like I'm heading for an interview: a white shirt with flower cuffs, paired with navy cigarette pants and my camel duster coat. My scarf too, because it's cold. It's an outfit I wouldn't dream of wearing to the *Gazette* because I know Simon would mock me mercilessly if I showed up with it on – but one I felt was important for me to wear. To show her I have been doing better. Until, of course, all this.

I open the door. It bangs against the wall more dramatically than I hoped and I'm inside, smelling all things crappy coffee shop. Plastic. Rubber. Burnt grinds, which crawl under my nostrils and make my eyes water. There aren't any customers and the seating area is deserted, bar a few cheap-looking steel tables and mismatched red chairs, the floor covered in black lines from where chairs had been dragged across it. I smooth down my handbag straps and breathe in deep, stepping towards the waitress ahead of me.

She's standing behind the counter, wearing too much eyeliner and tapping a pencil rhythmically to the beat of music coming through her earphones. Her hair is red now, cut just below her chin, though not much else about her has changed. Heidi, all these years later.

Finally, she looks up. She doesn't look too surprised to see me but she does drop the pencil in her hand, pulling out her earphones soon after.

'Jenny,' she says. 'How did you find me?'

'Does it matter?'

She shrugs, folding her arms across her chest. 'Maybe. Why are you here?'

'To talk.'

We stare at each other. Eventually, Heidi rolls her eyes and retrieves her earphones from the counter, tucking them into her shirt pocket.

'Fine,' she says. 'Do you want a drink?'

'Sure.'

'Take your pick,' she adds, motioning to the tables behind me, before disappearing through the door at her back.

I walk across the scratched-up floor and settle on the table with the fewest brown stains, removing my coat and scarf. Heidi returns a few minutes later, carrying two mugs and a pot of coffee. She pours out both and pushes one towards me too fast, so it sloshes a puddle on to the table where I'm sitting. Heidi makes no effort to clean it up or offer me something to wipe it with. She simply sits opposite me, dragging her chair across the tiles and putting my teeth on edge.

'Milk?' she asks.

'Black is fine.'

'Good.' She says. 'I'm out of milk anyway.'

Heidi dumps a few sugar sachets into her own mug, without bothering to stir them in.

'Say, that's a fancy outfit,' she says next, leaning back in her chair and staring at me appraisingly.

The comment unnerves me. Not an outright insult but no doubt meant as one.

I ignore it and Heidi smiles and removing an e-cigarette from the same pocket she'd tucked her earphones into earlier. Now we're up close, I see it's not the only thing about her that's changed.

Heidi was always grungy but only artificially so. A manufactured grunge, which is now more authentic; her eyeliner smudged more than I remember and a sheen on her nose caused by days spent making hot drinks for other people. Her clothes are different too. No longer ripped but paper-thin, like the material has been slowly rubbed away, her shirt today is see-through enough to notice she isn't wearing a bra and her Ugg boots are mangled so much her feet slope sideways.

'You own this place?' I ask, conscious of the silence. 'Why?'

'I fell into it,' she says, inhaling several times before returning the vape back into her pocket.

'But your parents . . .'

'We don't speak. As soon as I was twenty-one, I was someone else's problem as far as they were concerned. Told their friends I ran away to save face when in reality they got me a flat, wrote me a cheque, and left me to fend for myself. *Cowards*.'

Heidi finishes her sentence with a snarl. I don't know what to say, so reach for my coffee and take a sip. It's already lukewarm and tastes like it came from a jar but I swallow hard and place the mug back on the table, careful to avoid the puddle.

'When did you get married?' Heidi asks, now signalling to my wedding ring.

'Three years ago.'

She smirks. 'Didn't take you too long, then.'

'Too long to what?'

'Move on.'

My shoulders rise. 'I'm not here to trade insults—'

'No,' she says calmly. 'I know why you're here.'

It's obvious from the tone of her voice that Heidi is referring to the emails and I'm in no way taken aback. Tony and I were receiving them. It makes sense she would be too.

'How many have you got?' I ask.

'Don't say anything. I mean it, keep quiet. They don't know, keep it that way,' she replies and I nod almost stoically.

'They're exactly the same ones Tony and I have been getting,' I reply.

At this, Heidi looks surprised. 'You've talked to Tony?'

'Yes. Have you tried to find out who's sending the emails?' I ask, because I know Heidi's smart. That if any of us could figure out who the sender is, it would be her – but she shakes her head, looking irritated.

'You can't trace a Gmail account, Jenny. Everyone knows that.'

'And you didn't tell anyone . . . about what happened?'

She scoffs. 'And, go to jail? Of course I didn't.'

I feel my cheeks warm and can't think of a response. Heidi leans back in her chair and considers me for a few moments, tracing the edge of her coffee mug with her index finger.

'Can I be honest?' she asks.

'Sure.'

'I didn't think the emails would bother you that much,' she says. 'We don't want what really happened that night getting out, right? So the emails are a good thing. They're asking us to keep quiet about it.'

'For now,' I add ominously.

Heidi removes her finger from her coffee mug and grimaces. 'Have the police been to see you?'

I nod, panic drumming in my chest. 'Have they been to see you?'

'Yes.'

'When?' I ask.

'A few days ago.'

'Why?'

Heidi shrugs. 'Apparently they're interviewing all Phil's patients; the alive ones. Maybe it's because your file was stolen. Maybe not.'

'You know about my file being stolen?'

'I do.'

I'm unsettled by the information. And something else. 'Who came to see you, Heidi? The detectives? What were their names?'

'No, it was just the one guy. Keith, I think.'

The relief on my face must be palpable as Heidi narrows her eyes suspiciously. I don't care. I'm just glad James wasn't involved in that particular visit. That he hadn't spoken to her.

'What did he want?' I ask, shiftily now. 'Keith?'

'An alibi.'

'Do you have one?'

Heidi smiles. 'I was here. Couldn't sleep so I spent the whole night watching YouTube videos on my phone.' She nods to a plastic cube in the top left-hand corner of the room. 'Whole thing was caught on camera.'

'That's convenient.' The comment slips from my mouth before I can stop it.

Heidi smiles wider, picking coffee grinds from beneath her nails. 'I didn't kill Phil, Jenny. Why would I?'

I know she's right. Heidi liked Phil. He was one of the only people she did like.

'Well, neither did I,' I say miserably.

'The police think you did. Why is that?'

'Because my file was stolen.'

Heidi shakes her head. 'No. That can't be the only reason. Phil could have lost your file years ago. Left it on a bus or train or in a café or anything.'

'It's not the only reason,' I say grimly. 'The police think Phil and I were sleeping together.'

Heidi looks stunned. 'Why?'

'Because Sally told them we were close.'

She raises an eyebrow. 'I don't know, Jen. "Close" to "lovers" is a bit of a stretch . . .'

'It's not just that,' I interject. 'Before he died, Phil told Sally he wanted to make amends about something. Amends about a patient he failed. The police think that patient was me.'

What I'm insinuating is clear and Heidi looks unsettled. 'It might not have been her either, Jenny.'

'But the amends Phil was trying to make . . . they had to have been about that night.'

'You don't know that,' Heidi replies.

'My file. The emails . . . What else could it be?'

'I know what the emails say,' she adds impatiently. 'I just don't think Phil regretted what he did.'

Heidi stares at me challengingly and I have to look away because I disagree.

77

I do think Phil regretted it. Maybe not right away but over the years, I could see how it would start to eat away at him. Why he may have wanted to come clean rather than continue to cover up my mess.

'He regretted what happened,' I say quietly. 'I think he wanted to put it right.'

Heidi continues to stare at me. 'And how would he do that?' she replies. 'She's been dead for nine years. Don't tell me that before he died, Phil grew an interest in the occult.'

I sigh and shut off, saying nothing in return. It's my bad side. My worst side. Another thing Phil taught me.

He said I had an avoidance type personality but I can't afford that this time, not with my Hillside file still missing. I need to get ahead of this. Be proactive and find Phil's killer before anyone else can and I need Heidi's help. Heidi's clever. She would be able to find things – information, documents – I wouldn't be able to discover alone, and no one has more incentive to keep this secret than I do. It makes sense that we should work on this together, despite our chequered past. The scary part will be asking her.

'Phil was trying to make amends to someone,' I repeat, my leg shaking beneath the table. 'That's what Sally said. I think whoever it was, wouldn't accept the amends he wanted to make. That they killed him for it.'

Heidi squints. 'If you say so. But, why would that person steal your file?'

'I don't know, but what if we found out?'

Heidi looks uncertain. She takes the e-cigarette out of her pocket and places it back in her mouth, gnawing at its nib contemplatively.

'We're not detectives, Jenny,' she says finally, puffing vapour towards me. 'Where would we even start?'

'Tom.' I say, confidently. 'I have his address. I was going to go see him next anyway.'

Heidi's eyes flare with suspicion. 'How did you find him? How did you find me?'

'That's not important . . .'

'Then you won't mind telling me.'

I drop my gaze to the edge of her side of the table. 'My husband is a detective. He was working with Keith on Phil's murder case before my file was found to be missing. I found both your addresses inside his briefcase.'

Heidi's eyelids flutter with interest. 'What's his name?'

'James,' I reply, with a lot less enthusiasm than I would normally.

He slept in the spare room last night, after returning from the police station with an evidence kit and insisting I do the DNA sample and elimination prints right there and then. I think he wanted to see how I would react; maybe he thought I would break down in his arms and tell him what he's so convinced I'm hiding – but that didn't happen. I let him take the samples without question or comment and lay awake for hours after listening to his snores from the other side of the hall.

I don't blame him. I lied to James for years. He must feel hurt, betrayed, confused – and he doesn't even know the whole truth yet. He must have his suspicions, though. Otherwise he would never have had that article. The one I'd since stolen from him.

'Well, was there anything else in his briefcase?' Heidi adds now, as if reading my mind. 'Anything I should know about?'

'Just your names. Your addresses,' I say, fidgeting on my chair uncomfortably.

Maybe it's wrong not to tell Heidi about the article and

yet, I can't bring myself to. She wouldn't help me if I did. If she knew just how close James was to the truth already.

I don't tell her about Sally's key, either. The replica of which Roberts had shown me. Why mention it? Why worry her? I'm sure Roberts only did it to get under my skin because it's not likely, after all this time, someone still has it.

Heidi doesn't appear to know I'm lying. She looks relieved and exhales more vapour, while I lean my forearms against the table, forgetting all about the coffee puddle in front of me, and soaking my sleeves in the process.

'Fuck.'

Heidi smirks while I try to mop up the damage, flicking a tea towel that had been tucked in her waistband towards me. 'OK, fine. I'm in.'

I stop wiping at my sleeves and grab the tea towel from her. 'Are you serious?'

'Unfortunately yes,' she says producing her phone and types something into it. 'What about Nick? Was he in the list of addresses you so conveniently found inside your husband's briefcase?'

'No.'

'Then we should find him,' she says surreptitiously, still typing.

It makes sense. If we're looking for people wronged in the events of that night – the ones still alive – then, Nick was near the top of the list. However, I can't imagine he'd be smart enough to pull this off; nor be someone Phil would want to make amends to – but if Heidi thinks he's a plausible suspect, I should listen. Maybe I'll go and see him, after ruling out everyone else first.

2.15 p.m.

I get back to the office after my meeting with Heidi. We'd agreed she'd look for Nick and do some other digging; see what she can learn about the police investigation, or anything else that's relevant. We'd exchanged numbers and agreed to call each other if anything came up, though I told her not to text me because I jump now every time my phone goes off. I can't do anything more without speaking to Simon first, though it's another conversation I'd happily avoid.

He's in his office, transcribing one of the interviews that ended up as illegible shorthand at the bottom of my desk bin a few days ago. Simon tossed it in there himself, declaring he'd do the interview at a later date, because none of my work is good at the minute. I'm far too distracted by everything going on.

I knock on his door. Seconds later, a voice sounds through it.

'Come in.'

I walk into the office, which smells of sweet alcohol and one of the plug-into-the-wall air fresheners Simon uses to mask it. It lets out another *pfff* as I pass it and close the door behind me.

Simon gestures for me to sit opposite him, which I do. He stops typing and folds his fingers together, looking me up and down.

'What's with the get-up?' he asks. 'Job interview you want to tell me about?'

I realise I'd forgotten to change my outfit on my way back into the office. I hadn't been wearing this when I arrived for work this morning.

'No,' I say blushing slightly. 'I had lunch with James's mum. Somewhere nice.'

He nods. 'Wonderful. How can I help?'

'I need some time off.'

Simon pauses. 'How much time?'

'Two weeks.'

'Starting when?'

'Tomorrow.'

I gulp and Simon leans back in his chair, deliberating.

'It's very short notice, kid.'

'I know.'

He thinks about it some more, rubbing his eyes as if he has a migraine.

'Fuck it,' he says eventually. 'Fine.'

I blink. 'Really? Will you be able to—'

'Manage?' He laughs. 'To be honest, we're better off without you at the minute.' He gestures to the stains on my sleeves. 'Can't even hold a coffee the right way up, by the looks of ya.'

'Thanks, Simon.'

He holds his hand up. 'Don't thank me, kid. I know you're going through . . . stuff. Just deal with it, whatever it is. Then come back and do your job fucking properly.'

I nod and look to him for reassurance. For some reason, he fails to meet my eye.

Chapter 8

Before

21 January 2007
10.15 a.m.

I'm not hurt. Heidi's rage, though seismic, didn't inflict any lasting damage. It's hard to know whether to be relieved about that or not. She isn't being removed from Hillside, even after attacking me and a supposed zero tolerance for violence policy, so I guess, in a fucked up way, I wish she'd hurt me more. I don't know what you'd have to do to actually be kicked out of Hillside. Kill someone, probably.

Margaret escorts me down through the basement and leaves me at Phil's office door. I walk inside to find him standing by the filing cabinet, searching for what I assume to be my file.

'Jenny,' he says, prising it out. 'Do you think you're well enough for the session today?'

'Yes.'

Phil smiles and closes the cabinet drawer. 'Excellent. Take a seat.'

I do as he says and Phil sits opposite me, retrieving a pen that had fallen into the seam of his chair.

'So, do you have five words for me?'

I fight the urge to laugh; unable to entirely comprehend that, even after what happened with Heidi yesterday, the five words are what Phil is most concerned about.

'Yes,' I reply because it's true. I have them.

The words came to me last night while I was lying on a bed in the medical ward, listening to the moans of someone in the early stages of heroin withdrawal. It was an unpleasant noise. Hideous, if I'm being honest, but one I sympathised with nonetheless. It was the voice of how bad it felt to be in this body. How bad it's always felt, ever since I can remember.

Phil smiles before leaning forward eagerly. 'Great,' he says. 'Let's hear them.'

I take a deep breath and tell him.

7.23 p.m.

After our meeting, Phil writes me a new prescription. It's a surprise. I haven't been put on so many drugs before; just the daily Sertraline my GP prescribed years ago, which never seemed to make much of a difference. Phil warned me there may be side effects to this prescription, that I could feel worse in the first few weeks, and I said that was fine. I'm used to feeling like the worst so it's worth the risk to feel better. If better is something that's possible.

I'm in the reading room now. Heidi's in quarantine – I think, indefinitely – so I don't have to worry about running into her. I wanted to be alone anyway and no one ever comes here. Not since Irene left.

I want to be alone because Mum visited me earlier, hours after my meeting with Phil, and my dark thoughts turned darker once she left. They always do. Her visits are often the highlight of my day, because it's always good to have someone in your corner, even one as dark and dingy and decrepit as my own, but once she leaves, the grey cloud returns and I feel deserted. Vulnerable. Lonely, in the presence of everyone else.

It was the first time I'd seen her in two weeks. She'd been in Mauritius visiting my aunt and her family and it was weird, seeing her again; the trip one we were supposed to take together, though I'm glad she went without me. It can't be easy, having a daughter like this.

I knew from a young age that I was different. I was four, maybe five years old when I realised I didn't fit in with the other kids, and that not everyone had melancholia wrapped in a more general unease at their centre. I wasn't expecting it. To me, that came as a surprise.

My teachers worried. They'd call Mum in and ask her why I never smiled and she'd sit next to me, in whatever teacher's office, a confused but also mortified look on her face – because there was no reasonable explanation. 'Single-parent syndrome' some of the more hateful teachers called it, which wasn't fair. I knew my dad for a while, though I never knew what he meant to Mum. What they meant to each other. They'd always been strangers as I'd known them. It was hard to imagine them being anything else.

Dad and I would have scheduled bi-yearly visits – sometimes he would turn up, sometimes he wouldn't – and, aged fifteen, Mum asked if I wanted to continue our relationship. I said no. My dad was always a stranger to me too, and I was just as surly a little kid. I'm sure he felt the same.

There's a knock at the door.

I look up and see Tom, standing nervously in its frame, a newspaper clutched in his hand.

'Hi,' he says. 'Can I join you?'

85

'Of course,' I reply, knowing it would be rude to say anything else.

Tom is another of Phil's patients, one I haven't seen in a while. He'd recently been given permission for an extended home leave. *A trial run*, Phil calls it.

Tom's older than me, in his late twenties. He's also married, but we have a lot in common and we're friends, I suppose. Seeing as I haven't cleared the air with Tony since our squabble in the garden yesterday and Alicia hasn't left her room since she got out of quarantine, he's my only friend in here at the moment.

Tom walks inside and sits next to me, his chair dragging against the floor. It's a weird set-up, the reading room. Half carpet and half linoleum. Moon-shaped desks and plastic chairs on the right-hand side. Threadbare, donated sofas on the other.

'Are you all right?' Tom asks me once seated. 'Tony told me what happened with Heidi. Can't say I've had the pleasure of meeting her yet. How's your neck?'

'Yes, I'm fine,' I say. 'It's fine. How was it at home?'

'It was good. Really good.' Tom smiles and puts the newspaper on the table in front of us, thumbing through it until he lands on the puzzles section.

Tom and I like doing crosswords together. It's a tradition we've had for a while: one that started a few weeks ago, when I asked Tom to help me with a clue and we ended up completing the entire thing, which was the first time I'd been able to do so without cheating.

I don't know why I like puzzles so much. I guess it's because they give me a sense of achievement when really, I've achieved very little if nothing at all.

Tom smooths down the newspaper and produces a felt pen from his pocket.

'I saw your mum on the way in,' he says, and I nod, trying to hide my discomfort.

I don't like talking about Mum with other people. Not because I don't love her, but because I've put her through so much.

I miss her now, the familiar stab of guilt directly in my gut, and I stare through Tom without realising, making him reach self-consciously for his scar. Another thing about Tom: a fondness for puzzles isn't all we have in common.

Tom has a scar too. It's less hidden than those on my wrists, a slightly hooked line that runs along the right side of his face, made a little less offensive by the thick rim of his glasses. No one knows how he got it. Like Tony's toe, what prompted the act remains a mystery. Tom's official line is that he got it in a car crash. I imagine he tells Phil differently.

I'm about to apologise for staring when there's a knock at the door and Tony limps into the room. Tom gets up from his chair in order to let him sit down at our table and Tony pats his back gratefully.

'I was looking for you both everywhere,' he says. 'Why are you in the reading room?'

Tom and I both shrug, but inside, I feel glad Tony was looking for me at all. That, after yesterday, he still wants to be friends: people wanting to be friends with me is always something I've found hard to believe.

'Why are you looking for us, Tone?' I reply. 'What's wrong?'

'Nothing – but I have some news.'

'What is it?' Tom asks, and Tony wrings his hands excitedly.

'Phil's getting a new patient. Sally just told me.'

I crunch the numbers in my head. Tony. Tom. Heidi. Nick. Alicia. Me. That's six. There are already six of us.

'But Phil already has six patients,' Tom says before I can, evidently thinking the same.

'So he's getting a seventh patient?' I ask.

'No,' Tony says. 'It means that one of us is leaving. Soon.'

I look to Tom, who shakes his head.

'It isn't me,' he says. 'I saw Phil a few hours ago, when I checked back into Hillside. He told me I would be staying for another couple of weeks, at least.'

Tony nods to confirm Tom's story but the expression on his face tells me bad news is coming. That I won't like whoever's leaving Hillside or, perhaps, who's coming into it.

Chapter 9

After

21 January 2016
3.30 p.m.

I meet Tony in a storage unit on the Ealing Industrial Estate a few hundred yards down from the office. I rang him just before talking to Simon because what Heidi and I plan to do directly concerns him. It's something he needs to know.

I discovered the storage unit last year, Simon passed out inside it on a particularly drunk day I doubt he remembers. I don't know who it belongs to, and the unit itself is nothing special – a hall-sized steel box filled with a dozen wooden crates, random household furnishings and a mysteriously endless electricity supply – but I thought it would be an ideal place to come during my fortnight off work, without James having to know anything about it. He can't know anything about it. He's already suspicious enough.

It's cold in the unit. A couple of degrees cooler than outside and outside was cool enough. Shaking, I turn on the torch of my phone and see Tony a few yards down from me. He's shivering also and I quickly approach him, wrapping my scarf around his neck without a second thought.

'How long have you been here?' I ask.

'A few minutes,' he replies, but by the blue of his lips I can tell it's been longer.

I leave Tony hugging my scarf and walk over to the cobwebbed light switch and turn it on. It doesn't help much. The bulb is dulled and covered in a thick layer of dirt, and I go into the unit's kitchen and dragging out the portable heater I'd also found there last year. I plug it in it slowly fires up, the fan inside clicking upon every rotation.

Tony points a quivering finger to it. 'Is that safe?'

'It's fine,' I say, dragging the heater closer towards him.

Tony arches his body around it, cupping his hands as if it were a fire. I pull up an abandoned patio table that, just like the light bulb, is covered in black grit – but it was sturdy enough to support Simon's weight for several hours last year. I reason that it should support Tony's and mine for at least a few minutes.

I sit on the table's edge. Tony soon joins me, wiping dirt from its surface with his palms.

'Thanks for meeting me,' I say.

He shrugs. 'It's fine. I was on a half day anyway.'

I doubt that's true but nod gratefully. 'What did you tell your wife?'

'Ella?' he asks. 'She's in bed ill. The pregnancy . . . it hasn't been an easy ride. I didn't have to tell her anything.'

'She's pregnant?'

Tony's eyes light up, the corners of his mouth rounding. 'Yeah. We're having a baby.'

I know it's always been a dream of Tony's to have children, and I smile too.

'Congratulations. That's really great.'

'Thanks,' he replies, knocking his arm gently into mine. 'What about you? What did you tell James?'

'I . . . I didn't tell him anything.'

90

Liquid seeps from one of my nostrils and I wipe it roughly on the sleeve of my coat. Tony produces a tissue from his pocket and hands it to me, his smile gone and his expression guilty.

'I'm sorry I didn't reply to you, Jenny,' he says. 'Right after the first email. I freaked out. I never thought . . . I mean, why would someone do this? Why would they kill Phil? Why now?'

'That's what we're going to find out,' I say. 'Heidi and me.'

Tony raises his head and looks around the storage unit. 'Is she coming here? Heidi?'

'No,' I reply and I can tell he's disappointed.

Tony and Heidi were friendly back at Hillside. Friendlier than she and I ever were.

He nods, anyway, looking slightly confused. 'But you're going to see the others?'

'Yes.'

'Tom?'

'Yes.'

'Nick?'

I gulp. 'Maybe.'

Tony doesn't look pleased. He looks like he wants to object but doesn't think it's his place. 'Then I'm coming with you.'

'You don't have to . . .'

He grabs my hand, which seems too intimate for the friends we are now and I shake mine from his grip under the pretext of pushing my hair behind my ears.

'You're not talking me out of it, so don't even try,' he adds. 'Work is pretty flexible. I can pretend I'm taking Ella to some baby stuff and take a few hours here and there.'

'Thank you.'

'It's fine, Jenny. I want to help.'

I don't know how to reply so say nothing and we're both quiet for a few moments, nothing to be heard besides the heater's inconsistent clicks.

In the silence I realise I need to be completely honest with Tony. He's putting everything on the line to help me. It's only fair he knows what we're truly up against, and alongside the emails and Sally's key and my file being stolen, the news article I found in James's briefcase is a big part of that.

It means, in some capacity, the police are aware of what happened nine years ago. The question is, whether James has told any of his colleagues about it.

'Tony, I need to show you something.'

'What?'

Without further comment, I reach into my bag's zip compartment, pull out the article and hand it to Tony. Nervously, he takes it and starts reading.

The article is dated March 2007. The headline: *Hillside Death Ruled Suicide, Inquest Finds* – and below it, a black-and-white picture of a young woman. An eighteen-year-old, whose hair we both know was blonde.

Tony reads the article in its entirety, which takes him a few minutes. When he's done, he hands it back with a tremor in his hand that wasn't there previously.

'I don't understand . . .'

'I found the article inside James's briefcase.' I say. 'His work briefcase.'

I see Tony put two and two together. I wish I could forget the expression on his face when he does.

'So he . . .'

'He suspects.' I clear my throat. 'I told you what Sally told the police, right? That Phil was trying to make amends

92

about something before he died; amends about a patient he failed?'

Tony nods.

'After the police found out my Hillside file was missing, Lancey and Roberts and perhaps even Keith thought the patient is me: that I was having an affair with Phil, but I know James; he never would have thought that. He would have been looking for something else. Something still involving me; because of the file. Something like this.'

Tony shakes his head. 'But, this article? James hasn't shown it to anyone else?'

I think about my interview with Lancey and Roberts. What Tony had told me earlier on the phone about his, because it had been the same detectives who came to interview him about Phil's murder, a few days ago. Neither time, did Lancey or Roberts mention what happened nine years ago. Neither of them mentioned Olivia.

'I don't think so. Not yet.'

'Do you think he will tell them?'

I think about James. About him sleeping in the spare bedroom. 'I'm not sure.'

Tony flounders for a sentence but says nothing. Presumably, because he can't think of what to say. Tony doesn't know James. We hadn't been friends for a while before this but it's my fault. Everything about what happened many years ago was my fault entirely.

'It doesn't matter if he tells them, Jenny,' Tony says finally. 'What happened . . . it was an accident.'

'It wasn't an accident, Tony.'

'It was,' he replies firmly, passing me back the article which I take and put in my bag.

Tony's wrong. What happened wasn't an accident. A mistake, perhaps. One I regret fiercely and think about every day but can never take back, because the effects of it are too wide-reaching. It's the reason the article I found in James's briefcase makes me far more nervous than anything else. The reason I can't walk away from this, when in many ways, that's all I want to do – because I killed Olivia, and Phil helped me get away with it. So did everyone else.

PART TWO

Chapter 10

Before

23 January 2007
9.06 a.m.

Alicia is the patient being released from Hillside. That's what Tony told Tom and I two days ago, but I don't quite believe it. You don't go anywhere. Not when you're as sick as Alicia. She isn't at breakfast this morning, however, and I start to worry that Tony may have been right so I finish eating and walk along to her bedroom, to make sure she's still here.

Alicia has her own room. Besides Nick, she's the only patient who does. It's because she needs round-the-clock surveillance and isn't trusted to shower or sleep or go to the bathroom without trying to expel some calories. But when I get to Alicia's room, it's not her I find inside it.

Heidi is standing next to Alicia's bed, her zebra-print suitcase lying flat on the ground behind her. Confused, I look around the room for Alicia's belongings: her woollen throws and her Lena Zavaroni poster and the inspirational quote canvases that her dad brings with every month she stays here: *Peace is not the absence of conflict but the ability to cope with it. Progression not perfection. It does not matter how slowly you go, as long as you do not stop* – but Alicia's things are nowhere to be found.

In the corner of my eye, I see Heidi's own posters – My Chemical Romance and Fall Out Boy and Panic! at the Disco – rolled up like telescopes and let out an involuntary shudder.

'Do you want something, Jenny?'

Heidi is looking into Alicia's wardrobe but she must sense me in her peripheral vision. It's the first time we've spoken or even seen each other since she attacked me three days ago.

'A wardrobe and no hangers?' she adds. 'I mean, what is the fucking point?'

'This is Alicia's room,' I say and Heidi smiles.

'Not any more. They moved old bag of bones out this morning and moved me in, since we're no longer allowed to share.' She turns her head to me and winks. 'Thanks for that.'

I feel my cheeks burn.

'Do you know where Alicia is now?'

'The medical ward,' Heidi replies and I quickly turn to leave.

'Jenny, wait.'

I pause and reluctantly turn around again.

Heidi walks towards me and I notice there's something in her hand. 'I must have picked this up with my stuff,' she says. 'My mistake.'

Suspicious, I take the paper from her and, in my own palm, I recognise it immediately. It's the page from the dirty magazine. The one Heidi had stolen it from me.

I ball the paper in my fist and heart beating hard, set off for the medical ward because I need to get the truth for myself. It's hard to believe Phil would even consider releasing Alicia. She's the sickest of us all.

I reach the medical ward and throw the dirty magazine

page into the first medical waste bin I see, trying to forget about both it and Heidi – because it unsettles me: the thought of her sticking around. Then, I go to find Alicia.

It doesn't take me long. She's in one of the beds at the end of the ward, her woollen throws strewn shroud-like across her and her eyes firmly closed. There's a tube running up her nose, which is held in place by a shred of tape just below her nostril, and she looks even thinner than she did last week; her mouth is turned down as if in discomfort or distress and fur-like fine hair lines her cheekbones.

Restraints pin Alicia to the bed. Velcro cuffs, like those on trainers, wrapped around her arms and legs, and it's upsetting to see her like this, although maybe it shouldn't be. Perhaps I should have seen Alicia like this sooner because despite her round-the-clock surveillance, I've yet to see her gain weight.

'What are you doing here?'

Alicia's eyes, once closed, are now open and she's staring right at me; her possessions scattered like debris around her.

Startled, I sit down on the chair next to the bed. Then, awkwardly, I nod to the tube up her nose. 'Does it hurt?'

'Not really. The restraints are a motherfucker, though.'

Alicia smiles. So do I.

'Do you want me to take them off?'

'Just the leg ones,' she says, her eyes a mixture of anxiety and excitement. 'Sally always does them loose, so I can just pretend I wriggled out.'

I stand up and release Alicia's ankles from the restraints. The Velcro makes a terrible ripping sound but, once undone, Alicia rolls her ankles gratefully.

'I take it you heard that I'm leaving?' she asks.

I nod and sit back down. 'I did. Do you know where you're going? When?'

99

'No. Phil said he wants me to stay here until I'm "*strong enough*" to be moved. Then he's shipping me off.' She pouts moodily, like a child. 'I wish they would just leave me alone.'

'Alicia, if they left you alone, you would die.'

'So?'

Despite my own two previous attempts on my life, I'm shocked. Also, slightly embarrassed that Alicia would admit so openly that dying isn't the worst thing and awkwardly I try to console her.

'It might be better in the new place. You might even get better there.' It's the wrong thing to say. I know it as soon as the words leave my mouth.

Alicia's eyes burn with anger and distress. 'I'd rather die than get better, Jenny.'

'You don't mean that . . .'

'Why? Because wanting to die is your thing?'

'No. It's not my thing any more.' My answer surprises me I don't know why I said it as well. If it's true. Either way, it seems to surprise Alicia.

'Isn't that wonderful?'

It's a sarcastic response. One which slices the air like a hot knife through butter and I twist on my chair, knowing it was a mistake to come.

I look down at my hands and I don't say anything else until I hear a noise. One that isn't immediately familiar. Part-rustle, part-squeak. I look around the cubicle to see what could possibly be causing it, and soon realise it's Alicia.

Now free from the restraints, she's lifting her right leg up and down, up and down – like she's working out. Like she's exercising, and I stare at her, horrified. Even more embarrassed than I was before.

'Why are you doing that?'

Her leg stops moving beneath the blanket. 'What?'

'You know what,' I reply, my heart starting to beat like a hammer.

Alicia looks stunned by my challenging her and doesn't respond. We sit in silence and eventually she lifts her leg again. Up and down and up and down, again and again and again. Fucking pointless, fucking pointless, I think to the same rhythm and I reach out and pin her leg to the bed.

'Stop.'

The silence returns, the only sound my increased intake of breath as panic pings inside me. Before either of us can say anything, I drop Alicia's leg like a hot plate and leave the room – because I know I crossed it: the unspoken line of how involved you can allow yourself to be in the saving of another person.

4.39 p.m.

What happened with Alicia haunts the rest of my day like an unwanted shadow. I have no activities so I lie on my bed, shame washing over me in waves because I know I should never have grabbed her like that. No matter how much I felt like doing it. Even though it was pointless, what she was doing. Even though I was only trying to save Alicia from herself.

Someone knocks gently on my bedroom door and I reluctantly sit up.

'Come in.'

Sally walks into the room and there's someone behind her. My new roommate, I have to presume; dust now collecting where Heidi's stuff used to be.

Sally smiles. 'Jenny, this is Olivia Brennan. You'll be sharing this room together for now.'

I look at Olivia. She's pretty. A rosy complexion and long

blonde hair, wavy and braided like it'd been slept in overnight. Her eyes, blue. Her frame a little thicker than my own
and her face a hell of a lot nicer.

'It's nice to meet you, Jenny.'

Olivia's voice is small but solid, with gravelly undertones.
She waves at me now, and shyly I wave back. 'It's nice
to meet you too.'

We exchange awkward glances and Sally swiftly walks
out of the room, returning with a battered black suitcase.

'Apologies for the delay,' she says to Olivia. 'We had some
trouble with a few girls hiding things in their suitcases. That's
why we had to check your belongings.'

Olivia laughs. 'That's fine. No drugs, no dildos, I promise.'

Sally laughs, putting a hand to her mouth and quickly
swallowing.

'I'll leave you ladies to it. Jenny, can I trust you to show
Olivia to the cafeteria for dinner?'

'Sure.'

'Great. See you both later.'

Sally gives my hand an extra squeeze on her way out.
Once she's gone, I fiddle with the elastic of my socks, feeling
Olivia's eyes on me all the while.

'Is Jenny what you like to be called?' She asks and I stop
fiddling and I look back up at her.

'Jen's fine too. Most people go for Jenny.'

'Not Jennifer?'

'Not really. Only my mum calls me that.'

Olivia smiles like I just said something overtly saccharine.
I feel my cheeks redden.

'How old are you, Jenny?'

'Nineteen,' I reply.

'I guess that makes me the baby. I turned eighteen last
week.'

'Happy birthday,' I say and Olivia smiles, twisting a strand of golden hair around her finger.

'Thanks.'

I feel my chest fall, relieved that Olivia seems a lot friendlier than Heidi had been. Than Gina had been before her.

Olivia meanwhile, looks me up and down. 'You seem too normal to be here. You know that Jenny?'

It's a statement more than a question and I'm not quite sure how to respond. I could show her my wrists. Maybe hers look similar.

'So do you,' I reply eventually, unsure I believe it.

Chapter 11

After

I pull up on the kerb outside Tony's house, beeping my car horn twice and he eventually walks out, locking his front door behind him. Sat on my passenger seat are two stuffed animals I bought yesterday to celebrate Tony's baby news: an elephant and a lion. They seem like stupid gifts for a new born now but I'd purchased them on Simon's recommendation, having texted him and asked for advice because I couldn't exactly ask James.

I don't think we're speaking. He came back late last night, slept in the spare bedroom yet again and was gone by the time I woke up this morning. The distance between us is evident and I think it will persist until the end of this: if it does indeed have an ending. Or, at least until James gets the all-clear from work, having been temporarily suspended for the conflict of interest he had unknowingly committed.

The passenger-side door opens and Tony climbs in. A grin spreads across his face once he spots the toy animals and he leans over the seat to hug me.

'Jenny, you didn't have to . . .'

'I wanted to,' I say, subtly pushing him away because I'm anxious, and when I'm anxious I don't like to be held.

I'm anxious because Tony and I are going to see Tom. He's the only person who saw what happened the night Olivia died that I haven't yet spoken to, so it makes sense to visit him first. He lives in Cambridge now; a fact Tony found surprising but I didn't. Like Tom, I too had plans to escape Sutton. Tom had just been more successful at making these plans stick.

Tony removes his arms from my shoulders and fastens his seatbelt, holding the stuffed animals safely on his lap. I drive away from his house. My satnav says it should take a little over two hours to reach our destination but it takes a bit longer than that with me taking a wrong turn on several occasions and Tony, keeps speaking over the navigation. Eventually, though, we arrive in Cambridge and I park outside a lofty high-rise in the city centre.

'Tom works here?' Tony asks, and I nod.

It's a grand building which houses multiple companies, including Tom's accountancy firm. His home address was inside James's briefcase too but I didn't want to go there. His wife may have been there, for one, and it's private: what we have to discuss.

I get out of the car, as does Tony, and together we walk into the lobby, which is immaculate: an expensive-looking marble floor and pieces of furniture that must cost more individually than the interiors of the *Ealing Gazette* put together. The quiet hits next, and the heels of my boots clack self-consciously as I make my way to the reception, the squeak of his trainers confirming Tony is following closely in my wake.

We reach the desk and the receptionist looks me up and down. On instinct, I do the same back, wincing at the severely tight bun pulled to the crown of her head.

'Can I help you?' she asks.

I clear my throat. 'Hi, yes. We're here to see Tom Naughton. He's expecting us.'

Her eyes dart to Tony. 'And who should I say is waiting?'

'The Mattersons,' I say quickly. 'Gill and Frank.'

These were the first names that popped into my head. I'd forgotten to inform Tony about this part of the plan but it's important Lancey and Roberts don't find out we're here speaking to Tom, which means we can't leave any kind of trail.

My palms get sweaty as the receptionist calls up our request, but I'm hoping Tom's politeness will compel him to come and greet the strangers we're pretending to be. A few seconds pass. Then, a voice cracks through the speaker.

'I'm coming down.'

The receptionist points across the lobby. 'Take a seat. He'll be with you shortly.'

Tony and I walk over to a pair of lavish-looking armchairs. Tony removes his phone from his pocket and starts texting while I fidget restlessly, watching the numbers of the lift change as if it were a sport. Eventually, they drop all the way to zero and a man steps out from between the opening doors.

It's Tom. I recognise him immediately and watch as he scans the lobby, his eyes landing on Tony and me. He stares for a few moments and I'm certain he recognises us too.

Especially when he flicks his head in the receptionist's direction and strides towards us, his soles clacking against the marbled floor as mine had done moments ago.

'Jenny?' he asks once he reaches us. 'Tony? It's you, isn't it?'

I nod and we stand to greet him. Now close I see stubble where Tom had previously been clean-shaven and his scar, which – like mine – has faded over time but is still visible; puckering softly down the right-hand side of his face and is hidden almost perfectly by his glasses.

Tony rushes forward and hugs Tom while I hold back. They soon break apart and Tom and I hug in a more polite and reserved manner.

'It's great to see you both,' Tom says, stepping away from me and blinking. 'Are you here about Phil?'

'Yes.'

Tom nods and turns to face the receptionist. 'I'll be back in an hour, Maddie.'

'No problem,' she says, tapping her nails against her computer keyboard while Tom directs us from the building.

I exchange glances with Maddie the receptionist once more before leaving; figure she's around thirty years old, though she could be younger or even older than that. People often assume I'm younger than my age – there's not an off-licence where I'm not asked for ID, nor a cashier convinced I'm over twenty-one – which is ironic, because even twenty-eight feels too young for me. I feel a hundred years old, and like no one will believe it.

1.45 p.m.

Tom's on his second espresso shot of the hour, looking how I imagine I have since learning of Phil's murder and reading the emails that came thereafter. Unsettled. Anxious. We're sat out the front of a coffee shop on Cambridge high street. It's around the corner from Tom's office and we sit outside because all the seats inside were taken and none of us were keen to move elsewhere. Students and tourists walk past us in flurries, and it seems unbelievable to me we're sitting here all together. After all this time.

At first, we chat idly. Tony probes Tom about being a father since Tom already is one himself. He has a daughter who turns four next month, a fact neither Tony nor I knew before today and a reminder that we know so much about each other and yet so little. There's an awkward moment where Tom asks if I have any children. I tell him no and the conversation quickly moves on.

Eventually, Tony wanders off to take a call from Ella, leaving Tom and me alone. I sip my latte, which has gone cold over the course of catching up and Tom finishes his second espresso, dabbing a napkin against his lip.

'It's good to see you, Jenny,' he says, lowering his napkin. 'Really, it is.'

'There's a reason we're here, Tom. Why we came to see you.'

Tom nods stoically. 'I know there is.'

'The emails . . .'

'Yes. I'm getting them too.'

I'm not surprised. It's proof of what I've long assumed. Tom receiving the emails means that everyone who was there the night Olivia died is being targeted. That the killer knows the truth isn't what we told it to be. My hand starts to tremble and I quickly seat my latte.

'And you didn't tell anyone what happened?' I ask.

Tom looks alarmed. 'No. Of course not,' he says and his answer confirms something else. If none of us told anyone what really happened to Olivia, there are only two ways Phil's killer could have found out. Either they read it in my Hillside file, or Phil had told them by way of making amends, right before they killed him.

Neither prospect sits well with me and I feel the familiar

flare of panic, which I quickly push down. I've come to talk to Tom for a reason and panic won't help me now.

'Have the police been to see you?' I ask.

'Yes. They came to see me yesterday.'

'Lancey and Roberts?' I ask and Tom nods.

'Did they tell you about my file being stolen from Hillside?'

'Yes,' Tom says, looking uncomfortable.

We both shift in our seats. 'What else did they say?'

'Mainly, they asked me things. How well I knew you.' He pauses. 'And if I could remember what happened to Sally's electronic key.'

The key. Keith clearly hadn't mentioned it to Heidi but I do find it curious Lancey and Roberts would mention it to Tom, when they hadn't done the same to Tony. Indeed, Tony told me everything that Lancey and Roberts asked him and the key was never mentioned.

Was it bias? Tony's schizophrenia making him a non-credible information source? Or is it merely the movement of time? Are the detectives narrowing down the other keys in existence day by day? Is Sally's key, the one that in 2007 went missing, the only key to Phil's office left unaccounted for? The only one that possibly could have been used by Phil's killer in their escape from Hillside that night?

The thought makes me shudder. I try and mask it from Tom.

'Really?' I ask now. 'What did you tell them?'

'That I didn't know anything about it. That I hadn't seen that key in years.'

His answer doesn't surprise me. I genuinely don't know where the key ended up, and I'm sure Tom doesn't either. There was a lot of confusion that night; Sally's key was just the beginning of the awful events that unfolded.

'What do you think happened to the key?' I ask. 'After?'

'I just assumed Phil took it, to avoid any more trouble,' Tom replies, which is a scenario that seems plausible.

Up until three days ago I'd never heard Sally's missing key mentioned after that night and if it hadn't been picked up by Phil, I'm sure it would have been eventually because Phil wouldn't have stopped searching for it. Not after the damage it caused.

If Phil did take Sally's key on the night Olivia died, it also means it was probably in his office the night he died. That anyone could have taken it from him; although not just anyone. It had to be someone Phil would have let in to his office first.

Conscious of time passing and Tom going back to work soon, I forget about the key. At least, for the time being.

'Did the detectives ask you anything else?' I ask.

Tom nods shakily. 'They wanted an alibi, and I said I was at home with my wife Katie, which she confirmed. They also asked me for a DNA sample and my fingerprints and I . . . I shouldn't have given them to them.'

I stare at Tom, shocked.

'I didn't kill Phil,' he adds quickly. 'It's just that, I lied. I lied to the detectives, Jenny.'

'What do you mean?'

'Yesterday, the police asked me when I saw Phil last and I told them it was years ago – but I lied. I actually saw Phil recently.'

'When?'

'In December. A few weeks before he was killed.'

Air leaves my body. I gasp audibly but try to present it as a cough while Tom grimaces watching me.

'Jenny, that isn't even the worst part.'

'What is?'

'The second time I met with Phil, it was at Hillside. In

his office.' Tom laughs nervously. 'I'm not an idiot. I know there's a chance my DNA could still be there. Then if the police find it, they'll arrest me.'

I want to offer Tom reassuring words but I can't. Lancey and Roberts will absolutely arrest him if there's a DNA match – and I wouldn't blame them because it is suspicious: Tom being in contact with Phil so close to his death. It's even more suspicious, that they'd seen each other twice.

'The second time?' I ask. 'You saw Phil twice in December?'

Tom nods. 'Well, the first time, Phil came by the office to see me. He was Christmas shopping in Cambridge and knew I worked here; I'd told him about it years ago, but anyway, he asked me to swing by Hillside that same weekend because he wanted to talk to me about something. I wish I didn't now, but I agreed.'

I shake my head, perplexed. 'What did Phil want to talk to you about?'

'He wanted my advice. My financial advice, nothing personal.'

'What about?'

'He had a few questions about inheritance tax.'

'What does that mean?'

Tom grimaces yet again. 'It means that in the month before he died, Phil was arranging his will.'

I'm stunned but try to hide it. 'Well, a lot of people write wills. Phil was old, Tom.' I said, shakily. 'He was retiring.'

'A lot of people write wills, Jenny. How many of them turn up dead a few weeks later?'

'So, you think Phil knew that he was going to die?'

Tom shrugs. 'It's a hell of a coincidence, if he didn't. That's all I'm saying.'

It's true, it's a coincidence, and it's not beyond the realm of comprehension to think that Phil knew his life was in danger. Did he know that by making the amends he wanted to, it might be? If he did still have Sally's key, did Phil let his killer into his office that night, knowing that such an outcome was likely?

It's a possibility. One I have to consider, even if it troubles me a great deal.

A gaggle of young women walks past where we're sitting, their loud, excited voices carrying in the wind as they chat happily among themselves. Tom stares after them reflectively and I tense in my seat, uncomfortable at the thought of asking Tom yet more probing questions because I have to make sure he's telling me the truth. I have to make sure I know everything Tom does, before deciding who to go and see next.

'Why did you lie, Tom? Why not just tell Lancey and Roberts about your meeting with Phil in December? Before they asked you to submit your DNA?'

Tom swallows nervously. There's a long, uncomfortable pause.

'Honestly? I panicked. I knew me reconnecting with Phil so close to his death would look suspicious, and I didn't want the police asking more questions. Especially not after the emails.' His cheeks pinken. 'I also borrowed Katie's car to drive down there – I cycle everywhere, trying to go green – and I'm not on her insurance. If I told the police about that meeting, they would have wanted to know everything about it and I didn't want to get her involved, Jenny. She has a lot on her plate with Eve and everything.'

'Eve's your daughter?' I ask.

'Yes.'

I try to look Tom in the eye but this time his eyes flutter down, away from me.

'And the will?' I add. 'Will the police know about that if you don't tell them?'

'Yes,' Tom nods quickly. 'God, of course. Phil's lawyer will have told them by now.'

'What about his money? Who was he leaving it to?'

'Charities, mostly. Mental health ones,' Tom says, and I believe him. It sounds exactly like the kind of thing Phil would do.

Tom reaches out for his empty espresso and puts it to his lips, while I try to process everything he's just told me. Seconds later, Tony returns to the table and pulls out his chair.

'Braxton Hicks – a kind of false labour,' he says in explanation, sitting down. 'Nothing to worry about. So, what did I miss?'

Wordlessly, I stare at Tom, wondering how best to explain it.

3.23 p.m.

We're in the car driving home, having said goodbye to Tom shortly after Tony came back to the table. The roads are busy, which gives me plenty of time to fill Tony in on everything Tom said in his absence.

Further down the road, we reach yet more standstill traffic so I pull up the handbrake and switch off the engine before my knee starts cramping. Tony raps his fingers against his door handle in the absence of the engine's hum.

'So, what you're saying is that Phil . . . knew he was going to die?' Tony asks.

I shrug. 'I think he thought it was a possibility. That Phil knew whoever he was trying to make amends to would react angrily to what he was going to tell them.'

'And you think what Phil was trying to make amends about was something that happened that night?'

'Yes,' I reply, though not convincingly. I can tell Tony isn't too convinced either.

'I don't know, Jenny. I think we need to consider the possibility that Phil was trying to make amends about something else.'

I don't know how to respond. I don't want to appear dismissive of Tony's ideas, like it sounds Lancey and Roberts were. After all, he was helping me out of a mess of my own creation – but with the indicative tone of the emails and my file being stolen, it's ridiculous to think this could be about anything else.

Then again, who? Who would care about the truth of that night enough to kill Phil because of it? Certainly not Olivia's family; most of them are dead and, as I learned right before she died, the rest she was estranged from.

Nick, perhaps? He wouldn't care about Olivia, but he would care about the lies we told that night. How he was punished for them.

The traffic starts moving again and Tony and I drive for a little while without saying much else. We stop at a newsagent in a village we pass through to buy some snacks and coffee and creamer for the unit.

Half a mile later, Tony turns to me and I can sense from his posture that it's important, whatever he has to say.

'Jenny?'

'What?'

'All this amends stuff,' he says, scratching under his chin. 'The emails and everything; it doesn't make me think about Olivia. It makes me think of Alicia Davies.'

I'm surprised. Of all the names I'd expected to come out from Tony's mouth, Alicia's would have been the last.

I don't know why he'd bring her up now. I don't remember anything about Alicia that makes me think she'd be connected to Phil's murder, but Tony must know something. What would Tony know about Alicia I don't? Tony and Alicia were never close, but I guess she and I were; another dead friend of mine.

'What makes you think that, Tone?' I ask, unnerved.

'I saw something once.'

'What?'

'An incident,' he says. 'Between Phil and Alicia's dad.'

Alicia's father. I recall him vaguely but don't remember him having any problems with Phil. In fact, I remember him as an extremely quiet man. I wouldn't have expected him to have problems with anyone.

'What happened?' I ask and Tony nervously clears his throat.

'One day,' he says. 'I was in Phil's office for a session and Alicia's dad came bursting in. He all but forced Sally to buzz him in, she told me afterwards – and he was angry, Jenny. Really angry.' Tony pauses, looking perturbed by the memory. 'So, he started yelling, chucking things around the room and calling Phil a liar and I thought he was going to hit him, until Sally came back with a few more nurses and they all dragged him out.'

'Alicia's dad did that?' I ask incredulous.

Tony nods. 'I know he doesn't look the type but, that day, even I was scared of him.'

The story is unsettling but not one I think is relevant here. Alicia had died years after she left Hillside, it wasn't Phil's fault and it certainly wasn't any of ours. So I can't even begin to think of a reason why Alicia's dad might steal my file, or send those emails.

I think about Alicia, our one and only fight, and I almost smile at how ridiculous it seems now; me, grabbing her leg.

Back then, however, it was everything, and we wouldn't make up until a few weeks later. About hour or so before I killed Olivia.

I shrink in the driver's seat. Thinking about Olivia still hurts and I'm not sure it ever won't. What I did to her wasn't an accident, but before that we were friends and I regret what happened. I regret it very much. Still, I'm not sure how likely a lead Alicia's dad is. It's hard having a kid with a mental health condition, and all that argument with Phil proves is that Mr Davies had, at one time in his life, lost his temper. But, hasn't everyone?

'Did you tell Lancey and Roberts that story?' I ask Tony now. 'About Alicia's dad in Phil's office?'

'No,' he says quietly. 'Until now, I hadn't even remembered it.'

4.15 p.m.

Tony and I arrive outside the storage unit. Together, we get out of the car and walk inside to find Heidi's already here. She's sitting on the dirty patio table, her feet dangling several inches above the ground. As we walk in, she jumps off the table and wipes the butt of her jeans. I'd called her last night and said we'd be here around this time today, though I didn't expect her to actually turn up.

Tony walks past me and wraps his arms around Heidi, the carrier bag from the newsagent spinning around his wrist.

'Jenny said she went to see you,' I hear him say as they break apart, his voice slightly muffled by Heidi's puffer jacket.

She nods briefly and takes the bag from Tony's hand, rifling through it and tossing him the creamer. Tony catches it and Heidi sits back atop the patio table, the plastic bag dangling from her wrist.

'So, how did it go with Tom?' she asks. 'Learn anything new?'

Briefly, Tony and I tell Heidi what Tom had said. That he'd been receiving the emails too; how he'd seen Phil recently, and that Phil had been in the process of writing a will weeks before he died. I also show Heidi the news article I'd pulled from James's briefcase because I was wrong not to earlier and tell her about the police asking questions about Sally's missing key. She takes both developments better than expected.

'I wouldn't worry about the key, Jen,' she says, after a few puffs at her e-cigarette. 'There's probably a fucking thousand of those things in existence.'

'What about Tom? Do you think we should be worried about the police finding his DNA in Phil's office?'

'That's Tom's problem.'

'Heidi,' I say warningly and she sighs.

'Fine. It's all of our problem – but what can we do? The police might find his DNA there. We'll cross that bridge when we come to it.'

I know she's right and that we have to concentrate on what we can do now. Where we go next.

'Why are you here anyway?' I ask her. 'I thought you weren't coming today?'

'I wasn't . . . but I found something interesting. Thought I should share it with the group.' Heidi tucks her e-cigarette back in to her pocket. I stare at her curiously.

'What?'

'We're looking for people with some kind of axe to grind with Phil, right?' she asks. 'Well, I discovered that someone filed a negligence claim against him. Back in 2007.'

The negligence claim. I remember James mentioning it a week or so ago but I hadn't thought of it since. There'd been too much else going on for me to dwell on it.

'I know about the claim,' I say, quickly. 'Kind of. James told me about it before he was pulled from the case.'

'Well, thanks for sharing,' Heidi says sarcastically. 'Anyway, you know who made it.'

I shake my head. 'I don't. James didn't tell me who it was.'

Heidi rolls her eyes. 'I mean that *you know them*, Jenny. You know the person.'

Tony and I exchange nervous looks.

'Who was it?'

'It might be a bit of a dead-end but do either of you remember Alicia Davies's dad by any chance?'

Heidi frowns. Tony gasps and slowly, each hair on the back of my neck begins to stand.

Chapter 12

Before

28 January 2007
8.29 p.m.

I walk into my bedroom. Olivia is here. She's sat cross-legged on her bed and is painting her nails; her head bent in concentration and her tongue peeking out of the corner of her mouth. I watch as she sweeps the head of the nail brush gently across her thumb, thinking about what to say to her.

'Hey, Jen; I thought your mum was visiting?' she says without looking up.

'She's sick,' I reply stiffly, not wanting to be mean to Olivia but not wanting to be nice to her either.

It's been a long day. I had a meeting with Phil this morning and we mostly talked about my new meds and how I'm responding to them. Phil seemed encouraged by my progress and I agreed with him at the time – because, in certain ways, I do feel better. Lighter, than I had previously – and, until today, Olivia had been a big part of that, because I like Olivia. It surprises me how much.

I think I still like her now. I'm just upset because after my meeting with Phil, I tried to find her and Tony and where I found them was in the garden smoking with Heidi.

From Tony, it felt like a betrayal. Olivia was clueless as to what had gone on between Heidi and I before she arrived but Tony saw what she did: he was the one who pulled her off me – but at least Tony abandoned Heidi after the garden. Olivia spent the rest of the day with her and the rest of the evening, until visiting hours.

'Bummer,' Olivia says now, in a good impression of Sally's accent. 'Want me to do your nails?'

'No,' I say quickly. 'I'm fine.'

Olivia raises one of her perfectly shaped eyebrows. 'Come on, Jenny. I'm good, I promise.'

Olivia stares at me and I soon feel myself nodding.

'OK.'

She smiles and pats the mattress of the bed just ahead of her. 'Excellent. Take a seat.'

I follow her instructions, crossing my legs in imitation of hers. Up this close, I can see there's a hole in her nose where a piercing has been removed from it.

'Right, for Jenny I think . . . blue,' she says. 'Midnight blue, I think.'

I nod uncertainly. Olivia reaches into the make-up bag sitting between her legs and produces a different pot of nail varnish from the one she'd just been using. I'm relieved to see the colour is grey rather than the startling blue I'd envisioned.

'You know, I saw you earlier,' she says, grabbing for my right hand and bringing it to her lap.

'Sorry?'

'In the garden. I saw you go back inside.'

I blush. 'Oh, it was too cold—'

'You don't like Heidi,' she says, interrupting me. 'That's fine. You don't have to tell me why, Jenny. That's your business.'

Cautious about how much Heidi may have told Olivia

about me and in lieu of any further conversation, Olivia begins painting my nails and what soon becomes clear is that she knows what she's doing. That, to Olivia, this is more than just a hobby. It's a skill.

'You're really good at this,' I say.

'Thanks,' she replies, without smiling or acknowledging the compliment in any other way.

Olivia paints silently for a while and screws the lid back on the nail polish, blowing across all my fingernails. After that, she sits back, licking the edge of her lips where they'd become cracked and I think I knew the reason. The central heating in Hillside takes a lot of getting used to.

'My aunt, Karen, does this,' she says now, 'paints nails professionally. She's a lot better than I am. She has her own nail place and everything.'

I nod uncertainly because it's the first time I've heard Olivia mention her aunt. It's the first time I've heard her mention any family at all. She's yet to have anyone come to visit her at Hillside and she's been here for almost a week.

That would be fine. Some people don't get visitors – I presume, because they pushed everyone on the outside away – but Olivia's different. Olivia seems like the kind of person who would have a different visitor every evening. The kind of person who would get a lot more visitors than most.

'Oh,' I say, realising I haven't replied for a while. 'Well, you could definitely work there too.'

She shakes her head. 'No, I couldn't. You need training for that kind of thing.'

I nod awkwardly, unsure of how to respond, and Olivia picks up my left hand, lowering it to rest on her thigh. She then begins rolling up the sleeve of my jumper and, alarmed, I try to roll it back down.

'No, don't—'

'It's paint, Jenny,' she says insistently. 'You have to let it dry.'

My sleeves aren't in the way. I don't see why Olivia needs to pull them up and then I realise, Heidi must have told her about my scars. Of course, she did.

I don't protest further. Olivia continues rolling up my sleeve and feels the scar on my left wrist before she sees it. Slowly, she reaches for my other hand and rolls up that sleeve too, turning both my arms over.

It's the first time I've looked at my scars in a while, and they look better. They're healing much faster than I imagined they would. The scar on my left wrist is the messiest of the two; a jagged, diagonal line, but I'm left-handed so I guess that makes sense. My right-hand scar is far neater. In bad light, maybe you wouldn't even see it.

Olivia stares at my scars as well, though her expression is difficult to read. Disappointed. Almost amused – and I motion to pull my sleeves down but Olivia intervenes, wrapping her hand around my left wrist and preventing me from doing so.

'Were you trying to kill yourself?'

I'm startled by the brutal honesty of her question. 'Oh, I—'

'Were you?'

'Yes.'

'Really?'

'Yes.'

Heat pricks at my skin. Olivia smiles and tuts, as if she had just caught me doing something inappropriate.

'Well, you did it wrong.'

'Excuse me?'

Olivia smiles wider, dragging her finger vertically through the scar on my left wrist, miming a crucifix-like cross.

'You cut down instead of across,' she says. 'You could never have killed yourself like that. You'd be lucky to even nick an artery.'

I stare at Olivia and wonder how she knows that. Olivia, who doesn't have a scratch or burn or bald patch on her.

'How do you know that?' I say vocalising my query and initially, she doesn't respond.

Olivia does this sometimes. She'll be her usual, happy self and then she won't be. She'll go quiet and look off into the distance. *The thousand-yard stare*, Tony and I call it.

'It's how my mother killed herself,' she says quietly a few seconds later and I straighten up, horrified.

'I'm sorry . . .'

'Don't be. It was ages ago. She slit her wrists just like you, but she cut down instead of across, so she had more success with it. In fairness, it wasn't her first attempt.'

Olivia laughs. The thousand-yard stare is gone but a sadness remains in her eyes. I guess because some things are hard to have a sense of humour about.

I don't know what to say. Olivia rolls down my sleeves carefully, so they don't snag on the protruding scar tissue.

'OK,' she says. 'All done.'

'Thank you. They're amazing.'

Olivia shrugs and starts fiddling in her make-up bag. Nervously, I clear my throat.

'So, Karen? Is she your mum's sister?'

I know I shouldn't ask. That Olivia hadn't wanted to pry into my business and I shouldn't pry into hers – but she'd seen my scars, and I get the sense sometimes that Olivia wants to talk about something. That she wants to tell me the reason no one's been to visit her yet.

Olivia zips up the make-up bag and nods. 'Yeah. I lived with Karen before I lived here.'

'And, do you think she'll come to visit?'

'No.' she says. 'I don't think she will.'

The thousand-yard stare returns and I feel too nervous to ask Olivia anything else. In equal parts, I find the mystery of Olivia fascinating but also scary.

A few seconds pass and Sally walks into the room, opening the door without knocking. She sees us sitting on Olivia's bed together and doesn't smile or wave as usual. She looks worried. Shaken. Two expressions I've never previously associated with Sally's face – though Olivia doesn't seem to notice.

'Hey, Sal,' she says brightly, like she hadn't just been sad and I envy her that. The ability to switch off her dark feelings, and her natural ease with other people, which is something I've always wanted.

Sally continues to look worried.

'Is everything OK?' I add, and Sally shakes her head.

'Have either of you seen my key to Dr Walton's office?'

'Is it missing?' Olivia asks.

Impatience broadens Sally's face. I think for the first time ever. 'Have you seen it?'

'No,' Olivia replies. 'Sorry, I haven't. Jenny, have you?'

'No, I'm sorry.'

Sally looks distressed and hurries from the room. Olivia and I stare at each other and, quickly, I get off her bed.

Chapter 13

After

28 January 2016
10.12 a.m.

Tony and I are on the way to Bagshot. It's a small village on the other side of Surrey where Alicia's dad lives, according to Heidi.

She'd managed to find his address, alongside a few other things: his first name and also his criminal record, which includes a string of antisocial behaviour charges and a year-long suspended sentence for ABH. None of it sounds like the Alicia's dad I knew but it does match the man Tony had described. The angry man in Phil's office.

I chew anxiously on the remains of my nail varnish; isle-like flakes of midnight blue, left over from Christmas, while Tony sits stony silent beside me. He's been quiet this morning. It could be that, unlike our trip to see Tom, he's just as nervous about this visit as I am, because Tony had seen Alicia's dad – Roger Davies – at his worst. I'm nervous because Alicia was my friend. Another one I'd failed.

She died a few years ago, in the same institution Phil sent her to after Hillside. It was 2012, I remember, because I found out about Alicia's death exactly one week before my wedding to James. The news hit me harder than I expected it to – made me wobble, for the first time in years – although James didn't know what was wrong. I think he assumed it was cold feet and there was no way I could correct him, having already omitted too much.

It was Gina, my first Hillside roommate, who told me. She and Alicia had stayed in touch over the years and Gina just so happened to be living in Ealing at the time of Alicia's death. She recognised my name in the *Gazette* and rang me at work to tell me the news, asking me to meet for a drink that night but I wasn't interested. Back then, I didn't want anything to do with my Hillside past, though I should have known it would catch up with me eventually. The past has a habit of doing that. Just like it had done to Phil.

I think it's possible Roger Davies killed him. I wouldn't have agreed to go visit him if I didn't, even if I struggle to believe his motive as a credible one. Was Phil trying to make amends to Alicia's dad because Alicia had died? Because he failed to save her? And did Roger Davies, in a rage, kill Phil for it? Was he punishing us now with the emails, because we survived instead?

There's only one way to answer such questions and before too long the satnav rattles in its holder, telling me we've arrived. I double-check the house number I scribbled roughly on the back of my hand this morning and unclip my seat-belt. Reluctantly, Tony does the same and we get out of the car.

Mr Davies's house isn't in a good state nor is it in a bad one. The garden looks damp and weed-ridden though not entirely uncared for: newly-paved concrete slabs lead up to the front door and a bucket of salt sits outside it, no doubt to make the slabs less icy. Cautiously, I approach the door and Tony trails behind me, dragging his feet. I knock several times. No one answers.

'I don't think . . .' Tony begins.

'Just wait,' I reply, knocking a little harder.

We wait less than a minute and the door finally groans, creaking open to reveal a frail old man I recognise, if only faintly.

He's wearing a denim shirt underneath a knitted waistcoat and a bow tie, paired with navy corduroys and brown brogues. His hair is startlingly white and his shoes a little shabby, but otherwise he's impeccably dressed.

'Roger Davies?' I ask nervously.

'Yes?'

'My name is Jenny. I used to be friends with your daughter—'

'I know who you are,' he says abruptly. 'What do you want?'

'I was wondering if we could talk to you? Please?'

His eyes wander over to Tony and settle back on me. 'Fine,' he says. 'I suppose you'd better come in.'

He beckons us inside. Tentatively, I step past him and into the house, followed closely by Tony. He shuts the door after us and then turns around, pointing a shaky hand towards the opposite end of the hallway.

'Sit in there. I'll be just a minute.'

Without another word, Mr Davies disappears through a door to our right, leaving Tony and me standing in the hallway. I prefer to think of him as Mr Davies. Roger seems too intimate; certainly, too informal for our visit, given we're here to talk to him about his dead daughter and to accuse him, possibly, of murder. Tony and I catch each other's eye. Then, we move through the door to which Mr Davies had just pointed to.

It's a depressing room. Clean, but only because it's so bare; a capacious and empty space. At the centre of the room sits a matching sofa/armchair set, hunched around a wooden coffee table; the only mess a pile of letters and some old newspapers stacked upon it. A HDTV is attached to the furthest wall, collecting dust and looking thoroughly out of place.

I walk over to the sofa and sit down. Tony sits beside me and Mr Davies returns a few minutes later, carrying a tray with a plate of biscuits, a jug of water and three plastic cups upon it.

'Do you need help with that?' Tony says, standing up.

'No. I can manage.'

Mr Davies places the tray right beside the papers and letters. Next, he leans forward and pours water into each plastic cup.

'Help yourselves,' he says settling in the armchair and eyeing us cautiously.

Tony takes a cup, draining it in pretty much one gulp. Mr Davies waits for him to finish before speaking.

'So, why have you come to see me? What do you want?'

I look to Tony for assistance, but he shrugs and wipes water from his top lip.

'I have a few questions,' I say.

'About Alicia?'

Her name echoes around the room like a ghost. Tony shivers violently beside me.

'And other things,' I add elusively.

'OK, then. Get on with it.'

The old man's abruptness takes me by surprise. Again, Tony says nothing, so I swallow nervously and shuffle towards the end of the sofa.

'Do you remember Phillip Walton, Mr Davies? Did you hear that he died?'

'Of course,' he says. 'Dr Walton was murdered at a mental health facility my daughter attended. Even if she hadn't . . . it's national news. The whole country is talking about it.'

I feel scolded. Foolish, and suddenly unsure of myself and what I'm doing here.

'But the police have been to visit you, haven't they?' I add, undeterred. 'To question you about his murder?'

Mr Davies's eyes roll across me like gentle waves. Slow. Suspicious. 'Yes. They have.'

'And that's because you filed a negligence claim against Phillip Walton in 2007? That's why they wanted to talk to you?'

'How do you—'

'Alicia told me.'

It's a lie though it seems to work. The suspicion knotted between his brow loosens.

'Did she?'

'Yes.'

Mr Davies nods and sips at his water pensively. He doesn't intimidate me as he had done in the beginning and sitting in front of him now, the idea he killed Phil seems even more ludicrous – but he does have a criminal record. And, according to Tony, a temper.

'Mr Davies, did you file the negligence claim against Phillip Walton because he removed Alicia from his care?' I ask and his shoulders drop.

'Yes.'

'Is that also why you argued in his office? Why you had to be escorted out by the Hillside nurses?'

Mr Davies looks stunned and places his water back on the coffee table with an audible sigh.

'Did Alicia tell you that too?'

I nod and to my surprise, he smiles.

'That girl. She never could keep a secret. You have to understand . . .' He looks at me for a prompt, his smile slowly wilting.

'Jenny.'

'He nods again. You have to understand, Jenny, that Alicia was my daughter. Any parent in my position would have done the same. You saw how sick she was, and she wanted to get better but Walton never gave her the chance to do it at Hillside under his care. She just needed time and, apparently, his was too precious.'

I hesitate before speaking next. The Alicia I knew didn't seem to have any interest in getting better – in fact, she never did – but I don't want to contradict Mr Davies's claims. Nor imply I knew his daughter better than he did.

'And, what happened after that?' I ask, carefully. 'Why did you end up dropping the claim?'

He sighs. 'I realised that taking Walton to court wasn't going to change his mind about treating Alicia. Nor would it make her any better.'

Mr Davies's eyes start to water. Uncomfortable, I lower my own and Tony coughs loudly beside me, making me jump.

'I'm really sorry, sir, but could I use your bathroom?'

Mr Davies exhales wearily, his eyes still glistening. 'The room next door.'

Tony nods and walks out. Once he's gone, Mr Davies wipes his eyes and turns to me.

'To save you time, dear, I had nothing to do with Phillip Walton's murder. Neither did you, I'm guessing?'

I shake my head. 'Why would you—'

'The detectives.' He smiles weakly. 'They came to see me a couple of weeks ago and asked me about you. I remembered you briefly from some things Alicia said, but I never thought you would show up at my door.'

My throat tightens. Mr Davies adjusts the collar of his shirt.

'I got confused at first, actually,' he adds. 'I told them you were dead – but, of course, that was the blonde girl.'

'Olivia?' I ask.

'That's her name. Nasty business, all that. Especially what happened with her parents.'

It's a passing remark but one that jars, because Olivia didn't have any parents. Not when I knew her.

'Why? What happened with her parents?' I ask nervously, hoping Mr Davies can shed some light.

He picks up one of the cups and takes a sip of water before doing so.

'The day after the girl – Olivia – died, I saw Walton and her parents in the medical ward at Hillside. I was visiting Alicia at the time – they hadn't moved her yet – and from what I could infer, the couple received a phone call the previous evening saying Olivia was in the medical ward and another call from the police that day, saying she was dead. They were confused, naturally, and also furious.'

My stomach starts to churn because I know what Mr Davies is saying has a chime of truth to it. Olivia was in the medical ward the night before she died. I'd helped put her there.

'And, what did Phil say?' I ask. 'To her . . . parents?'

'At first, he was just trying to calm them down. They seemed strange, this couple. Argumentative. Like they were on drink or drugs or something – and I remember they refused to budge until Walton told them what was going on, so he did. Then, the man started bombarding Walton with questions, though he didn't seem half as upset as the woman. He was saying things like, "*Are you sure it was a suicide? How do you know it wasn't an accident? Why would a beautiful young girl like that kill herself?*" And then . . .'

'And then what?'

'A very weird thing happened. Walton turned to the man and said, "*I think you know why*" – and the man shut up

131

after that. Didn't say another word, while Walton spoke solely to the woman.'

I sit back, I nod slowly, and trying to collect my racing thoughts.

As telling as his story may be, Mr Davies is wrong about a few things. For one: the couple Phil was speaking with couldn't have been Olivia's parents, but I know who they probably were. Phil must have been speaking to Olivia's aunt Karen and Karen's boyfriend, Malcolm – and I know a secret about Malcolm. A big one.

I don't speak for a long time, such is the whirring of my brain.

Eventually, Mr Davies gestures to my wedding ring. 'When did you get married?'

'A while ago,' I reply and he smiles.

'Congratulations. I would have liked to see Alicia get married one day. Her mother would have liked it especially.'

I'd met Alicia's mother a few times. Her dad came and saw her most regularly, but I do remember there were days when he came with a woman who had Alicia's face; a plumper version of it.

'Is Mrs Davies around?' I ask awkwardly and Mr Davies shakes his head. 'She's in a care home,' he says. 'Alzheimer's. Fiona deteriorated rapidly once Alicia passed. She kept wandering off all by herself and trying to find Alicia, you see, because she couldn't understand where she'd gone. There was also the trouble with a few local teenagers. Young punks, they were. They'd tease her and all sorts and, in the end, the home was the best place for her.'

I nod, assuming the 'trouble' Mr Davies refers to is the reason behind his ABH and other charges. He was trying to protect his wife. He was trying to protect his daughter. He didn't kill Phil. There's no way he could have done it.

Now, I think Malcolm did.

My silence returns as I obsess about Malcolm and everything Olivia had ever told me about him. Mr Davies must mistake my further silence for discomfort, as he leans forward and taps the coffee table reassuringly.

'Don't worry, dear. Alicia and her mother had their fun together during those last few months. When we were all home together.'

I'm confused by the statement. Bewildered, because Gina told me Alicia never made it home. That she died in the place she was moved to after Hillside.

'I'm sorry, Mr Davies; when you say Alicia came home . . . do you mean here? To this house?'

'Yes. She was home for quite a few years in the end.'

'So, you're saying Alicia got better? That she gained weight?'

'Yes, but not too much,' he says defensively, and horror – ominous feeling – crashes over me in waves. I look in the direction of the door. Tony still hasn't come back.

'But if Alicia gained weight, if she . . . recovered, then how did she die?'

I regret asking the question as soon as I've asked it. Mr Davies swallows hard.

'Alicia could be a very unhappy girl at times, I'm sure she didn't mean to but—'

'Yes?'

A chain flushes. Mr Davies bows his head.

'She hanged herself, dear. There was nothing I could do . . . when I found her.'

I can't be here. I need to get out, whether or not Tony's with me, and abruptly, I get to my feet.

'I'm sorry, Mr Davies. I can't—'

I reach the doorway just as Tony is returning. Without a

single word, I push past him and run outside, unable to stay there any longer.

1.01 p.m.

It took a few minutes for Tony to join me in the car. He said he had to smooth things over with Mr Davies after my swift exit and started badgering me with questions as soon as we drove away from the kerb. '*Why did you leave? What happened?*' I don't answer him. Instead, I speed dangerously along the M25, as if I can outrun the truth – though I'm not surprised Gina had lied. Embarrassed, possibly, I hadn't realised it sooner because Gina is a compulsive liar. Why would she tell me the truth?

'Pull over, Jenny.'

'No, I—'

Tony rests his hand on the handbrake in a pseudo-threatening manner. 'Pull over. Now.'

Reluctantly, I concede. There's a lay-by a little further up the road so I signal left and pull up on the edge of the carriageway. Tony climbs out first. He bangs on the bonnet of my car, making me jump.

'Out.'

I unclip my seatbelt and walk around the car, away from the oncoming traffic, to meet him.

Tony is leaning against the passenger-side door, and I sit on the silver bollard opposite, trying to stop my legs trembling.

'What the hell happened back there?' He asks.

'Do you know how Alicia died?'

Tony looks surprised by my question but shrugs. 'Starvation, I'm guessing?'

'She killed herself,' I say, almost aggressively. 'She hanged herself.'

'That's what upset you?'

'It didn't upset me. It was just a shock.'

It's a lie and Tony must know it. Hearing that Alicia killed herself did upset me. A lot. I'm not sure why but knowing she completed suicide, even years after the fact, feels dangerous to me. It feels triggering; a stirring of the grey cloud my mind had all but forgotten.

Tony digs his shoe into the ground, mud licking up his trainers.

'Do you think he killed Phil?' he asks. 'Mr Davies?'

'No,' I say. 'I don't.'

'Neither do I.'

'I think Malcolm did.'

Tony looks confused. Concerned.

'Jenny, who's Malcolm?' he asks, and I have no option but to tell him the secret I know.

I hadn't thought about it until Mr Davies told me the story about Phil in the medical ward, and I guess I must have blocked it out. It's not surprising. Over the years, I'd blocked out a lot of things Olivia told me, but she had told me this.

She'd told me the secret about Malcolm and I assumed she hadn't told anyone else at Hillside but I was wrong. Mr Davies's testimony proves for certain she told Phil too, and I know it changes everything – because Phil knowing the secret means there was a way he could try and make amends to Olivia by sharing it with the right person; an apology for all the other ways he failed her. It's a way I thought of making amends myself, once. Back when I still thought of Olivia, in the earlier years after I'd killed her.

Tony listens patiently while I explain what I know and at the end, looks shocked.

'I had no idea,' he says and I scrunch my nose.

'Olivia asked me not to tell anyone.'

He nods. 'So, you think . . .'

'I think that Phil was trying to make amends to Olivia by telling Karen what she told him. I think he was trying to convince Karen to go to the police or, I don't know, leave Malcolm?' I pause, thinking about my file and the swirl of Phil's handwriting. How I had rarely seen him without a pen in his hand. 'That's it.'

Tony looks worried. 'What is?'

'I think Phil wrote Karen a letter, telling him what he knew and that he believed Olivia. I think Malcolm got to it first and, feeling threatened – like when Phil challenged him at Hillside – he wrote Phil back pretending to be Karen, and asked him to meet at Hillside that night.'

It all makes sense, the more I think about it. A letter would explain why there was no unusual calls or emails found on Phil's devices by the police. And, if the meeting was arranged weeks before Phil's death, around the same time Tom said he was arranging his will, there wouldn't be a letter trail for the police to find either.

Tony nods in what seems like agreement. 'It's possible. But why would Malcolm take your file?'

'Maybe he knows Olivia told me too. Maybe Malcolm stole my file to keep me quiet but got more than he bargained for. He got the truth, about how Olivia really died.'

The thought makes me nervous. If Malcolm does know the truth, what might he do with it? Has he thought of a way to turn this all back around on me? Or is it merely leverage; an incentive for us to keep each other's secrets?

Tony stops leaning against the car and straightens up.

'So, what do we do now?'

'We find him.'

'Are you sure you're OK to do that?' he asks. 'I mean, after Alicia . . .'

'I'm fine, Tony,' I snap, and immediately feel bad for doing so.

3.03 p.m.

Tony and I get back in the car and call Heidi. We tell her Alicia's dad was a dead-end, as she'd suspected, and I ask her to find Malcolm. Where he is now, and what he's been doing in the years since I'd last thought of him.

Heidi seems unhappy about this. She insists finding Nick should be our priority but I convince her we should trace Malcolm first because I can't even think about Nick right now. Reluctantly, she agrees, promising to do all she can to find him before moodily hanging up.

I drop Tony off at his house and decide to head home instead of back to the storage unit, because it's been a long day and I'm tired, thoughts of Alicia buzzing through my subconscious like a fly I'm in able to swat.

On the way, I notice a black car driving behind me. It takes every turn and corner I do for a few minutes.

I don't recognise the car. It's sporty with a number plate that's not familiar but it makes me nervous and I speed up, eventually losing it by taking a different route home. Fear lingers in my chest even after the car's gone, and I try to convince myself it wasn't really following me. That I'm just being paranoid; the barriers of my mind made precarious by everything the day had bludgeoned them with; barriers that, normally, keep the grey cloud out.

Finally, I pull up at my house. As I suspected, James isn't here – but the Insignia is. Unfortunately, so are Lancey and Roberts.

Chapter 14

Before

29 January 2007
5.12 a.m.

There's a light on in the hallway. It creeps under our bedroom door, alongside the sound of footsteps. I look to Olivia's bed but she's still sleeping soundly, so I try to ignore the light and fall back asleep. Nonetheless, curiosity soon overcomes my caution and I get out of bed and open the door.

Margaret is standing a few metres along the corridor, talking to someone on her mobile phone. She spots me and immediately hangs up, shaking the phone in my direction.

'Wake up your roommate. You both need to go to the canteen.'

I squint, my eyes still adjusting to the brightness of the hallway light. 'But w—'

'No questions. To the canteen.'

Margaret pushes past me and into the bedroom. I hear the flick of a light switch and Olivia's vocal protests and quickly follow Margaret inside.

Olivia is now awake and sitting up in her bed, her cheeks reddened slightly.

'Do you know what time it is?' she asks sleepily.

'We have to go,' I say to her before Margaret can start again. 'Just get ready?'

Olivia nods and we both put our shoes on, leave the room and head to the canteen. Margaret stays behind and it's clear from the sound of rustling that she's searching through our belongings. I'd heard the nurses had done the same with Heidi's after I left the room the day I got her sent to quarantine, though I can't imagine what they'd be looking for now.

Olivia yawns and rolls her shoulders. 'Sally's key. I guess she didn't find it.'

I feel silly for not thinking of it myself. Of course, they were trying to find Sally's key; the one she was looking for last night.

Olivia grabs my right hand and we walk through the other corridors which are still darkened, her hand noticeably warmer than my own. I go to bite the nails on my other hand but Olivia slaps it down.

'No,' she says. 'I just painted those.'

I laugh. She laughs, and together we reach the canteen. It's soon obvious we aren't the only ones who've been woken early.

All six of us are here. All Phil's current patients. Heidi, Tom and Tony sit at one of the tables, Heidi and Tony in their pyjamas like Olivia and me, while Tom is wearing jeans and a jumper.

Nick is sitting by himself at a table on the other side of the canteen, and he's clearly asleep, his head slumped against the table, and his arms slack against the bench he's sitting on. I haven't seen him for a few weeks. Not since he gave me the vodka bottle.

Olivia walks forward and sits down on the bench next to Tony. Nervously, I follow her and sit next to Tom. Heidi is on his other side while the bench right in front of me sits empty.

'What's going on?' Olivia says to no one in particular. 'Is this about Sally's key?'

'We have no idea,' Heidi replies grumpily. 'Sally threw me out of my room this morning before I had the chance to ask her.'

'Ryan came and got Tony and I,' Tom adds. 'He wouldn't say why either but Sally told me she was looking for her key yesterday. She said she hung it on her peg in the buzz room to use the toilet and that when she got back, it was gone.'

It takes me a few minutes to place Ryan before I remember he's the new nurse. I'd seen him on duty a couple of times.

'It has to be the key then,' Olivia says, stifling a yawn, 'which isn't fair. Anyone could have taken it. It doesn't necessarily have to be one of Phil's patients.'

There's a murmur of agreement from everyone at the table.

A few seconds later, there's a loud screeching noise and we all turn around to see Nick slowly rising from the bench.

He walks towards us and sits on the other side of Olivia, opposite me. It's the only vacant seat at the table but I know that isn't why he sat there.

I watch Nick observing Olivia, his eyes sliding to her chest because her pyjama top is slightly see-through. He isn't doing anything wrong necessarily so there's nothing to warn Olivia about. I want to warn her all the same and I think about doing so. Then, Nick kicks me under the table.

I think it must be an accident until I feel him do it again; the toes of his trainers banging into my shin once, twice, and two more times after. I don't know what to do. Nick smiles while the others talk, oblivious to what's happening.

He kicks me a few more times but I don't say anything. I don't think it hurts enough for me to mention.

Chapter 15

After

28 January 2016
5.12 p.m.

I let Lancey and Roberts into the house. It's the only thing I can do. I don't know where James is but I bet they have a pretty good idea. I think they knew he would be busy this evening, and thought it the perfect time for a second visit.

It seems cowardly but I don't tell them that. I lead the detectives to the kitchen where, crossing over to the sink, I turn round to face them.

Roberts pulls out one of the dining chairs without invitation and lowers himself into it. Lancey stays standing, leaning his back against the doorframe with a suspicious expression I hadn't seen on his face last time – and I wonder what prompted it. What the detectives know now that they didn't before.

Roberts clears phlegm from his throat, wiping his nose between pinched fingers.

'How are you, Mrs Nilson?'

The question isn't one I'm expecting and I curl my fingers into the palm of my hand.

'It's Jenny, and I'm fine. What do you want?'

'We have a few more questions, and we were in the area. Thought we may as well pop in.'

He says it calmly, like a lion circling its prey, and I look towards Lancey, who shifts guiltily against the door jamb. *They must know something* I think to myself. *Something I hadn't heard already.*

I'm in no mood for an interrogation. The visit to Alicia's dad, hearing of her suicide and my paranoia about being followed home have left me rattled, but I know Lancey and Roberts aren't going anywhere so they may as well get on with it and ask whatever questions they want.

'OK,' I say now, slowly crossing my arms. 'What do you want to know?'

They exchange glances. A few seconds later, Lancey straightens up.

'Do you know who Nick Crewe is, Jenny?'

I feel both of them scanning my face for a reaction. 'Yes.'

'Who is he?'

'He was a patient at Hillside when I was there, but I didn't see him a lot. He was kept in an isolated unit. I never even spoke to him.'

It's a bold lie. I definitely spoke to Nick at Hillside, more times than I'd have liked, but I know I need to close down such questions because talking about Nick is dangerous territory. It's part of the reason I keep knocking Heidi back when she insists we should concentrate on finding him.

Lancey's eyes turn steely and I can tell he's my enemy too, just as much as Roberts. 'Well, Nick Crewe thinks he knows you. Quite well, actually.'

'That's because he's insane.'

'Aren't we all?' Roberts adds conspiratorially, and I know what he really means. Not '*we*' as in '*he and I*', but '*we*' as in '*me and the crazy people. The former inpatients of Hillside*'. 'Nick Crewe had quite a lot to say about you.'

'Like what?' I ignore Roberts and stare directly at Lancey, knowing Nick's word can't be something the police would take seriously without any supporting evidence. Nick is a convicted felon. Not to mention, a former Hillside patient.

'We'll get to that,' Lancey replies, 'but we need to ask you a few more questions.'

'About?'

'About the key and lanyard lost by Hillside nurse Sally Edwards in 2007. We showed you a replica of it last time.'

The key again. Somehow, it keeps coming up.

'I don't know what happened to Sally's key.' I say shortly. 'I told you that last time.'

Lancey and Roberts exchange further glances and I feel like screaming in derision. 'Jenny, Sally Edwards told us you stole it from her. Back in 2007.'

His words hit me like whiplash, I lean back, trying to digest the information.

I don't know why Sally would tell the police I stole the key from her. It's not true, for one. I didn't steal Sally's key – not at first – and she certainly can't think I have the key now. She didn't even know I had it for the brief time I actually did.

The timing of the police asking me about the key also seems suspect. They interviewed Sally weeks ago, yet they didn't tell me this last time, when James was still present.

'Did you take it from her back then?' Lancey asks.

'No. I didn't.'

'So, you're saying Sally Edwards is lying?'

'Yes. Or, she's mistaken.'

Lancey pauses. Then, looking uncomfortable, clears his

throat. 'But if Sally Edwards is lying, Jenny, if she's mistaken; why did Nick Crewe tell us the very same thing?'

I'm dumbfounded into silence.

'There has to be a reason, doesn't there?' Lancey adds. 'A reason why Nick Crewe and Sally Edwards both believe you stole her key to Phillip Walton's office back in 2007? A reason why your Hillside file was taken from the same office on the night Phillip Walton died?'

I can feel Lancey turning up the pressure. Trying to get me to crack, as Roberts has done from the beginning.

'No,' I reply, determined to prevent that from happening. 'Nick and Sally are lying.'

'Are they, Jenny? Or are you?'

I shake my head and clutch the sink behind me so hard, my fingers start aching.

It's frustrating, knowing Lancey and Roberts are spending all this time pursuing me with Phil's killer still out there, and I briefly consider telling them about Malcolm – but, no. I need to find out more about Malcolm myself first.

'This is crazy,' I say finally. 'I haven't seen that key in nine years.'

Roberts coughs pointedly. 'Speaking of crazy: would you like to tell us why you stopped picking up your prescription for quite a number of antidepressants three months ago?'

'Paul,' I hear Lancey say warningly and my fingers slide off the sink altogether.

'To help us with our enquiries, we pulled your medical records,' Lancey says, his voice softer than it had been.

'You're not allowed to do that . . .'

'I think you'll find we are,' Roberts says and I know he's probably right because my Hillside file went missing from the crime scene. They'd have wanted to know, and it would be within their rights, to find out as much as they could about its contents.

'Would you like to answer the question, Jenny?' He adds. 'Have you stopped taking your medication, or are your medical records lying as well?'

My blood runs cold. But of course. Of course, the detectives would try to use this against me. 'No comment.'

The atmosphere in the room changes.

Roberts claps his hands together. 'Right. I think that's enough for us all to take a little trip down to the station together.'

'No, that's—'

I stop talking when I hear keys rattle in the door. Alarm registers on Lancey's face and I can tell that, like me, they're surprised. They weren't expecting James to come home so soon.

I hear the front door open and we're all silent as the sound of footsteps fill the hallway. Roberts stands from his chair and Lancey turns around. Seconds later, James walks into the kitchen.

His expression is cautious if unsurprised when he enters; Roberts and Lancey's appearance no doubt confirming what he must have thought when he drove up and saw the Insignia parked outside. I'm confused to see he's wearing a suit jacket and also a tie, which he only wears to work on rare occasions; and he doesn't say anything. Not yet.

Lancey steps aside to let him through and James walks further into the kitchen, tossing his keys on to the worktop right beside me. They land with the pissed-off thunk of metal hitting wood.

'Chief know you're here?' His voice is quiet. Almost a whisper, but there's a shake and fury to it that's undeniable.

'He does,' Roberts says, and I can tell from James's expression he's surprised.

'So, it was just me you neglected to tell.'

Lancey looks remorseful. Roberts doesn't. He swaggers forward, significantly reducing the space between himself and James. Lancey eyes them both warily.

'We don't have to run anything past you, mate. We're just trying to do our job.'

James laughs. 'Your job? To come to my house and harass my wife?'

'It's our job to talk to the suspects of this inquiry. It's your choice who you marry.'

'That's enough, Paul,' Lancey says, reaching for Roberts' shoulder but Roberts pulls it from his grasp.

James's face hardens. 'She isn't speaking to you again,' he says. 'Not without a lawyer. Get out of my house.'

Roberts looks like he's going to say something else but Lancey grips him by the shoulder yet again.

'We're going,' Lancey says, his eyes falling back on me. 'We'll be in touch.'

Roberts pushes Lancey's hand off him and storms out of the kitchen. Lancey looks at James apologetically but follows Roberts from the room. The front door slams a couple of seconds later.

'That cunt.'

'James.'

I shake my head and James pulls me into a hug. One he abruptly ends.

'Those bastards. They knew I wouldn't be here and what Paul said . . . I'm going to make a complaint,' he says, still holding my shoulders. 'He shouldn't have said that.'

'Don't.' I say, trying to calm him. 'I've heard worse.' I gesture to his suit jacket. 'Were you in court?'

'No. I had a meeting.'

James doesn't say more than that but I can tell by his

tone exactly what the meeting was about. He releases my shoulders, stepping back from me.

'And?'

'I'm not being fired,' he says, sinking into one of the dining chairs. 'Not even suspended. A bit more desk duty, but I'm allowed to work on other cases. The chief knows I was completely unaware you were Walton's patient when I took the case. He believes I was just as blindsided as the rest of them.'

It's a relief to hear, if a bit awkward. I never wanted James to have to suffer for my mistakes, and I feel bad about the many problems my past has already caused him; each one a knife to my gut.

I sit down beside him. 'James, I'm sorry.'

He sighs. 'If you were really sorry, Jenny, you'd tell me the truth.'

I'm shaken. I've just survived one interrogation and I wasn't expecting another. I don't think I can handle it.

'I told you the truth,' I say stiffly. 'I don't know anything.'

'No, you're hiding something.'

'I'm not,' I repeat, but this time even I don't believe it.

James stands up and walks away from me, disgusted. Like he can't bear to sit beside me for one more second.

'I know you took the article from my briefcase, Jen. The one about Olivia Brennan's death.'

'I didn't.'

'Please, don't lie. You're the only other person who knows the code.'

I mouth words, unsure of how to reply because James is so close to the truth now. A truth that would push him away from me for ever.

James puts his fingers to the back of his head. 'Olivia

Brennan,' he says, gentler this time. 'Does she have anything to do with this?'

Weakly, I shake my head. 'Olivia killed herself. That's it. There's nothing else to know.'

'Then why did you take the article?'

'Because I didn't want you to have it.' It's an honest answer. One that trips off my tongue before I can stop it.

James's eyes widen. 'What does that mean? Why not?'

As much as I want to, I can't tell him. There's no way he would forgive me if I did.

Chapter 16

Before

29 January 2007
5.38 p.m.

I'm sitting in the lounge with Tom, trying to play a game of Scrabble. Heidi, Tony and Olivia are outside smoking but I wanted to stay inside and Tom agreed to stay with me. We've already gone through all the crossword puzzles we could find, having been here a while.

It started this morning. The early wake-up call. The canteen. Nick, kicking me under the table. Sally and Ryan arrived shortly after that and took us all down to Phil's office, where he was waiting with questions.

Each of us denied stealing Sally's key. All six of us. Heidi, Tony, Tom, Nick, Olivia and me. Phil looked disappointed; warned us that if we were lying, we'd be found out and the consequences would be severe. Still no one spoke up, so they questioned the rest of the Hillside patients. They all denied stealing it too.

We've been on this lockdown of sorts ever since. More nurses were called at midday and every room in the building searched, though it seems they haven't found Sally's key yet. They hadn't found Heidi's secret lighters either, so I don't put much faith in their searching skills.

My eyes dart towards Nick who's sitting in the corner, suspiciously quiet for once. Tom sighs and picks up a letter tile, tossing it lazily into the centre of our already constructed words.

'Should we stop?' he asks. 'I'm sick of this now.'

'Me too.'

I stop looking at Nick and focus my attention back on Tom, whose own eyes are now wandering. They settle on a group of addicts in the corner. I can tell they're addicts because they're the quietest, twitchiest group in the room.

Tom nods towards them. 'You'd think that Alicia would have been brought down here too. They've obviously emptied the rest of the medical ward.'

'Mmm,' I say, dumping my own letter tiles on to the board between us.

I hadn't seen Alicia since our fight last week. She isn't Phil's patient any more but she is still in Hillside, her only treatment being the food they're forcing inside her.

'It's not fair how they're keeping her,' Tom adds. 'Tied down like that.'

Feeling awkward, I pretend not to hear him.

I feel bad about what I did: grabbing Alicia's leg and storming out straight afterwards. Maybe I should go to the medical ward and apologise or maybe I shouldn't. I was just trying to help Alicia get better, and the nurses tying her down – although Tom disagrees with it – they're just trying to help too.

I continue to ponder my Alicia dilemma as Heidi, Olivia and Tony re-enter the lounge. I look towards Nick again and see that he's watching Olivia, as he had done this morning.

Tony waves to me. Seconds later, Sally appears behind him and taps his shoulder, signalling for him and the others to take the nearest seats.

Sally then takes a deep breath and addresses the room. 'You can all leave. Go straight back to your rooms until visiting hours start.'

Tony sticks his hand in the air. 'Did you find it, Sally? Your key?'

'No,' she says quietly. 'We didn't.'

Tom and I exchange nervous glances. Heidi leaves the room first and she's followed by the other patients and Nick, who won't look in Olivia's direction now Sally's here.

Tom and I clear away our Scrabble game while Tony and Sally talk about something. Olivia is standing right outside the lounge door. Presumably, waiting for me.

Eventually, Tony pats Sally's shoulder and leaves. Tom and I follow him but when I go to walk past Sally, I feel her hand pulling me back.

'Jenny. Can I speak to you for a minute?'

I turn to Sally, who looks fraught, her eyes tired and ringed in red. Sally looks over my shoulder towards the others.

'Go on. Jenny will be there soon.'

Olivia, Tom and Tony wander up the corridor, leaving Sally and me alone. I stare at her nervously, wondering what this is about and worrying if Heidi has finally found a way to get me in trouble.

'How are you?' I ask.

'Oh,' she replies. 'I've had better days.'

Sally's bottom lip trembles and I feel a sympathetic rush towards her. Someone stole her key. Sally's the victim in all this, but she'll be blamed, I'm sure, if they don't find it, and they've already searched all day.

Sally must be thinking the same as she stares past my shoulder, looking disorientated. She doesn't even mention what she said she wants to talk about.

I clear my throat. 'Did you want something, Sally?'

She nods, her eyes once again focused on me. 'Yes. Your mother's sick again. She won't be able to visit tonight but she sends her love.'

I can't help but be disappointed. Frustrated, in a way, because I miss Mum and, selfishly, the comfort she provides. Conversely, I'm also relieved that what Sally wanted isn't anything worse.

'Right,' I say. 'Is that all?'

'No. Dr Walton wants to see you in his office tomorrow afternoon.'

'Alone?'

'Yes,' Sally replies and I feel a pounding at my ribcage. My heart beating harder inside it.

'Is this about your key? Because I swear—'

'Jenny, no. It's not about that.' Sally smiles but it doesn't reach her eyes. She grabs for my hand and squeezes it in a reassuring fashion, which does nothing to suppress my concerns.

'Sally, am I in trouble?'

'No,' she says, but I get the sense she's lying. Or, not quite telling me the truth.

6.56 p.m.

I don't get much more out of Sally. She tells me my meeting with Phil will be at three o'clock tomorrow afternoon and that I should be in the buzz room five minutes beforehand, where one of the nurses will meet me to escort me down to the basement. She won't tell me what the meeting is about. I'm left to worry about that as I walk back to my bedroom.

I run through multiple scenarios and hypotheses in my

153

head. Was Sally bluffing? Is the meeting about her missing key, after all? Does Phil want to talk about something else? Alicia? Had she told them what I'd done to her? How I had grabbed her leg? Or, had someone found the dirty magazine page in the medical ward bin and traced it back to me? As I walk, I also notice a pain in my shin. A dull ache from where Nick had kicked it hours ago.

I get back to my room and Olivia is already there. Yet again, she has no visitors and for the second day running, neither do I. She's looking in the mirror but she doesn't seem embarrassed when I walk in. She continues to stare at herself and starts playing with her hair, looking at her reflection with great interest. I suppose I would too, if it were mine.

I sit on my bed. Olivia stares at me through the mirror.

'What did Sally want?'

'I have a meeting with Phil tomorrow afternoon.'

She turns her head to face me in person. 'Why?'

'She wouldn't say.'

'Her key?'

'Apparently not,' I reply, hoping Olivia won't pick up on my inner worry and she doesn't seem to.

She turns back to the mirror, looking at herself once more.

'I never noticed him before,' she says quietly.

'Who?'

'Nick,' she says, staring at me through the mirror yet again. 'How long has he been here?'

'A while. He's kept separately . . .'

'Is he?'

'He's meant to be.'

'Well,' Olivia says, 'he was pretty close to me this morning.'

I recall this morning. Vivid images of Nick looking at

154

Olivia and smiling to himself while giving my shins a bashing.

Olivia walks over to the windowsill and sits on it.

'Jenny, can I ask you something?'

'Erm, sure.'

'Nick . . .' For the first time since we'd met, her voice falters. 'He's a creep, isn't he?'

'What do you mean?'

'Does he . . . touch you? Do things he shouldn't?'

I freeze, feeling annoyed at Olivia for asking me the question.

Yes, Nick does things he shouldn't. Spits gum out on the carpet. Sneaks in contraband items. Steals food from the canteen and games from the lounge. Touches me, without asking. He's never hurt me though, not really, so to tell Olivia about him touching my thigh a few weeks ago when he gave me the vodka seems silly. To tell her about how he kicked me this morning seems even more absurd. Olivia and I patients in a psychiatric hospital. It's a good thing, we're not the worst ones in it.

'No,' I say. 'Of course not.'

Olivia looks relieved. I don't expect her to believe me so easily and I feel bad for lying.

'Good. That's good. It's just . . .'

'What?'

'Nick reminds me of someone. Someone unpleasant.'

Olivia's thousand-yard stare returns. The vacant, if slightly haunted expression – and I consider asking who Nick reminds her of though swiftly, I think better of it. If Olivia wanted to tell me, she would have done already and just like why her aunt won't visit her, it's clear she doesn't want to talk about it.

Still on the windowsill, Olivia reaches out for the teddy

Heidi left behind and clutches it to her chest. It feels like a private moment and I'd look away if Olivia weren't staring straight at me, her blue eyes wavering.

'Jenny?'

'Yes?'

'You're sure Nick's never done anything to you?' she asks. 'That you're not scared of him?'

'I'm sure,' I reply, because if Olivia worries about Nick, I'll have to worry too – and I don't want to do that.

In between the times I have to see Nick, I'd rather just forget all about him.

Chapter 17

After

29 January 2016
12.21 p.m.

I'm in the storage unit. Tony can't make it. He told me he was ill via text after ignoring several of my phone calls, so it's just me alone. A fate I seem to be getting used to.

James left the house after our fight last night. He told me he was sleeping at his parents' and stormed out. I don't blame him. He knows I'm lying. He just wants to know why I won't tell him the truth – but whatever his suspicions, I know the truth is worse. That's why I can't tell him.

I shiver violently. It's cold in the unit. Normally, I would drag out the portable heater but since it's only me here I don't feel the need. I sit on the patio table, swinging my legs back and forth; waiting for Heidi to ring.

A lot of bad things happened yesterday but all I could think about after James left was the story Alicia's dad told me. The one about Phil and Olivia's parents, as he called them. It's proof, I'm certain, that Malcolm is behind what's happening. Phil's murder. The emails. My file being stolen.

Briefly, I think about yesterday's other events. Lancey and Roberts questioning my prescription. Sally and Nick corroborating each other's claim I'd stolen Sally's key nine years ago and that I still have it today. All that can wait. I need to know about Malcolm. I need to know where he is. I need to talk to him.

The door of the unit creaks. It starts to open and my heart lurches – but it's only Heidi, once again showing up unannounced.

She has a tote bag wedged under her arm, the kind you might pick up in a supermarket, and is wearing her red puffer jacket and black lipstick. It seems a lot, considering what's going on at the moment.

The door closes behind her and I rub at my chest. 'You scared me.'

'Did I?'

She smiles but it's no laughing matter. 'Yes. How did you know I was here?'

'Intuition,' she says, her eyes darting around the unit. 'Where's Tony? Isn't he the Watson to your Holmes?'

'He's ill.'

Heidi's brow knits furtively and it's not hard to see why. Tony has always been more sensitive than the rest of us. He'd been OK so far but I know it's probably not good for him: all this digging up of the past. I don't think it's all too good for me either.

'What do you want, Heidi?' I say grouchily. 'Why are you here?'

'I need to tell you something. A few things, actually.'

I sigh and make to jump off the table just as my phone buzzes in my back pocket. A soft pinging sounds from Heidi's jacket a second later, and we stare at each other, alarmed.

Sliding off the table, I draw out my phone and see it's another *urgent* email. The first we've received in a while.

Stay low. Almost over.

I look at Heidi. She's checking her own phone and looks shaken, so it's clear she got the email too.

It doesn't make sense. The other emails suggested that if we followed their instructions, nothing would ever begin. But *Almost over* suggests an ending of sorts. A final conclusion to whatever is going on – and it rattles me. I can't pretend otherwise. If it was Malcolm who killed Phil and sent the emails, how does he plan to end this?

Phone still in hand, I call Tony to check on him but he doesn't answer. Meanwhile, Heidi paces the floor of the unit, chewing at her nails. It's unusual to see her this out of sorts. It makes everything feel worse somehow.

Eventually, Heidi stops pacing. Her left foot, however, jiggles continuously against the ground.

'Can we get out of here?' she says. 'Go for a drink?'

'A drink with you?'

A wry smile crosses her face. 'A drink with me is the least of your worries right now.'

And I can do nothing, only agree with her.

1.55 p.m.

I take Heidi to the Pig's Head. She goes to the toilet and I order two pints, making it back to our table first. The pub is empty besides us and a suited man. He's a few tables down, speaking hurriedly into his phone with a posture that tells me he's not where he's supposed to be. You notice these things when you have it too: a guilty conscience.

It's much warmer in here than it was in the unit and I take off my hoodie. Underneath, I wear only the T-shirt I slept in last night, leaving my wrists exposed. With Heidi still in the bathroom, I look at my scars for the first time in a while.

They're still there. Still noticeable. Faded and purple in my skin. Faithfully sewn. Vertical wounds that have never quite healed; the one on my left wrist dragged downwards like a frown, the far more obvious of the two.

'What a dump.'

Heidi climbs on to the stool opposite mine, untangling the straps of her tote bag and lowering the red jacket from her shoulders.

She nods at the full pint in front of her. 'That for me?'

'Yes.'

'Take it,' she says, pushing it across the table with a sigh. 'I'll be right back.'

Heidi gets up and walks to the bar, returning a minute later with what appears to be a glass of Coke, though I smell the booze wafting from it as soon as she sits down. She picks up the drink and takes a generous sip, her black lipstick smearing the glass.

I take a sip of my own pint and place it cautiously back on the table.

'So, what did you want to tell me?' I ask.

'Malcolm,' she says. 'I found him.'

'You did?' My stomach twists.

'It was hardly a challenge. Fucking Facebook.'

'Where is he?'

Heidi slides her phone towards me. I pick it up and see a screenshot of yet another newspaper article. This one from the *Brisbane Journal*.

The headline is 'Nailed It'. The picture, a middle-aged couple smiling and holding two glasses of champagne outside a store called 'Karen's Nails'. Fretful, I zoom in on the picture until I can read the caption below it: *Karen (left) and Malcolm Burgess (right) celebrate their first successful year of business, May 2011.*

My stomach, once twisted, falls.

'It wasn't him, Jenny,' Heidi says. 'Malcolm didn't kill Phil.'

'But he could have—'

'He didn't. He and Karen emigrated to Australia in 2009. They've been there ever since. They haven't been back to visit, either.'

That I could have been wrong about Malcolm seems impossible because I had been so sure, but it wasn't him. As Heidi's information and the *Brisbane Journal* article proves, it couldn't have been.

I stare at the picture anyway, and it surprises me how much Karen looks like Olivia. She's in her late forties in this photo – so, older than Olivia will ever be – but underneath the peroxide-blonde highlights and aggressive tan, I see her: the girl who by my actions is dead.

My eyes find Malcolm next. He looks different than I'd always imagined him; thinning hair and a reddish nose, which tells me he hadn't yet acclimatised to the Brisbane weather. A slightly rounded stomach. I see also as my eyes fall down him. He's just a man, and not the monster I envisioned. The one whom Olivia had described.

Heidi wrenches the phone from my hands, her eyes scanning my face.

'Why did you want me to look into Malcolm, Jenny?' I can't think of a reply right away so sip at my drink instead.

Though I told Tony the truth about Malcolm, I'd been more elusive on the phone to Heidi yesterday. I had my reasons. Firstly, because I told Olivia I wouldn't tell anyone and I'd already told one person by the time I gave Heidi a call. Secondly, because while I've always trusted Tony, trusting Heidi is something I'm still working on, despite her keeping my biggest secret for many years.

'It doesn't matter,' I say finally.

'It matters to me,' she replies, the apprehension in her eyes turning aggressive. 'I want to know what made you think he could have killed Phil?'

'I can't tell you. I'm sorry.'

There's an awkward pause. Heidi drains the rest of her glass and I hear the ice rattle against her teeth. I take a few more sips of beer and before I know it, have finished the pint. James used to work as a bartender and told me once that beer is the ultimate palate cleanser. He was right. Bad tastes, as well as my memories of Malcolm and everything Olivia had told me about him, seem to wash down a little easier with the amber liquid.

Heidi drops her glass to the table and pushes it to one side while I take a generous sip of the pint she hadn't wanted. That fourth email was a lot to take in. I doubt Heidi will judge me for it.

'So, what else did you want to tell me?' I ask. 'You said there were a few things?'

'I don't think I should tell you anything now . . .'

'Heidi, this isn't a game.'

'I never said it was,' she says tetchily, though her temper quickly falls. 'The second thing I need to tell you is about Nick.'

'I don't want to talk about Nick . . .' I begin but Heidi cuts me off.

'Tough shit. We're going to.'

'You found him?'

I take another sip of beer.

'I did. He's living just outside Sutton now. Some trashy estate, in a flat he doesn't pay for, not that it would surprise anyone. Anyway, that isn't what I need to tell you.'

Heidi reaches inside her bag and produces a piece of paper. She passes it to me and I soon see it's a bank statement. With the alcohol starting to take effect, the numbers spiral on the page.

'What . . .'

'It's Nick's most recent bank statement.' Heidi says. 'Don't ask me what I got it from. I'm good at finding things. Let's just leave it at that.'

I stare at her, aghast. It's completely illegal for Heidi to have this without Nick's permission and I know our investigation has changed as a result. We'd get into trouble now, if anyone were to find out about it – and I can't help but feel angry at her for taking such a risk without consulting me first.

Heidi doesn't seem too concerned. She picks up her empty glass and swirls the ice around it, water now pooling at its bottom.

'You shouldn't have done that, Heidi.'

'Well I did. Now, do you want to know the interesting part?'

'What interesting part?'

'The petrol garage next to Hillside,' she says. 'Do you know it?'

'Yes. I bought flowers for Phil from there. After he died.'

Heidi squints suspiciously. 'Nick bought something there too. Guess what day?'

'The day Phil died?'

She nods and my legs start to tremble. 'So, this is evidence Nick was right next to Hillside on the day Phil was killed?'

'It is.'

I look at the bank statement again and see Heidi's telling the truth. According to this, Nick made a purchase at the petrol garage next to Hillside on the same day Phil was murdered. He was definitely in the immediate area that day, and my thoughts turn to Lancey and Roberts. How insane it is that, even after this, I'm still their number one suspect.

'How do the police not know about this?' I ask Heidi now and she shrugs.

'The police aren't looking at Nick, Jenny. They're only interested in you.'

'So you think it's Nick? You think Nick killed Phil? That he's sending the emails?'

Heidi nods again. 'There's no way it can be a coincidence. Nick has motive to want to see Phil and the rest of us punished. We're the reason he was thrown out of Hillside, remember?'

'We are,' I say, slowly, 'but Nick doesn't know that.'

Heidi shrugs. 'He knows it now.'

I take another sip and contemplate whether Heidi could be right. Did Phil feel bad for lying about Nick that night? Is Nick the Hillside patient Phil was trying to make amends to? Does Nick now know fully what we did to him? Is all of this, what's happening, his response?

The thought of seeing Nick again makes me feel sick and light-headed, and shakily, I lower my pint to the table.

'It doesn't matter,' I say. 'I'm not going to see him.'

'Jenny, you don't have a choice. You read the email. *Almost over*. If it is Nick doing this, he obviously has a plan and whatever it is, you can bet we won't like it.'

Heidi eyeballs me murderously. I can't help but see the funny side.

'Is that why you asked me to have a drink with you? So, I would get drunk and agree to visit Nick?'

Heidi shakes her head. 'No. The getting drunk is for my benefit.'

'Why?'

She doesn't answer. She leaves her seat and returns a few minutes later with a tray carrying two more drinks for her, another pint for me, and four shots of a clear spirit which she places squarely at the centre of our table.

'I ordered some food too,' she says. 'It's coming in a bit. You're paying for it.'

'OK,' I say, draining my second pint and grabbing for my third.

Heidi picks up one of her drinks.

'Heidi, about Nick . . .'

'Not now,' she says. 'For a few minutes, let's just talk about something else.'

I nod and we fall into a reasonably comfortable silence. The man at the corner table wanders out of the seating area to go and sit at the bar. I watch him for a bit while Heidi drains her glass.

'Do you remember the five words?' she asks.

I look at her. 'The ones Phil asked us to come up with?'

Heidi nods, laughing under her breath. 'That was so fucking dumb. Five words. As if five words could explain the nuances of a person. A sick person, at that.'

She reaches for her second new drink, though it takes her a few attempts to get it in hand.

'Did you do it?' she adds.

'Do what?'

'Come up with them?'

'Yes,' I say.

She smiles. 'What were they?'

'I don't remember.'

'That's a lie,' she says challengingly, and she's right: it is.

'Fine. *I'm alive but not really.* Those were my words.' I take another sip of beer, feeling embarrassed. Exposed.

Heidi narrows her eyes. '*I like to feel pain*,' she says. 'They were mine.'

I think of Heidi's burns and remember my reaction to first seeing them. My shock. I had my own scars then of course, but pain itself had never been the purpose of them. The pain was merely a vehicle for me getting out of my life. For Heidi, pain was the destination, and I've never quite understood it.

'Is that true?' I ask. 'Do you?'

'No,' she says, 'and Phil knew I didn't.'

Heidi picks up the four tequila shots on the tray and pushes two of them towards me. She looks surprised when I don't protest and instead take one, splashing a little over my fingers; the alcohol stinging cracked callouses in my hand, caused by the cold weather.

We clink and down the first and I shudder. Downing the second, I shudder less.

'Can I ask you a question?' My words come out slurred. Like my brain is sending the instructions but someone else is operating my mouth.

Heidi laughs. 'Now's a better time than any other.'

'Did you know that Alicia killed herself?'

Slowly, her smile drops. 'Yes.' Her bleary eyes flicker, curious. 'Why? What did you think happened to her?'

'Gina, my Hillside roommate before you, told me she died in treatment.'

'What a bitch,' Heidi replies, a look of horror and almost admiration on her face.

Thoughts of Alicia's suicide start to sour under my skin,

just like they did yesterday afternoon, and I rinse the taste of tequila from my mouth with another sip of beer. This time, the dark thoughts don't go with it.

'Why do you think she did it?' I ask. 'Alicia, I mean?'

'It's hard to say.'

'Try. Please.'

Heidi considers the question, swaying on her stool precariously enough for me to worry she might fall off it – but she doesn't. She grabs the table's edge and steadies herself just in time.

'Alicia was ill, Jenny. And, when you're ill, nothing else matters but that.'

Her reply sobers me and I lower my third beer to the table, feeling ill myself. Heidi finishes the rest of her drink.

'I still feel bad about it,' I say quietly. 'What happened to Olivia.'

Heidi sighs, reaching for another drink she doesn't have. Once she realises, she flags down the barman with her fingers.

'You did what you did, Jenny. We've all done what we've done and we just have to learn to live with it.'

I grimace at the brutality of her words. Heidi hiccups and removes her vape from the jacket she's sitting on, chewing at its nib torpidly.

'But, in all seriousness,' she says, between puffs, 'why did you ask me to find Malcolm?'

Even in my drunken state, I don't tell her. Instead, I offer something I know has more value. 'I'll do it. I'll go and see Nick.'

Heidi looks surprised but also pleased. The barman finally reaches our table and from there, things get fuzzy.

Chapter 18

Before

30 January 2007
9.52 a.m.

I eat breakfast with Tom and Tony. Olivia's in the basement with Phil and Heidi is nowhere to be seen. Nick isn't here either. Tom and Tony are talking about Sally's missing key and the likelihood of it being found after two days of being missing. I don't add much. I'm thinking about later: my own meeting with Phil and what it could possibly be concerning.

'What do you think, Jenny?'

Tony is looking at me expectantly and I shrug, too distracted by my own worries to care much about Sally's. For some reason, he looks annoyed by this.

'What's wrong with you?'

'Nothing,' I say. 'I'm fine.'

My answer doesn't seem good enough for Tony and he frowns, piercing a particularly juicy grape with his spork. It's unlike Tony to frown at all and I wonder if he's having one of his bad days, the likes of which I hadn't yet seen.

Unsettled, I look down into my cereal trying to defuse the situation. Still, I feel Tony's eyes on me.

'You have to give it back.'

'Give what back, Tone?'

'Sally's key. I know you stole it.'

'Excuse me?'

Tony's eyes narrow. Tom puts his hand on my arm, though he quickly removes it.

'Jenny, he's confused . . .'

'I'm not confused,' Tony says, his own arms gesturing wildly. 'She's a danger, Tom. A danger to herself and everyone else.'

I know Tony doesn't mean it. That he's confused and this is just a bad day but still, my eyes burn. I don't want either Tom or Tony to notice so I leave my tray on the table and run from the canteen, my heart thumping as I hurry through the corridors, trying to reason my way out of the grey cloud, like Phil has been teaching me.

It stings all the same; knowing that somewhere in Tony's landscape there lurks a low opinion of me. That he too can see the darkness inside me he'd always denied existed.

I end up in the reading room. I didn't want to go to my bedroom, knowing Olivia will be back from her session with Phil any minute, so this was the first place I thought of. It's somewhere I can be alone but I open the door and see that isn't the case. Nick is already inside.

He's sitting in the corner to my right, both his hands down his pants and breathing heavily. It makes sense: the dirty magazine page I'd found in here weeks ago must have been his, and bizarrely what occurs to me is how angry he'd be if he knew I stole it. There's anger in his face now. A fury, heaviness, in his brow as he masturbates. That's what he's doing, and it's disorientating to see him here doing this while I'm trying to stop my thoughts spiralling.

The wind of the door hits the back of my legs as it closes behind me. I don't move and Nick looks up, the elastic of his joggers making a lip-smacking sound as he removes his hands from inside them.

'I'm sor—'

'Don't leave,' Nick says, interrupting me, and for some reason, I don't.

My stomach tightens into a hard ball of anxiety but I stay rooted to the spot. I don't know what makes me do it. Fear? An impulse to submit myself to the needs of other people? A curiosity about what will happen if I don't, because Nick's dangerous but I'm dangerous too? That's what Tony said, at breakfast.

Nick smiles a menacing, small-toothed grin. He stands up and walks towards me and I know I've made a mistake. I reach for the door handle but Nick is faster, rushing forward and pushing me into the wall that was previously to my left. Now, I'm pinned right against it.

The light switch digs painfully into the top of my spine and I try to wriggle away, but Nick won't let that happen. He holds me in place like he wants me to suffocate though in the back of my mind, I know what he actually wants. His erection against my hip is all the proof I need.

Terrified, I shrink away from it but Nick is insistent and continues pressing me into the wall with his body; the wall or me or my bones, close to breaking. I try to scream but I've never screamed before. I don't know how. My attempt comes out as a whimper. It only excites him more and I stop fighting. Defeated, I roll my head back against the wall so that, whatever happens next, I only see ceiling.

A victory exhale. Nick's hands move to the front of my jeans. There are three buttons at the crotch and he takes his time undoing them. A tear slides down my face. The door opens.

We're standing so close, I hear it hit Nick in the back and dare to straighten my head. Pain flashes through his eyes, like the blur of a passing commuter train, and crumbles the concrete of my bones. Speedily, I wriggle from his grasp and button my jeans up again.

Olivia is in the room now, her cheeks cherry red and eyes stormy. Nick doesn't seem to care much. He laughs and pushes past her to get out. A few seconds later, I hear the echo of his whistle reverberate through the corridor, like nothing had happened at all.

I try to walk out too, get away from the situation, but Olivia puts her arms around me.

'Jenny, stop.'

I flinch. She looks remorseful and quickly lets go.

'That's not the first time he's done something like that, is it?' she asks.

I know I can't lie this time. That she wouldn't believe me, if I did. 'He's grabbed me a couple of times. That's it.'

The colour leaves Olivia's cheeks. She presses her lips together and steers me towards one of the tables in the centre of the room. I sit down and notice I'm trembling fiercely. Olivia trembles too but doesn't sit down.

'OK, you wait here,' she says. 'I'll run and get Tony and then I can get one of the nurses to come down.'

'No, don't.'

The panic of my voice slows Olivia and she reaches for one of my shaking hands.

'Jenny, you have to report this.'

It's not what I want her to say. So I have no response for her.

Olivia lets go of my hand and sits down.

'You have that meeting with Phil this afternoon, right?' she says gently. 'You can tell him in private. That way, no one else will know what happened. I won't tell anyone.'

I notice that, in his rush towards me, Nick knocked a book from one of the tables on to the ground. I stare at the book now, its belly pressed to the floor but its back and front cover visible. *The Butcher Boy*. The book from which Irene's joke was stolen.

'Jenny?' Olivia repeats. I hesitate before looking back up at her.

'I don't know,' I say, finally. 'What can Phil do about it?'

Her eyes widen. 'Are you serious? Jenny, Phil can do everything about it. He's in charge.'

'He wouldn't believe me.'

'Why wouldn't he? Why would you make something like this up?'

It's a good question and maybe Olivia's right. There's a chance Phil will believe my versions of events but also one he might not. Olivia's confirmation wouldn't necessarily be enough, either. We're women in an institution for the mentally disturbed. Why would anyone listen to us?

'You have to do this, Jenny. You must know that you can't be the only one Nick's doing this to?'

Olivia drops her head and retreats into the quiet place I'd seen her go into many times. The thousand-yard stare. A tear rolls down her cheek a few seconds later, and I reach for her shoulder.

'What's wrong?'

'I'm just . . . angry, Jenny,' she says and I believe her. She's crying. But she looks mad too.

I also believe that if I told Phil what happened, he wouldn't take any action. In my gut I know. What happened wasn't bad enough.

Chapter 19

After

30 January 2016
8.59 a.m.

I wake with a start and a hangover in a room that's unfamiliar. As I sit up, things start to come back to me. The email. The Pig's Head. The tequila. Heidi, convincing me we were too drunk to travel and should get a hotel in Ealing and me, drunk enough to agree with her. She isn't here now but the mascara stains on the pillow beside me confirm she was at one point. I look around, head spinning, and try to locate my phone.

Mercifully, it sits unharmed on the bedside cabinet and I crawl towards it, reading through the text messages I vaguely remember sending to James last night. The ones telling him I was out with the *Gazette* team and would be crashing at Simon and his wife's place. It's a lie, not even a good one, so I can't be angry to see he's read the messages without replying to any of them.

I put my phone down and take stock of the night before – that my hair is still attached to my head and my teeth all accounted for; a reflex of my previous, clearly entrenched, misgivings about Heidi. I try to recall what we talked about. Malcolm, being a dead end. Alicia. Nick – and I agreed, I think, to go see him. Another smart move on Heidi's part. I never would have agreed to it sober.

I shudder and my phone pings. I shudder even more once I pick it back up.

It's an email. Another, like the others, although this one has no words. No subject line. The sole entry in this email is a picture attachment. My stomach turns as I open it.

It's a photo of something long and red and snake-like, a black nub at its bottom. It's Sally's key, I'm sure of it; sitting in a dirty white sink I don't recognise. A key that, before this picture, I'd last seen nine years ago.

I ring Heidi. I worry she may be crashed out at home sleeping off her hangover but, thankfully, she answers.

'Jenny. How's the head?'

She sounds tired, her voice a few octaves lower than normal, and I start to suspect something is amiss. That she didn't receive the email I just did.

'Did you get it?' I ask nervously.

'Get what?'

'You didn't?'

She exhales deeply into the receiver. 'No. What are you talking about?'

'The email?'

'Wait – you got another one? What did it say?'

I lower the phone to my lap, breathing quickly.

If Heidi hadn't received the picture email, it probably means Tony and Tom hadn't either. That this email was only intended for me.

It can't be a good sign. Not considering the email sent yesterday – *Almost over* – and that both Sally and Nick told the police I stole her key, back when it first went missing. I realise, almost in an instant, that someone is trying to frame me for Phil's murder. Someone wants to make it look like I stole the key. That I killed not only Olivia but Phil too. Is that someone Nick?

I think back to what Heidi told me in the Pig's Head, about the bank statement which places Nick near Hillside that day, and it's beginning to seem more likely. He was in the area. He has motive – and it makes a sort of sense. Phil would have been scared to tell Nick the truth of that night. The real reason he got kicked out of Hillside; so scared, that he probably would have had drafted a will first. Besides, I already know Nick's lying. He knows full well I didn't steal Sally's key back at Hillside. He did.

I hear Heidi tapping at her phone.

'Jenny? Are you there?'

'Yes,' I say, unnerved. 'The email didn't say anything. It's just a picture.'

'A picture of what?'

'Sally's key,' I say, and there's a thick pause.

'Impossible,' Heidi replies. 'You're sure that's what it is?'

'Positive.'

'Then delete it.'

Quickly, I do.

'I already have,' I say, and down the phone, I hear her gulp.

'Jenny, I need to tell you something else.'

'What?'

'It's Tom. He's been arrested.'

The room swirls violently. My head spins and I know, in that moment, Nick will have to wait. Before anything, I have to help Tom because he had helped me before. All those nine years ago.

I hang up on Heidi before she can say anything else and reach for my bag, for Lancey's business card, because I need to fix this. Whatever Tom has been arrested for, I know it's in some way my fault.

Lancey answers his phone. He sounds surprised to hear from me but we agree to meet at St Augustine's Christian Church in Surbiton. It's the church where they held Phil's memorial and the first place I thought of because it's in the opposite direction to the Sutton police station, which means there's no chance James will see us. Reluctantly, Lancey also agrees not to tell him or anyone else about our meeting.

I pack up my stuff and get ready to go to the station, catch a train and collect my car at the other end; all the while regretting the decision I'd just made to meet Lancey at the church, because Phil isn't the only person who was memorialised there – and the grey cloud: I can feel it coming back.

Chapter 20

Before

30 January 2007
5.23 p.m.

I don't tell Phil about Nick. I don't tell him anything. He tells me things. Horrible things I wish I could take back hearing.

Currently, I'm with Sally in the buzz room. She says we don't have to talk. That we can just sit here in silence and I can go back to my room whenever I'm ready.

'I don't know what to say, darling,' she says after that.

There's a reason why Mum has been sick. A reason why she hasn't been to visit. She was in Phil's office when I arrived there earlier, still shaken from what happened with Nick. I knew immediately something was wrong because Mum looked much worse than the last time I'd seen her, which was scarcely a week ago.

Phil asked me to sit down and Mum told me how she hadn't been feeling well for a while. How she was reluctant to admit it to herself. Finally, she went to the doctor and they told her news which was worse than she imagined. They told her she had cancer. A bad kind. The worst kind – and only has weeks left to live. Months, if she's lucky.

A short, sharp crack through my centre. That's how it

felt to be told the news. To be told that, whatever happens with my own recovery, Mum won't live to see it. It's a shock. Why wouldn't it be? My mum – the one, stable constant in my life – to be fine one minute and dying the next? Dead, before the year ends, and there can only be one reason.

Sick with worry. It's an expression for a purpose and one that fits here. Mum worried about me my entire life and this was the result. Now, she's sick too and she won't be getting better.

I don't know what to do with the information. It spills out from me like water, my body run awash with grief and yet it's invisible. It feels inconceivable she'll be gone soon. Unfathomable, and it was scary to see her cry. It was the first time I'd ever seen her do it.

Mum cried. Phil cried. And, finally, I did. It felt important to be the last one, not that it helped much. I didn't know what to say. How to comfort her. For my whole life, it had always been the other way around.

7.02 p.m.

I eat dinner in the buzz room with Sally, just her and me alone, and head back to my bedroom after, feeling numb and trying to process this information I want nothing to do with whatsoever.

The shock is wearing off but the acceptance hasn't yet kicked in, so it's hard for me to know how to think; feel; behave. I do know I don't want to tell anyone. I don't want anyone besides Phil and the nurses and me to know. How can I tell anyone else my mother is dying? How do I accept it myself?

Olivia is in our room when I get to it, sat on her bed

with her legs crossed over each other. She sees me and scrambles to her feet and I don't want to talk to her – but I must. Otherwise, she'll know something's wrong.

She reaches me, her eyes large with concern. 'What happened?'

'What do you mean?'

'Your meeting with Phil? Why did it take so long? You were there for ages, Jenny.'

I step slightly back from her. 'It was just about my treatment. How it's going. Things like that.'

She frowns. 'That's all?'

I nod. 'Those kinds of meetings . . . they just take a long time,' I add dismissively, hoping she'll end it at that but she doesn't.

She stares at me for a few seconds and narrows her eyes. 'Have you been crying?'

'No.'

She must know it's a lie. I looked at my reflection in the buzz room mirror earlier, though it was hard to do. The crest of my cheeks were noticeably red. My eyelids, visibly swollen.

Olivia, however, doesn't contradict me. 'Did you tell Phil?' she asks. 'About Nick?'

'No.'

'Why not?' She adds, folding her arms squarely and there are several things I could tell her.

I could tell her that what happened with Nick was an inconvenience and Mum dying is a problem; one that Phil the Fixer can't fix. I could tell her that the last nineteen years of worrying about me had chipped away at Mum's well-being to the extent that she won't get to live another one – and I feel so bad about it, I deserve everything Nick intended to do to me. I could tell her that nothing matters now. Nick. The pills. Me, wanting to kill myself or wanting to get better. None of it.

'It's just easier not to,' I say, instead of all these things.

Stunned silence follows my answer. I look down and see Olivia's feet walk away from me towards her bed. They disappear from my view as I hear her climb on to it.

'You're making a mistake, Jenny. They're a creep, and then they're a criminal. You're a victim, and then you're a fool.'

I keep my head down, wrapping my fingers around my neck. Olivia tuts at me from across the room.

'You should have told Phil,' she says warningly. 'It will get worse now.'

I don't tell her but as far as I'm concerned, let it.

Chapter 21

After

30 January 2016
2.00 p.m.

I'm parked in the car park outside St Augustine's Church. I stopped by the house to grab something first and even so, arrive before Lancey.

I sit in my car, blasting the heat and holding my hands to the dashboard in a fruitless attempt to warm them. It's colder than it's been all week and numbness spreads through my fingers and toes; a fact worsened by the chill of my serotonin plummeting and the graveyard, a few metres to my left. It's always colder in graveyards, I find. I've been in far too many.

Mum's grave is inside this one, just metres from me now. I haven't been to see it in a while. In truth, I don't visit it as much as I should, because whenever I do I feel raw; like a bloody lump of meat just tenderised. I probably shouldn't have come near it today. Not with the grey cloud returning.

I find it hard to talk about Mum. James used to ask me questions about her but when he saw the mood such questions put me in, he stopped asking and I was relieved. My grief about Mum is so intrinsically linked to my grief about

Olivia that it's better not to talk about her at all – although talking about her, even after what happened, was something Phil always encouraged me to do.

Simon knows, of course. Being the nosy type, he had the information out of me twenty minutes into my first official day at the *Ealing Gazette* and he could understand, relate, having lost his own wife early. Thankfully, he didn't ask many questions beyond that. Simon isn't the gushy, talk-about-feelings type.

It's at least another fifteen minutes before the blue Insignia pulls in beside me and beeps its horn. I turn off my engine, get out of my car and climb in the passenger-side door. I notice Lancey still hasn't had a haircut, and his eye bags are prominent when viewed from the side. It's warm in the car and I'm grateful my hungover breath doesn't make clouds in the air like it had done in my own.

'I thought Roberts owned the Insignia,' I say, pulling the door closed behind me.

'Paul can't drive at the minute. He chipped his heel bone golfing,' Lancey replies smiling, though his face quickly turns more solemn. 'What do you want, Jenny? Why did you phone me?'

'You have it wrong. You shouldn't have arrested Tom Naughton. He didn't kill Phillip Walton.'

Lancey looks less tired and genuinely surprised. 'How the hell do you know about that?'

I pause. I know I can't tell Lancey that Heidi told me about Tom's arrest, nor any of the other things we'd found out; like the bank transaction Nick made at the petrol garage near Hillside hours before Phil's murder, or the picture of Sally's key I think he sent me. They're both leads, though. Leads, the detectives should have found long before now.

'I saw it on James's phone when he was in the shower this morning,' I reply shakily, hedging my bets that Lancey is keeping James informed of the investigation, because I know James. Even though he's no longer working the case, he'll want to know what's happening in it.

It seems to work. Lancey nods abashedly, eyeing me with caution.

'And?'

'And . . . you have to let Tom go,' I reply. 'He doesn't know anything.'

Lancey stares at me for a few seconds. He then sighs, unclipping his seatbelt and pushing back from the steering wheel.

'When was the last time you saw Tom Naughton, Jenny?'

'What?'

'Tom Naughton. When did you see him last?'

'About a week ago.' I know I should lie but I don't have the energy. I'm lying about too much already.

Lancey doesn't look surprised. 'Why did you see him?'

'Because . . . we're friends.'

'That's strange,' Lancey adds. 'James told me he'd never heard of Naughton until he cropped up in this investigation a few weeks ago. Wouldn't your husband know who your friends are?'

My hangover is starting to kick in – a pounding behind my eyes, my brain aching like I'd gone through a windshield – and I squint into the distance, wishing I'd grabbed some aspirin from home earlier as well.

'Let Tom go,' I say. 'He didn't do this.'

'You're sure about that?'

'Yes.'

'Then why did he lie to us? Why did we pull a strand of Tom Naughton's hair from Phillip Walton's office carpet?'

Lancey looks regretful, like he'd just told me something he shouldn't – but the meeting, the will, the reason Tom is in custody is a story I already know.

'Tom saw Phil a few weeks before he died,' I say. 'That's why you found his hair at Hillside.'

Lancey doesn't ask how I know this, but I see something like recognition behind his eyes and assume Tom told him the same thing. Lancey, at least, believed him.

'You believe Tom, don't you? You don't think he did this?'

Lancey's eyelids batter uncomfortably. 'I think he knows something.'

'Something about me?'

Lancey nods and a sense of helplessness descends. It's quickly replaced by indignation and I dig my hand into the bag between my knees.

Lancey's hand closes around my wrist – around my scar. He must feel the coarse skin but he doesn't let go.

'Take your hand out of your bag, Jenny. Slowly.'

I do as he says. I remove my hand from my bag and cautiously, Lancey lifts the medication packet out of my hand. It's what I grabbed from home before coming here.

'What is this?' Lancey asks now, shaking the packet. The silver trays inside rustle like leaves.

'It's my medication.'

He stares at me inquisitively and I sigh.

'My prescription ran out in November, that's true – but I didn't have time to make a doctor's appointment. My boss's wife is a nurse, so she agreed to top up my prescription for me temporarily. Just until I had the time to arrange an appointment.'

Lancey still looks puzzled. 'Why didn't you tell us this before?'

'Because I know what Roberts is like. He would have insisted on getting Yvonne into trouble, and I didn't want that. She didn't do anything wrong. She was just helping me – but that's not the point. The point is that I'm still taking my meds. That I'm not crazy or deranged or delusional. I didn't go insane and kill Phil, if that's what you and Roberts think I did.'

We hold each other's gaze for a while. Lancey is the first to look away.

'I'm sorry for what Roberts said; about you being crazy: he shouldn't have done that. I had . . . words with him about it.'

Lancey throws the medication packet back to me and I catch it.

'Lancey-Chawatama,' he says. 'That's my full last name.'

'Excuse me?'

'My full name is Craig Lancey-Chawatama, but the chief thought that was too long and made me shorten it to just Lancey when I joined the force. The Chawatama comes from my mother's side. It's West African.'

Lancey pulls at the ends of his hair. I slide the medication into the bag beneath me.

'They're staunch Catholics, my mother's side,' he adds, 'and mental health problems . . . I won't get into it too much but mental health – that kind of thing – they just don't accept it. Growing up, I know if I said I was feeling anxious or depressed or struggling in that way, I would have been clipped around the ear or laughed down the street. So, what you just did – showing me your medication, just like that – it feels bold to me, Jenny. It feels brave.'

I hesitate, unable to decide whether Lancey is being genuine or mocking me further. The colour in his cheeks suggests the former, and I'm unsure how to respond.

'I didn't do anything to Phil,' I say, eventually. 'You're wasting your time looking at me.'

'But, you did something,' Lancey ripostes. 'That's why you look guilty as sin every time we talk.'

'No. You're wrong.'

'I don't think so.'

Silence fills the car. *This was a mistake,* I think to myself and decide to leave.

As I open the door, Lancey leans over me and pulls it shut.

'It must be traumatic,' he says. 'Us; bringing up Hillside again with your mother's death and Olivia Brennan committing suicide right in front of you.'

A chill descends on my skin. I thought Lancey was warming to me slightly with his story about his real last name, but I realise his being nice – calling me brave – was nothing more than an act. A trick to get information out of me.

'She completed suicide,' I say.

'What?' Lancey looks confused and I push the door back open.

'Olivia Brennan. She didn't commit suicide. She completed it. Suicide isn't a crime.'

I climb out of the Insignia and walk back to my own car, just as it starts raining. It patters against the roof of my car, pounding my head as I watch the Insignia drive away – but the hangover is the least of my worries.

The police still think I know something. They won't stop pushing until they find out what it is and Lancey mentioning Olivia's name means they're closer than they think to finding out the truth. I need this all to end and fast.

My phone pings. It's a text from Heidi. An address: *48 Creston, Gadsmore Estate, Sutton, SM1 EWD.* Nick's place. It has to be.

I have to go and see him. Lancey mentioning Olivia's name doesn't leave me with much choice, but Tony will have to come too. Even I'm smart enough to know there's no way I can go and see Nick alone, because I know what being alone with Nick means for most women. I doubt time had changed that much.

Chapter 22

Before

31 January 2007
8.23 a.m.

I wake up, hoping yesterday was a bad dream. That it was the new medication playing tricks with me, but I soon know that it isn't. The grey cloud in my head is smaller than I remember it ever being, but there's a grey in my heart and stomach now. One that medication can do nothing about, because Mum is dying. She's dying, and I'm not even there.

Olivia has already gone to breakfast. Usually she tells me she's going before she leaves, whether I want to be woken up or not, and it's obvious things between us have changed. I get it: she's mad I didn't tell Phil about what happened with Nick in the reading room yesterday, but I don't worry about that. I need to find Sally. I have a question to ask her.

I find Sally in the buzz room. She looks tired but smiles at my approach, rubbing her hand up my arm in a reassuring fashion.

'How are you feeling?' she asks.

I shrug. 'Is Phil in today?'

'Yes, darlin'.'

'Can I see him?'

Sally freezes. Her hand drops from my shoulder and her eyes go to the corner of the room.

'Sally, please. It's important.'

She blinks at me for a few seconds and finally nods. 'Come with me.'

I follow Sally to the basement door. From her pocket, she removes a set of car keys I don't recognise. She separates the black plastic I recognise as the basement door key from all the others in her hand.

'Your key?' I ask. 'You haven't found it.'

She shakes her head.

'So whose keys are you using?'

'Dr Walton's,' she replies. 'He's letting me borrow his key until my replacement arrives.'

'So, how does he get out?' I ask, confused.

Sally grimaces. 'Well, he calls the buzz room and I come down and get him.'

Self-consciously, Sally presses the key to the lock and I can tell it bothers her immensely that she lost her key; that someone may have stolen it.

The light turns from red to green and Sally lets me through the door, grabbing my hand as we make our way down the stairs. It's something she's done previously – but not for the last few times as if she thinks I once again have a reason to jump – and she's right. I have Mum. I don't have anyone else and what also occurs to me is that if someone did steal the key, they could jump without anyone else around. That Sally's mistake may be a deadly one – and that the lock should be changed. I don't know why the same thought hasn't yet occurred to Sally or Phil, or maybe I do. Hillside is only part of Phil and Sally's lives. They have other things to worry about.

We reach the bottom of the stairs. Sally buzzes me into Phil's office and he looks startled as I walk in.

'Jenny?' he asks, his eyes darting to Sally.

'She wanted to see you. I didn't have the heart . . .'

Sally trails off and Phil nods as if to say, *'That's fine, no problem.'* Sally smiles at us both and shuts the door, and it takes longer than usual for me to hear the soft pad of her feet climbing the stairs.

Phil gestures to the sofa ahead of him.

'I'm glad you came, Jenny. Please sit.'

I do as he says and Phil closes the file in his lap. He seems different, more nervous, around me now. Like I'm someone he's no longer sure how to handle, which is good. Which should make him more amenable to what I plan on asking.

'How are you this morning?' he says.

'I'm . . . OK.'

He nods, unfolding his legs and crossing them the other way.

'Good,' he says. 'That's really good. I'm aware this is a rare and delicate situation and if you have any concerns or questions—'

'Actually, Phil, I came to ask you for a favour.'

He stares at me. I find his expression difficult to read behind the thick lens of his glasses.

'Of course. If there's anything I can do to help . . .'

'Discharge me.'

'Jenny . . .'

'Discharge me to outpatient care. Alicia is still in the medical centre, right? Let her come back and see you again. Give her my place so I can go home and help Mum get better.'

A tragic look crosses Phil's face. It's similar to Sally's expression moments ago.

'I don't know what to tell you, Jenny . . . your mother isn't going to get better.'

'No,' I say, 'I know that, but better in the meantime. To help make her feel better. Help her around the house and things.'

Phil drags his chair forward and reaches out for my leg. I flinch and he pulls his hand back, as if petting a dog that tried to nip him.

'Your mother won't be at home much longer,' he says. 'She'll be in the hospice like we talked about yesterday, remember?'

'That's fine.' I swallow thickly. 'I can be in the hospice too.'

'No, Jenny, you can't. You have to stay here.'

'But, Phil—'

'Hillside is the best place for you to be at the minute. Your mother is of the same opinion as me.'

His words sting. Phil offers me a tissue, but I bat it away with my hand.

'We'll all help you and you will get through this,' he says. 'You're not alone here, Jenny.'

'Mum's alone,' I reply and Phil lowers his head.

'Your mother's not my patient; you are,' he says, sterner this time. 'I'm sorry but my answer is no.'

I glare at Phil and decide that in this moment I hate him. More than anyone else in the world.

Chapter 23

After

31 January 2016
10.37 a.m.

I'm on my way to Tony's house. I don't have any other choice. I tried ringing him after my meeting with Lancey yesterday and again all last night, but he's ignoring all my calls and texts, just like he did after the first email arrived.

It doesn't take long to get to Tony's from mine. I pull up on the kerb outside to see a heavily pregnant woman trying to get out of the car right in front of me. I hurry over to help her and she smiles gratefully, a good-natured gap between her front teeth.

I offer my hand and she looks at me with vague recognition, though we've never met before.

'Jenny?'

'How did you know?' I ask, pulling her to a standing position.

'Tony said you might show up.'

I let go of her arm and she pants slightly, her bump protruding alarmingly as it draws level with my own flat stomach.

'Thank you.'

'Don't mention it,' I say, waving her down.

'I'm Ella, by the way.'

'I know that too,' I reply and she smiles again, smoothing the front of her blouse. 'Is Tony here?'

'Yes. He's inside.'

Her smile drops, and I can tell from the expression on Ella's face that she's worried about him. I don't think James is worried about me. Tired of me, probably.

He didn't come home again last night. He texted, telling me he was working late and I replied saying that was fine; unsure of whether or not I believed him and obsessing too much about Nick to care. Perhaps James will leave, once all this is done. It would be easier, I think, than having to tell him about the grey cloud and how it's starting, once again, to break me.

Worry coagulates at the bottom of my own throat. I cough several times to clear.

'What's wrong with him?' I ask, and Ella shakes her head.

'Honestly? I don't know.'

'Can I go and see him?'

'Sure,' she says. 'It can't hurt,' and I gather from how nice she's being that Ella can't know everything. That Tony has never shared with her the awful things I did.

Ella tells me I can find Tony in the nursery upstairs; that I need only follow the smell of fresh paint. I do just that and soon find *Bubba's Room* – knocking three times before I press down on the handle and walk in uninvited.

It's a lot brighter inside than I'm expecting, the walls painted eggshell blue with clouds and a rainbow on the ceiling. Briefly, I remember Tony telling me that Ella teaches art to handicapped kids and adults, and I'm surprised how good she is.

There's a cot in the corner of the room and Tony is sitting on a chair beside it, staring out of the window. He's still wearing his pyjamas. Well, jogging bottoms and an old white vest, with yellow spilled down its front. He looks awful, with eye bags that match my own and Lancey's yesterday.

I walk further into the room and lean against the wall next to the window, just metres from Tony.

The corners of his mouth twitch. 'Why did you come here, Jenny?'

'You won't take any of my calls. I'm worried about you.'

'But you weren't worried before.'

I blink in surprise. 'What?'

'All those months I spent visiting you at Hillside,' he says. 'I gave you my phone number, more than once, and waited for you to call when you got released, but you never did. Why not?'

Tony exhales deeply. I take a step back.

The question feels unexpected; but no, it'd been there all along. A distance between Tony and me that I attributed to time having passed – when it was never that. It was always this.

'I don't know . . .'

'Yes, you do.'

I swallow hard. 'I just couldn't, Tone. How could I be friends with you without remembering all the horrible things I did? I couldn't be friends with anyone.'

It's true. The only real friend I've had since Hillside is Simon, and that's only because he wouldn't allow for anything else. Being my boss, it was easier to let him in. It hasn't been easy with anyone else. Even James was supposed to be a one-night stand.

The grey cloud and the tiredness and the fear all start getting to me and my eyes water. Tony stands up and pulls me into a hug, the flesh of his bare arm soaking up most of it.

Eventually, he lets go and sits back on the chair. I lean against the wall again and wipe my nose on the bend of my wrist, staring at the clouds and rainbow on the ceiling.

'Alicia painted,' I say. 'Did you know that?'

'Are you OK, Jenny?'

'I just keep thinking . . .'

'Thinking what?'

'That if people had just let me die when I wanted to, Olivia would still be here. Phil would be, too.'

I tear my gaze from the ceiling to look at Tony. He stares at me wretchedly.

'Jenny, I think you need to see someone.'

'I will,' I say quickly. 'Once all this is over. I promise, I will.'

Thankfully, Tony seems convinced.

'So what's going on? You said something in a voicemail about going to the estate on the other side of town . . .'

'Gadsmore.'

'That's it,' Tony replies. 'Who lives there?'

'Nick. There's some stuff we found out, Tony, and I think he did it. I think Nick killed Phil.'

'OK. Tell me everything.'

I tell Tony about the Pig's Head and the *Brisbane Journal* article. About Nick's bank statement, and the picture of Sally's key being emailed to me.

I also tell him about Tom being arrested, Heidi giving me Nick's address and my plan to visit Nick today so I can locate Sally's Hillside key, and end this, prove he killed Phil. I also need to find my Hillside file because who knows what

Phil had written inside it? Potentially, the truth about that night.

Tony's mostly quiet while I speak, asking the occasional question but otherwise letting me talk uninterrupted. When I'm done, he raises his hand.

'So, you don't think it was Malcolm any more?' he says. 'You think it's Nick?'

'I do.'

'You're sure it wasn't Malcolm?' he adds, and I get why. I had told Tony Olivia's secret. The one I refused to tell Heidi.

'I'm sure. He's in Australia. There's no way it could be him.'

Tony doesn't reply for a few seconds. Then, he sighs. 'Are you prepared to see Nick again, Jenny? After everything that happened?'

'Yes. I need to do this.'

'Can you handle it?'

'Yes.'

Tony stares at me reluctantly but slowly starts to nod. 'If we can't find anything in Nick's flat or we don't get the chance to search it, we leave. Straight away. Promise me, Jenny.'

'We'll leave,' I say agreeably. 'So, you'll come with me?'

'Yes. Just let me shower first.'

'And you're OK, Tone?' I ask, gesturing to his dirty vest.

'I'm fine.'

I don't question him further. Tony picks up a dressing gown that's lying over the side of the crib, and limps from the room leaving me alone and awful.

We drive to Gadsmore. Tony's mood seems to have improved since earlier but he's still quiet, his arms folded over the chest of his big duffle coat, as if holding himself together.

'Jenny?' he asks, a few miles down the road.

'Yes?'

'Did Nick ever attack you?'

My breathing hitches slightly. 'Yes.'

'Did he rape you?'

'No,' I say. 'Olivia interrupted him.' An endless pit opens up in my stomach, one that immediately fills with shame.

'Jenny?'

'What?'

'I'm sorry about men,' he says. 'What they do.'

'It's not all men, Tony . . .'

'It's enough.'

Tony sinks into the passenger seat, looks out of his window and falls silent once again. We stay that way for the rest of the journey.

Eventually, we pull up at Gadsmore. I see that Heidi had been accurate in her description of it in the pub two evenings previous. The estate is grimy; each building mossed-over brickwork that's at least thirty years old and what's left of the grass outside, urine yellow. Tony looks nervous and I get out of the car before he can talk me out of it. He follows me towards Nick's building.

The communal door to the Creston block is open and we climb the stairs to flat forty-eight. Hesitantly, I knock, and the door opens to reveal a face I hoped I'd never see again.

He looks old. Unfortunately, his is an image I've never

truly forgotten but it's difficult to recognise in the face of the man standing before me. Some things are the same. The skinniness; his cropped haircut and illegible neck tattoos, all as I remember them. But his skin is haggard now. Harder. It was a mistake for me not to be more cautious of Nick at Hillside. This Nick, I would have been scared of.

He raises an eyebrow at me gruffly. 'Hillside?'

I try to speak but stammer several times. Tony pulls me back slightly and steps past my shoulder.

'It's us, Nick. Can we come in?'

Tony's voice is colder than I've ever heard it and Nick eyes him warily. At Hillside, Tony was the only person Nick was afraid of. It seems time hasn't changed that much.

'Not here.'

Nick closes the door in our faces. He reappears moments later, squeezing out through a small gap in the door and carrying a blue plastic bag.

I step back, so as not to be too close to him.

'Can't we go inside?' Tony asks, eyeing the bag suspiciously.

'No, we can't,' Nick replies, locking his flat door. 'Are you coming?'

Tony shakes his head at me, but we're here now. If we leave, we might not get a second chance – and this has to end soon. I need this to end soon.

'Yes,' I say, reaching for Tony's hand and hoping he'll forgive me for going back on my earlier promise.

Tony pushes my hand away but nods at me forgivingly and together, we follow Nick outside.

We end up in the park passed by on the way up to Nick's flat. Nick drapes himself across the back gate and reaches into the plastic bag, removing a heavy blue plastic bottle and undoing the lid with his teeth.

He takes a few gulps and stares at us. 'You two, what do you want?'

I feel each nerve vibrating but steel myself, refusing to be afraid of Nick this time.

'The petrol garage down the road from Hillside,' I ask him. 'Do you know it?'

My voice sounds steady and I'm grateful for the fact.

Nick shakes his head. 'Nope. I haven't been that way for years.'

'You're lying.'

'I'm not,' he says, and takes another swig from the bottle.

'Do you remember my name?'

'Jenny?' He smiles, teeth yellower than the grass.

My neck itches like a bug just landed on me. I reach for it with my fingers, feeling nothing but skin.

'Jenny,' I repeat. 'The person you told the police stole Sally's key.'

'I didn't tell them you stole it. I told them you had it at some point.'

'The posh girl's the one who stole it. She gave it to me and I gave it to you.'

Tony turns rigid beside me.

'What posh girl?' I ask, frozen to the spot myself.

'The goth one.' Nick says. 'The midget. She stole the fucking key so I'd get her some cigarettes and lighter fluid.'

Nick takes another swig. I glance towards Tony who looks shocked. He's not as shocked as I am.

'Heidi, you mean?'

'I guess. I couldn't tell the police, though. She's fucking nuts, that girl.'

'I don't believe you.'

Nick shrugs and spits phlegm on to the ground. 'You don't have to. Phil did.'

'How?'

'I told him.'

'When?'

Nick scratches his head. 'Like an hour before I was kicked out of Hillside. Phil came to see me and asked me if I knew where the key was; said that if I told him what I knew about it, I wouldn't get in any more trouble than I was already in.'

The park starts spinning around me because I remember the day Nick was kicked out of Hillside quite well. It was the day after I killed Olivia, and I know what that means. If Phil was looking for Sally's missing key the day after Olivia died, it means Phil couldn't have possibly taken it from the Hillside basement the night that she did. It would mean Phil never had Sally's key. That someone else did and still does. They emailed me a picture of it yesterday.

The grey cloud circles as I try to reason my way out of this. Nick's lying. Nick did this. The bank statement proves he was near Hillside on the day Phil was murdered. Nick sent me the picture of Sally's key, and he has it now.

I just need to find it.

'Can I use your bathroom?' I ask in desperation.

Nick shakes his head. 'Not a chance.'

'I know you were at that petrol garage, that day, Nick. The one near Hillside; the day that Phil was killed.'

'And, I told you, I haven't fucking been there in years.'

Nick finishes the two-litre bottle of hard cider he's holding and tosses it on the ground.

I feel Tony reach out for me. 'Jenny . . .'

'Crazy fucking bitches,' Nick says, interrupting him. 'Always lying and getting me into trouble. The blonde bitch first; telling tales and I never touched her – and then, I got kicked out. Lying, crazy fucking cunt.'

Crazy fucking cunt. The blonde bitch. I step closer to Nick, coiled for attack but before I can do anything, Tony grabs my arm.

'That's enough, Jenny,' he says. 'We're leaving.'

Tony steers me in the direction of my car. I hear Nick call out after us.

'Dumb bitch. Fucking dumb, life-ruining bitches, the lot of you.'

I try to turn but Tony gets there first. He lets go of me and walks over to Nick, shoving him to the ground.

'Get out of here. Now.'

Nick looks shocked. Fearful, and scrambles to his feet.

Tony pulls me back to the car and, too stunned to protest, I let him. I climb into the driver's seat and as we drive off, look in my rear-view mirror to see Nick is stood still watching us.

12.03 a.m.

We're in the car driving back from Gadsmore. I feel shaken and I can hear Tony breathing heavily beside me. Moments later, he starts thumping his fist against the dashboard.

'Tony, stop.'

He hits the dash a few more times and leans back in the seat, breathing twice as hard.

'Your hand,' I say with concern.

'It's fine,' he says. 'We didn't get it. After all that, we didn't get the bloody key.'

'Do you think Nick still has it?'

His eyes bulge. 'Of course I do. You saw how Nick lied about Olivia, Jenny. All that other stuff; he was clearly lying

201

about that too. That's why he wouldn't let us inside his flat. He knows Sally's key's are in there.'

I don't tell Tony, but I don't agree.

I hate Nick and I want him to be guilty of this, but I'm not so sure anymore that he is.

'*Telling tales and I never touched her – and then, I get kicked out.*' That's what Nick said, which means he still doesn't know the real reason he was made to leave Hillside. It's clear Phil hadn't told him it was the five of us and not Olivia who was responsible. That Nick wasn't the patient Phil was trying to make amends to. Someone else was.

Of course, there are still red flags about Nick. Undeniable ones pointing in his direction.

His reluctance to let us inside his flat and him lying about being in the petrol garage near Hillside on the day Phil died. His bank statement places him there – or does it? Heidi had shown me the bank statement and after what Nick said about her stealing Sally's key first all these years ago, it's hard for me to know whether I can trust her.

A lot of things are murkier now than before I went to see Nick but one thing is clear: I have to find out more about Sally's missing key and what happened to it after I dropped it in the basement that night.

Someone must know. Someone who was there and is among the handful of us still living. Alongside the medics and everyone I'd asked already, there's only one more person I can think of. The person whose key it was. Who's convinced, even now, that I stole it from her.

Chapter 24

Before

31 January 2007
9.32 a.m.

Sally is escorting me back up from Phil's office. She's been quiet since collecting me. Then again, so have I. Stewing in my own fury; my plan to help Mum, to be with her for the last part, up in flames and it's all Phil's fault. Well, not all of it.

I should have known something like this was coming: Mum being sick, just as I was starting to feel better, because life works out for some people and it doesn't for others. I'd made my peace with that a long time ago but somewhere along the way, because of the medication and Phil trying to get into my head, I'd forgotten it. I'd forgot I was one of those people for whom life would never work out, and Mum's now paying the price.

Sally buzzes us back through the basement door and I walk with her for a while. Distracted by my own gloom, I don't even notice at first I don't know where she's leading me. We've already walked past the female dorms and the communal areas.

'Where are you taking me Sally?'

'Tony told me you and he had a bit of a falling out,' she says, tactfully avoiding my question.

Tony. I had forgotten all about what happened at breakfast yesterday. Before what Nick did and what Mum told me.

'I don't want to talk about it,' I say, and Sally seems to respect my wishes.

We keep walking. Somewhere in the distance, I hear the sound of laughter and feel angry. My worries aren't everyone else's worries and yet it feels they should be.

Finally, things start to look familiar, Sally having brought me to a place I don't know but which looks like one I do. It's the male dorms, and I have no idea why Sally would lead me here until Tony shuffles from one of the rooms, rubbing his hands together and looking genuinely upset.

'Can I talk to you?' he asks me now. 'Inside?'

Sally nudges me forward and wanders off, leaving Tony and I alone.

The atmosphere is awkward and I feel oddly detached from Tony now. I feel detached from everything now Mum is dying, but I decide to hear him out. I've hurt enough people as is.

'Fine.'

Tony walks back into the room he just emerged from, gesturing for me to follow. I do, and he closes the door behind us.

The room is almost identical to mine and Olivia's bedroom, but with everything in reverse, the furniture arranged in the exact opposite order.

Tony gestures to the bed I assume must be his but I don't sit on it and stay in close range of the door.

'That's fine,' Tony says, his cheeks pinking at my rejection. 'We can stand.'

'What do you want, Tony?'

'I wanted to apologise,' he says and sways where he's

stood, his balance compromised by the absence of his big toe.

I think about that toe. Where it is now. What happened to it after Tony cut it off, for whatever reason he did, and what it feels like, to lose a part of yourself forever. An essential part.

'I'm sorry Jenny,' he adds now. 'I'm sorry that I accused you of stealing Sally's key.'

'Why did you?'

'I was having a bad day. I got it into my head you had Sally's key, and once I had the thought, it kept popping back into my head. I kept seeing it over and over again.'

I don't respond. There's something about his stance that tells me Tony isn't quite finished.

'I also wanted to say that I'm sorry. I know about your mum, Jenny. I know she's sick.'

'How?'

'Sally,' he says, 'but please don't blame her. She was only trying to help.'

I know Tony's right. Sally would only tell him because she wanted to help me and yet I do blame her. I didn't want anyone to know. This wasn't her secret to tell, and I feel more anger inside me. An accumulation of all my bad parts.

I'm about to reply when the door opens and Tom walks in. He looks equally surprised and nervous to see me here.

'Can we have a minute?' Tony asks him. 'Sally knows she's here.'

Tom's eyes flicker towards me though he soon nods and walks out.

Tony's fall back on me once he's gone. 'You should tell Tom too, Jenny. You should tell Olivia. We're all your friends. We all care about you.'

'No. I don't want anyone else to know about this, Tone.'

'Jenny, I think you should . . .'

'No. Please don't tell them.'

I stare at Tony imploringly. He hesitates for a few seconds. Maybe longer.

'OK, I won't tell anyone. I promise,' he says finally, and my chest lightens in relief.

Tony reaches for my hand and squeezes it. I think he's nervous I might burst into tears but I don't feel like crying any more, because Tony's story about his intrusive thoughts – about me having Sally's key – has actually given me a plan.

If Mum's going to die, I will too. And, once again, everything feels simple.

Chapter 25

After

31 January 2016
5.23 p.m.

I didn't tell Tony about my plan to visit Sally. I dropped him off at his house, said I'd call him tomorrow and headed straight to Hillside.

I've been parked outside for hours, knowing Sally will have to walk in or out of the building at some point; the flower tributes to Phil that had previously smothered the brickwork long gone, which I find unsettling. Not even a month has passed since he died. It seems someone was in a hurry to get rid of them.

I shiver. The temperature has plummeted further since Gadsmore and despite my car heater's best efforts, I'm unable to keep myself warm enough without the engine running. I'm about to give up and go home when the Hillside doors open and a flash of blonde steps out.

Despite the cold, I get out of the car and walk towards her.

It's Sally. She's older; her face has a few more lines and her cheekbones aren't as high as they used to be, but it's definitely her – I know it is. She notices me standing on the pavement, a few yards away, and it takes her a few seconds to recognise me. Her face falls completely once she does, and it stings. I can't pretend it doesn't.

'Sally, hi. I'm . . . It's Jenny Parker.'

'I know who you are.'

Her voice is oddly formal. Less American and crisper than I remember it.

'Do you have a minute?'

She looks around uncertainly, as if she could find an excuse floating in the air. 'I'm sorry, I don't—'

'Please, Sally. It's important.'

We lock eyes and I can only begin to imagine what she's thinking right now: her feelings towards me, and how they've evolved over the years. Finally, Sally nods, holding her arms squarely at her sides.

'What do you want?'

'How are you, Sally?'

She shakes her head as if it pains her to hear me speak. 'Jenny, please. Tell me what you want or I'm leaving.'

Despite the negative things I know Sally told the detectives about me, I'm shocked by her abruptness here and wonder why she's turned on me like this. A car drives past and I wait for it to turn the corner before speaking.

'I need to know what you remember about the night Olivia died. About what happened after Phil led me and the others out of the basement.'

Sally shakes her head again. 'I don't want to talk about that . . .'

'Please, Sally. Do you remember any of the other patients or staff being in the basement on that night? Do you remember if your key was there?'

At the mention of her key, the water in Sally's eyes turns to ice. 'No. It was just the ambulance team and me. No one else was there. I'm quite sure of that.'

It's not the response I was anticipating or even hoping for. The key, whatever happened to it in the end, was definitely in the basement at the start of that night. Whether Nick was lying or he wasn't, someone had to have picked it up because it certainly wasn't there by the time police arrived.

'You're sure that you couldn't have missed seeing it?' I ask Sally now and she sighs.

'Yes. My key wasn't there, and I know that because I looked for it. Believe me.'

Sally makes to move past me but I step to the side, blocking her path.

'Jenny, I have to go—'

'Why did you tell the police I stole it? Your key I mean?'

Sally looks in the direction of Hillside, steadily avoiding my gaze.

'I don't know what you're talking about—'

'Yes, you do. Sally, the police think whoever took that key – whoever has it now – murdered Phil. Do you think I did?'

She makes to move past me but once again I block her path.

'Sally,' I say but my voice breaks.

Hesitantly, she looks up. 'Yes. I do.'

I step back feeling stunned. Hurt. Wounded.

'Why?' I ask, and Sally now looks equally hurt.

'Because, that day – that morning – Heidi Allman came to me and told me that you were the person who did.'

It has to be the truth. Unlike my scepticism about Nick's version of events, Sally has no reason to lie.

'She did?'

Sally nods and her face softens. It looks more like Sally's face, how I remember it.

'Of course, I didn't believe her. Not at first. I knew the two of you had a difficult relationship and I didn't think that you were capable of . . .'

Sally stares at me, her icy blue eyes searching my own. I try to hold her gaze, as not to reaffirm my guilt.

'So, what changed your mind?'

'You acted so differently after Olivia died,' she says. 'Dr Walton did too. He was always asking me how you were doing and demanded the nurses search your room every week for months after that; and I just knew the reason was because he thought you had my key. That you were still hiding it somewhere.'

I feel winded and take a few deep breaths, trying to process everything Sally told me.

Both Sally's and Nick's testimonies confirm Phil was looking for the key after Olivia died, which makes it impossible for him to have taken it out of the basement that night. They also confirm Heidi has been lying to me since I visited her in Uxbridge, and it throws everything she's told me into doubt.

I look back at Sally. She was the person who told the police Phil was trying to make amends to a patient before he died to begin with. She should therefore know, or at least have some idea, who he was trying to make them to.

'Sally, you told the police Phil was trying to make amends about something before he died.' I say now. 'Why did you say that?'

'Because he was,' she says.

'Did he tell you what about? Did he tell you who he wanted to speak with?'

'No.'

'But you told the police Phil and I were close? You implied—'

'I didn't mean it like that, Jenny. The detective, he twisted my words.'

Guilt crosses Sally's face and I remember the last time I saw her wear that expression. It was a few hours before what happened. A few hours before I killed Olivia.

'And you're sure no one else came into the basement after we left?' I add. 'You're positive?'

'No one else,' she says in a tired voice. 'Now, I have to go.'

'But—'

'I said I have to go.'

I step aside and Sally walks past me without looking back. I stand on the pavement and stare after her, contemplating the facts as they are now.

Heidi was lying. Maybe Nick wasn't. Phil didn't take Sally's key from the basement on the night that Olivia died, which means one of us – Tony, Tom, Heidi or me – did.

Chapter 26

Before

31 January 2007
6.30 p.m.

Nick has Sally's missing key. That's what I tell myself. He's the only patient with the nerve to steal it and without the conscience to give it back. The thought of seeing Nick after what happened in the reading room yesterday scares me, but I need the key. That, or something else to end my life with and this time make it permanent.

I search the staff rota for when Ryan is next on duty in the buzz room, because Nick likes Ryan more than the other nurses and has got into the habit of following him around. I don't think Ryan likes Nick. That makes me like Ryan.

He's working the late shift in the buzz room so I wait until the evening time to go there. Walking past the lounge, I see Tony talking to his sister and Tom deep in conversation with a bald, middle-aged man I've seen visit him a few times. I don't know who the man is but it's definitely not his dad because Tom's dad is an unpleasant-looking man with thick, dark hair.

I get to the buzz room. Nick is sitting on one of the sofas and though it's my plan for him to be here, I recoil at the sight of him.

Ryan nods in my direction and looks down at the comic book in his lap, which isn't surprising because Ryan is shy. Olivia often tries to talk to him and his answers are always monosyllabic, like Olivia's now are to me.

She hasn't really spoken to me all day. She's angry. She wants Nick gone, and I get that. I just don't get why she wants him gone so badly, though I certainly have my suspicions.

I walk towards Nick and sit next to him.

Ryan's head bobs up cautiously.

'Everything OK, Jenny?' he asks.

'Fine,' I say, and when Ryan looks back at his comic book, I tap my foot against Nick's.

'Do you have it?'

My voice is hushed. I practically mouth the words so Ryan can't hear them. Nick looks confused and then curious and I feel intimidated, remembering how his eyes looked the last time I stared into them.

'That depends,' Nick replies, sitting up. 'What are you looking for?'

'Sally's key.' I wait with bated breath.

A few seconds later, Nick nods. 'I might do. What do you want it for?'

'Give it to me and I'll tell you.'

Nick deliberates for a few moments, spitting the gum in his mouth towards the waste bin at the end of the sofa. It falls just short and he makes no attempt to collect it.

The phone rings in the little office cubicle at the back of the buzz room. Ryan drops his comic and hurries to answer it, meaning Nick and I can finally talk without the need to lower our voices.

'Sure, fine,' Nick says now. 'I was going to use it to raid Phil's office but I don't think I'm going to do that now.'

'Why not?'

'Phil's a cool dude. He said he'd write me a good reference, you know, when I get out here.'

I stare at Nick, wondering if I've got him wrong in some way. That I've misjudged him. Then, with Ryan's back still turned, he leans forward and runs his hand up my thigh. I slap my own hand on top of it, like a card game Tony had once shown me.

'Don't.'

I flare my eyes threateningly in Ryan's direction. Nick looks startled and releases my leg. I wonder if he'd have done the same had Ryan not been yards away, but it's not a thought I allow myself to linger on.

'Where's the key?' I ask.

Nick shrugs, sulkily. 'What do you want it for?'

'To jump, from the landing.'

I tell Nick the truth because I know he won't try to stop me; that he'd enjoy the drama and the thought of me in pain.

I'm right. The corners of his mouth turn up and he tells me exactly where he's hidden Sally's key, without asking for anything in return.

Chapter 27

After

31 January 2016
6.17 p.m.

I drive away from Hillside and go home, wondering what to do next.

I can't talk to Heidi. I can't trust her; but, try as I might, I still can't see her being Phil's killer. She couldn't have done it herself – she isn't strong enough, certainly not to overpower Phil and stab him seventeen times – and I can't think of any reason she'd want someone to do it for her.

I don't reach out to Tony either, and I can't reach out to Tom and am thankful for it, because if it wasn't Heidi who took Sally's key on the night Olivia died, it had to be one of them. Unless, of course, Sally's mistaken. Did she see everything that happened after we left the basement that night? Is there a vital clue still missing?

James's car is in the driveway and my heart sinks at the sight of it. I know there'll be more questions and I can't give him any answers. I don't know what will happen next.

I open the front door. The hallway is dark but the kitchen light is on and I walk towards it. I left my phone in the car so I wouldn't be tempted to answer if Tony or Heidi call me, but I wish I had it now, because walking down the dark hall is starting to scare me. Everything now has the potential to fill me with terror.

At last, I reach the kitchen. James is sat at the dining table, his shoulders hunched over and his fingers locked together.

'Hi.'

'Sit down, Jenny.'

Reluctantly, I walk around the table and lower myself into the dining chair opposite his.

James lifts his head and looks at me. 'Craig told me you spoke to him yesterday.'

It takes me a few minutes to comprehend Craig as Lancey's first name and I feel a stab of betrayal; the second in as many hours.

'He said he wouldn't tell you,' I murmur bitterly.

'He's not a priest, Jenny. He's not your lawyer.'

'Do you think I need one?'

'You might. Why have you been speaking to Tom Naughton?'

'We're friends,' I say shakily.

'Fine,' James replies, and I detect a whiff of impatience. 'Why haven't you been working for the past ten days?'

I'm astonished. 'How do you . . .'

James sighs. 'After Lancey told me about your meeting, I drove to your office to confront you about it – but Simon told me you weren't there. That you hadn't been for a while.'

He blinks at me and I sit back in my chair, biding my time and searching my brain for an excuse.

James must mistake my silence for apathy. Jaw clenched, he reaches into his pocket, pulls out a folded piece of paper and hands it to me. 'Open it.'

I stare at him uncertainly but eventually unfold it.

I see my own handwriting and a few lines in, realise what

216

I'm reading. It's my witness statement. The one I wrote for the police on the night Olivia died and it suddenly occurs to me what has been keeping James busy over the past few days. Why he hadn't come home last night.

'This is the case you've been working?' I ask. 'Olivia's suicide?' My voice has a detached quality to it. One that shouldn't be but is familiar.

James looks frightened and gets up from his chair, walking over to sit next to me. 'I had to know . . .'

'Know what?'

'What you're hiding.'

I don't respond. James produces more folded sheets of paper from his pocket and drops them on to the dining table.

'Tom Naughton, Heidi Allman and Tony Black. All of you were there. All of you wrote these witness statements telling the exact same story about what happened to Olivia Brennan. As did Phil Walton.'

I stare at the sheets of paper but don't open them.

James stares at me. 'It's common practice for witness statements to vary somewhat; usual, for people to report seeing different things despite having witnessed the same event – but these . . . they're identical. Do you understand what I'm saying, Jenny? They're too identical to be the truth.'

I stay rock still. Inside, I feel myself crumble.

James continues to look at me.

'Something happened the night Olivia Brennan died,' he says. 'That's why you stole the article from my briefcase. It's also why you're suddenly meeting up with Tom Naughton and why you want him out of police custody. You think it has something to do with Phillip Walton's murder. You think it's why your file's been stolen.'

My eyes sting. Fiercely, I wipe them.

'No, nothing happened. I don't think anything.'

'God, Jenny, yes, you do. I can see it in your eyes. I can't do this with you any more. You have to tell me the truth.'

James grabs my hand and shakes it. Hostage to his gaze and out of options, I tell a story. Some of it based on the true version of events and other parts modified because I can't lose him and if I don't tell him this now, I will.

He sits and listens patiently and at the end, sits back in his chair, looking sickened. It's the same way Tony looked after I told him the story about Malcolm.

'Why didn't you tell me this sooner?' James asks.

'Because I was afraid,' I say, which is the truth.

It may also be the biggest lie I've told him.

Chapter 28

Before

31 January 2007
9.28 p.m.

I retrieve Sally's key from where Nick said it would be: behind a loose tile in the art room's ceiling. As always, the coded door is left on the latch so I have no trouble getting inside and almost punch the air, such is my delight when I see the key and Sally's red lanyard lying there, ready for the taking.

My plan will work. I'm going to die, and it's freeing to know my remaining actions don't hold much weight, since I won't be around to see the consequences of them.

I tuck the key up the right sleeve of my jumper. It presses uncomfortably against my scar and I turn the nearest corner and almost bump into Heidi, who seems to be heading in this direction.

I'm horrified to see her and she looks confused to see me.

'What are you doing here?' she asks.

'Looking for newspapers. Tom and I—'

'I know. You do crosswords together. How cool.'

Heidi smirks and I glower at her, motioning to walk past.

'Jenny, wait.'

Reluctantly, I turn around because I can't risk her grabbing out for me and feeling what's beneath my sleeve.

'What?'

'It's Olivia,' she says. 'You need to be careful with her. She's got a dark side. She's dangerous.'

'More dangerous than you?'

Heidi opens her mouth but no words come out. Not for a few moments.

'Fine, don't believe me,' she says, finally. 'Just ask Olivia why she ended up in Hillside. What she did.'

I ignore Heidi's threats and push past her.

When I get back to my room, Olivia is still awake and it seems waiting for me. I'm surprised, given her coolness towards me last night and all day, and overly conscious of the key still tucked up my sleeve.

'Is everything all right?' I ask.

Olivia nods. 'I just wanted to say I'm sorry for how I've been acting today, Jenny. What you tell Phil is your business. Even if it's not in your best interests, it's up to you to decide what you tell him.'

My chest falls in relief. 'That's OK. Let's just forget about it. Go back to normal.'

She smiles. 'Let's do that.'

I smile back and Olivia climbs atop my bed.

I stare at her, confused. 'Did you want something else, Olivia?'

'I've just been thinking and . . . I have a plan.'

I shake my head, perturbed. 'What are you talking about?'

'About Nick,' she says. 'How to get rid of him.'

Chapter 29

After

1 February 2016
11.51 a.m.

James forgives me immediately after the story I tell. He also promises not to share it with anyone else because in that version of events I'd still end up in jail. Just not on a murder charge.

We spent the rest of the evening together. James ordered Chinese food and we had sex, which is the first time we'd done so since Phil's murder case began. I was surprised when he made the move and relieved he still felt capable of touching me. The relief, in a lot of ways, made it the best it's ever been.

He left a few hours ago. He got a call around 5 a.m. and ran out without showering, which is indicative of him being called to yet another murder.

Killing isn't as rare as people think it is. Sometimes it's not even that interesting, but I'm interested in every case James works. For ever looking for the killer I'd be willing to forgive.

I went back to sleep after James left and wake now, much later than I'd planned. It's light outside and I reach for my phone, before remembering I left it in my car last night. I turn on the TV to check the time.

It's almost midday and I feel a fleeting sense of panic as I always do waking up late because I know it's a sign things are getting bad again. I try not to dwell on it. I get out of bed and go downstairs to fetch my phone from the car, hoping I'd remembered to lock it last night and Car Thief hadn't been able to take advantage.

Thankfully, I did, and I find my phone in the drink holder, still in battery with several missed calls. All of them are from Tony.

He's also sent text messages and I scroll through them, my heart growing heavier with each.

> Hi Jenny, it's Ella. Hope you don't mind me texting from Tony's phone. He hasn't come home yet and he's left his mobile behind, silly man! Is he still with you? Xx

> Is he with you? Starting to worry. Ella xx

> Are you together? X

> Calling police now.

The last text was sent at 1 a.m. this morning. The last time I'd seen Tony was close to midday yesterday, when I'd dropped him off at his house after we'd visited Nick.

Concerned, I try calling Tony myself to see if I can get hold of either him or Ella, but the call goes straight to voicemail and I run back inside because it's too cold for me to stay out any longer. I close the door behind me and my phone buzzes in my hand. I have another text message. This one from Heidi.

> Don't call me. Everything will be fine.

Rattled, I call Heidi's phone but – once again – there's no answer and I dash upstairs to get dressed, planning to drive over to Tony's to see what's going on.

In the bedroom, the TV is still on a news channel and I quickly search for the remote in my sheets. Next, I hear something that makes me look up.

The police have declared a major incident at the Gadsmore Estate in Sutton. Detectives were called to the scene in the early hours of this morning amid speculation the incident could be linked to the ongoing investigation into the recent murder of a psychiatrist in the area . . .

I don't listen to any more. I throw on the clothes I wore yesterday and bolt out the door, leaving the TV playing.

12.42 p.m.

There's commotion when I arrive at Gadsmore. Several police cars and an ambulance are blocking the road just outside the park which Nick led Tony and me to yesterday. Dozens of people are stood in the street, most in their normal clothes but a few in their pyjamas. The lights of one of the police cars is still flashing though it makes no sound, and my heartbeat mirrors its flash as I pull up my handbrake and jump out of the car.

I rush towards the police vehicles and the officers standing beside them. It's raining, heavy enough to make it weird that all these people are standing around, but I continue towards the policemen undeterred. As soon as I get to them they start running the opposite way.

I'm confused until I see a parting of the crowd and a man emerging through it, struggling furiously while several police officers try to restrain him, with their colleagues running over to help. The man is Nick, yelling as he's dragged forward.

I stare at Nick. Long enough for me to see that the front of his shirt is stained red. Long enough for him to stop yelling and stare right back. We hold each other's gaze for what may be a minute or just seconds, my eyes constantly flickering to the red and wondering how it got there. Nick starts yelling again, lunging firmly in my direction.

'You cunt. You dumb fucking bitch.'

I'm startled by his aggression, and I don't think the officers – now, all ten of them – are enough to keep him from me, but Nick soon falls down. They pin him to the ground, and I run away from them all. Towards the building Nick had just been escorted from.

I hear someone call after me – 'stop, ma'am' – but I don't look back. I run up the stairs with my heart still pounding to the lights of the siren. *Oh no. Oh no. Oh no.*

I reach Nick's floor and see the door to his flat is wide open. Two police officers are stationed outside it, but one of them is on his phone and another is drinking coffee, so I run past them and I'm inside. Yesterday, I'd wanted to be.

The flat is messy. Plastic bags and bottles and trash all over the floor; the smell of forgetting to take the bin out not just once but repeatedly, like rotten meat and yeast. Amid the rubbish is Tony. He's lying on his back, in the corner of what I can only assume is the living room; his neck slumped to the side and a pool of red surrounding his body like a halo.

He lies still. Too still for someone who's supposed to be living and all air leaves my body. The whole room bends and compresses until everyone inside is a swirl.

I fall towards Tony but someone grabs my arm. A person with long and spidery fingers.

'Jenny, this is a crime scene.' It's Lancey, whispering in my ear. 'You're contaminating evidence. You need to leave.'

'For fuck's sake,' I hear Roberts shout. 'Who let her in here?'

Lancey tries to drag me back but I slip out of his grip and push towards Tony, because I have to be there for him. I can't abandon him this time.

Somewhere behind me, I hear the loud stomping of feet.

'Christ. Someone get Nilson in here. Now!'

I reach Tony and fall hard on to my knees beside him, several beer-can wrappers cushioning the blow.

He looks different. Off, like the smell of this apartment and I put my hand to his neck, desperate to feel a pulse. All I feel is my own blood pumping violently and a cold, hard crack inside me because I don't want this to be happening. Tony can not be dead.

I'm lifted. The whole room is upended and I'm being held by someone who grabs my arm as I try to hit out at them.

'We have to go, Jen. Things will get a lot worse if we don't leave right now.'

I'm surprised to hear James's voice and stop hitting out. I feel myself nodding and James lowers me to the floor.

Unsteady on my feet, James helps pull me from the flat, but on my way out I spot something and turn back around.

Something that Roberts is holding.

'Sally's key? You found it here?'

Roberts breathes hard through his nose and looks to James, who now has a grip of my shoulder. 'Get her out of here or I swear . . .'

'We're going,' James growls back, dragging me from the flat and into the stairwell.

The door shuts behind us and I bend at the waist, feeling like I'm going to throw up. James straightens me and grabs both my shoulders this time, looking around to see if anyone else is nearby.

'How are you here, Jenny? Why did you come to Gadsmore today? Did you know?'

It's cold in the stairwell and James's breath comes out like smoke, his features a mixture of fury and angst as his nails dig into me.

'What are you talking about?'

'Did you know Tony Black was coming here? Did you plan to meet him here?'

'No,' I say, shaking my head. 'No, I saw it on the news.'

James stares at me sceptically but finally lets go.

I think of Tony and, God, it hurts to think of him now.

What was he doing here? Why did he come back to Gadsmore without telling me? Why did Nick kill him? What happened before Nick stabbed him in the back?

I also think of Sally's key and realise I'd gone wrong somewhere. The dirty white sink was Nick's and he'd lied. He'd had the key all along because Nick killed Phil, as well as Tony. Surely, that's the only explanation left.

James walks past me and opens the stairwell door. He closes it again and then runs up and down the stairs to make sure we're here all alone.

'Promise me you had nothing to do with this, Jen. Promise me you had no idea Tony Black was coming to Gadsmore last night.'

'I had no idea. I swear.'

I think James believes me and he reaches into the breast pocket of his coat, pushing something into my fingers.

226

I stare at James, confused.

'I found them on the body,' he says. 'They were tucked into the back of his trousers. Luckily, the first responders didn't see.'

I know he means Tony's body and my hands start to shake.

It's dark in the stairwell so I have to squint to identify the items. A pair of gloves, I think, and paper; random pages folded haphazardly, their bottom halves stained crimson.

I remove my phone from my pocket and shine a light on them. Phil's handwriting is at the top of some of the pages and I realise what the papers are. They're pages from my Hillside file. The file that was stolen the night Phil died. What was Tony doing with them?

I switch off the torch on my phone.

'What—'

'Get rid of them,' James says quickly. 'If the guys upstairs found these on Tony, they wouldn't be able to take Nick Crewe to trial. Do you understand what I'm saying, Jenny?'

I nod, because I do. If my Hillside file was found on Tony it leaves room for reasonable doubt. Sally's key wouldn't be evidence enough to charge Nick with Phil's murder as well as Tony's – and James wants Nick to go down for it. Because of the story I told him.

I try to push them back.

'I can't do it. The blood . . .'

James grabs them and my hands and clamps them together.

'Jenny, you have to. Don't worry about the blood. You're covered in it anyway.'

I look down and see he's right: that red covers my front the same way it covered Nick's.

James tucks them into the waistband of my joggers and

covers me with his coat. He then hands me something else. A lighter, that now sits on my palm.

'I have to go,' he says. 'Just get rid of them. I'll see you at home later.'

He nudges me gently towards the stairs leading down and, before I can ask him any more questions, walks out of the stairwell back towards the crime scene.

I feel the gloves and paper against my waist and think to myself: Was Tony Phil's killer all along?

PART THREE

Chapter 30

After

4 February 2016
7.12 a.m.

I'm in the shower. It's the only place I feel safe at the moment. James was the notoriously long shower-taker but I have since surpassed him and if he notices he doesn't mention it. The water is blisteringly hot, scorching my back and still, a shiver at my core I can't shake – but, I stand in the shower, hoping the steam and heat can thaw it.

I did what James asked me to after Gadsmore and got rid of the items he found on Tony. I got back in my car. Drove to a petrol station for supplies and kept driving until I found a country road with no street lighting, where I burned Tony's gloves and my Hillside file and the bloodied jumper I'd been wearing; standing for several minutes in the freezing cold, wrapped in nothing but James's coat.

James told me I'd done well when he returned later that night, and said we wouldn't have to worry about it in a couple of weeks. I felt it was a callous statement to make but didn't pull him up on it. How dare I, after everything I'd done?

It's hard to believe Tony's dead. He had such life about him that it's hard to imagine him not living, but he's not. It's been three days since it happened, his death plastered all over the news which I ignore. It's too hard to go there so I don't, apart from at night when I'm supposed to be sleeping.

At night, I binge on the facts like an alcoholic on their drink of choice before a dry run. I Google Tony's name. I Google Nick's, and always get a head rush, like I've stood up too quickly.

I know that Tony was stabbed just twice in the back but left to bleed out for hours, the police only called after Nick's girlfriend came to the flat and found Tony's body and Nick a few yards away, balled up and rocking in a corner. I know that Sally's key was found hidden inside a sock at Nick's Gadsmore flat, with Nick's DNA and traces of soil on it. I know Nick admits killing Tony but continues to deny Phil's murder, and that the police found the knife used to kill Tony inside Nick's flat. It isn't a match for the one used on Phil.

Those last two facts, I didn't find online. I found them on James's phone, while he was sleeping. It seems Lancey is still keeping him informed. There was also a text from Lancey, asking how I was doing. Quite aptly, James left that one on read.

Sometimes, when I'm done searching James's phone and Google alerts for Nick and Tony, I look up Alicia's name, each time with a different buzzword beside it. Anorexia. Suicide. Noose.

Several times I've looked up Olivia's name. Simply because I can. I know Lancey and Roberts won't be spying on me or my phone's internet history any more, since they no longer suspect me of wrongdoing. They think Nick killed Phil.

I reach for the heat gauge of the shower and turn it up. Who do I think killed Phil? Does it even matter?

10.02 a.m.

Simon pulls me into a hug as soon as I arrive at the office. Ros busies herself with the photocopier to make it look like she isn't watching but she is and I can see why. For all his warmth and familiarity, Simon isn't usually the hugging type so I must look like I really need it. He holds me for a few minutes without saying anything at all, squeezing the back of my arms.

I'm back to work this morning. James doesn't approve. He thinks it's a bad idea and suggested I take some more time off. Like Tony before him, he also said I should see a psychiatrist, but to ask for help – to be helped – is a concept that feels strange now. I don't see the point. Neither staying at home nor a therapist can bring Tony back or tell me why all of this happened.

Finally, Simon releases me and I step back, smoothing the shoulders of my jumper from where his hug pulled them out of place.

'It's good to see you, kid. How are you feeling?'

'I'm . . . OK,' I reply and Simon smiles, rubbing his hands together. 'Oh, just wait till you see all the work I've got lined up for you. Just you wait.'

I know he's teasing but the thought of doing a lot of work, any work at all, seems less manageable than it did two weeks ago.

Feeling uneasy, I sit down in my desk chair and Simon's smile drops. He eyes me warily.

'You wouldn't know you had two weeks off, the eye bags on ya,' he says and I shrug.

'I didn't sleep much last night, but I'm good. Honestly.'

'Great. I can tell you the bad news then.' Simon snaps his fingers and sighs, pointing to the far corner of the room with a mutinous expression on his face. 'Starting tomorrow, I will no longer have my own office. Instead, you can find me over there.'

'Why?'

'Budget cuts finally found me. It was either lose that office to the recruitment guys next door, or lose the lot of ya. Not a decision I came to lightly.'

I try to laugh. It doesn't really work. Simon pats my arm like he might say something else but he doesn't. He shakes his head and walks away and I breathe a sigh of relief, knowing it's only work I have to get through now.

I log into my email without the terror I had become accustomed to facing, because in my gut is the understanding that the threatening emails won't be coming through any more. That what happened at Gadsmore was the '*over*' they'd promised – that Nick had promised, apparently – though it doesn't feel like an end to me.

My phone rings in my bag. I scoop it out in the hope it might be Heidi. I haven't spoken to her since she texted me the day Tony died but I have the feeling she could provide answers to the questions I have left. I've tried ringing her multiple times over the past three days but it goes straight to voicemail and my texts are all being left unread. I know she's fine. Heidi's too smart to have got herself into any serious trouble, and I wonder why she won't respond. What it is that she doesn't want to talk about.

To my surprise, it isn't Heidi calling me now but Tom. Another thing James had told me was that the police had dropped all charges against him following Nick's arrest, which soothed my conscience slightly and was, in my view, the only good thing to come out of what happened at Gadsmore three days ago.

I don't know why he'd call me now and I don't want to speak to him. I can't face whatever questions he might have for me, so I let my phone ring out, too much of a coward to answer.

Chapter 31

Before

4 February 2007
9.54 a.m.

I'm in Phil's office. Ryan escorted me down here half an hour ago and I haven't said much since. My anger towards Phil has faded since our last meeting, I just don't have anything to say to him. Phil has been equally quiet.

In a way, I feel sorry for him. He's clearly out of his depth dealing with me and, though he doesn't know it, his reputation as the Fixer will soon be in tatters. He could just about recover from discharging Alicia after failing to help her, but he won't get away with me jumping from the landing of his office a few short weeks later. There's no way people will call him the Fixer after that – and I do feel kind of bad about it. Not bad enough, though, to change my mind.

Phil removes his glasses and wipes them on the end of his shirt.

'What are you thinking about, Jenny?'

'Nothing.'

He frowns. 'You're getting on with your medication? You don't have any problems there?'

'Yes. It's fine.'

'And you're going to see your mother this evening, is that correct?'

'Yes,' I reply, the thought of seeing her not as comforting as it used to be.

She's in the hospice now. *When things start to happen, they happen fast,* the doctor said.

I'm being allowed trips out to visit her in the evenings, just like how she used to visit Hillside, and Margaret drives me. Sally can't and Phil either chooses not to or isn't allowed. My guess is that it's the former because it's not easy-going. It's hard; having to watch her get sicker, thinner, greyer – but I want to watch. All of it. It's not fair she should go through it alone, so I will watch. Right until the end. It's the only thing I can do for her now.

Phil nods and puts his glasses on. He taps his pen against my file, then raises it and rests its tip a few centimetres to the right of his cupid's bow.

'Do you have any plans, Jenny? Plans that could be harmful to yourself or others?'

I'm alarmed Phil's asked me this. Do I have a tell? Is it written on my face that I plan to die, once all this is over? I didn't think it was. I thought I'd been acting quite calmly, considering Sally's missing key is stuffed inside the teddy bear Heidi left behind in my bedroom and it has been now for days.

'Of course not,' I say.

Phil stares at me disconcertedly and I stare back, knowing that all this hurt and pain and anguish will soon be over if I can just hold my nerve.

'OK. That's good,' he says finally, and I leave his office, my plan still intact.

Ryan leads me back upstairs and I find Olivia and Tony in the lounge. Olivia looks happy to see me. She stands up and pulls me onto the sofa next to her while Tony sits in an armchair to her left.

Olivia is acting normally again now. She hasn't mentioned Nick since telling me about her plan to get rid of him a few days ago, so she might have already got over the idea and I'm glad. Of all the people at Hillside, Nick's now the last I plan on rocking the boat with.

Tony nods at me shyly. I'm glad we're friends again – I wouldn't want to die not talking to Tony – but it still feels a bit awkward between us since he knows about Mum, which is why I didn't want him to know. It'll be harder to shield my own plan from him now, so I have to be vigilant around him. Act as if I want to get better.

'Hi,' he says.

'Hi.'

Olivia grabs my arm. 'Heidi's coming down now. She has something important to tell us.'

My heart rate increases but I tell myself I'm being paranoid. There's no way Heidi can know I have Sally's key.

As promised, Heidi appears minutes later. She sits in the chair next to Tony's and I eye her cautiously. She does seem more reserved around Olivia than she is normally and I think back to what she told me the other day; about Olivia doing something bad to be sent here. I'm starting to think Heidi believes it.

'So, what do you have to tell us?' Olivia asks Heidi now, apparently oblivious.

Heidi shifts uncomfortably away from her. 'Actually, I was only going to tell Tony but since we're all here . . . I heard the isolation ward is needed for another patient and Phil is considering moving Nick into the normal ward.'

'You're serious?' Tony asks.

'Deadly.'

My arm tremors and slips from the sofa, like falling over in a dream. Tony shuffles uncomfortably on the armchair, playing with the tassels at the end of the armrest and Olivia sits dead still until, coldly, she turns to me.

'Do you have that thing this evening, Jenny?' She asks.

Tony and I eye each other awkwardly.

Olivia doesn't know about where I go every evening is to the hospice. Besides Tony, none of the other patients know mum's sick. They think I leave Hillside every evening for an alternative therapy not yet on offer here.

'Yes,' I reply. Olivia sighs impatiently.

'When will you be back?'

'I'm not sure. Why?'

Olivia doesn't answer right away. She takes a few seconds to think about it and stands up, a determined look on her face.

'Can you meet me in the lounge at ten o'clock? Will you be back by then?'

'Yes,' I reply, while Tony and Heidi look confused.

'Why?' Tony asks. 'What is this about?'

'You'll find out,' Olivia tells him, already turning to leave. 'Meet me in here at ten, Jenny. Don't forget.'

She walks out. Heidi seems relieved once she's gone and I think it has to be because of what she discovered. How Olivia ended up in Hillside. Despite Mum, and Sally's key, and everything else I'm worried about, I kind of want to know now what it was.

Chapter 32

After

4 February 2016
7.32 p.m.

James's car is in the drive when I get back from work. He's been getting home early every night this week. I open the front door and the sizzle of oil, the stench of meat, fills the hallway, turning my stomach. I walk towards the noise and the smell and find him in the kitchen, standing by the grill and wearing an apron. There are two pots boiling on the stove.

I can see why he's done it. He wants things to go back to how they used to be. I don't think now that they can.

My keys land on the dining table with a noticeable rattle. James turns down one of the dials on the stove and turns to greet me.

'How was your day?'

'Fine,' I reply, without asking James about his. I think it's better not to.

I hang my bag on one of the dining chairs and tie my scarf there too, rolling up my sleeves.

'Do you want help with the cooking?'

James shakes his head. 'No. It was your first day back. Sit down.'

I do as he says and sit in the chair I'd just wrapped my scarf around.

We both fall silent, nothing to be heard but the whirr of the extractor fan and the faint bubble of whatever vegetables are cooking. Several minutes pass without either of us speaking. Finally, James stirs the vegetables on the hob and turns to face me.

'What are you doing tomorrow night?' He asks.

'Why?'

'It's my cousin's eighteenth birthday party. You know, Samantha? I completely forgot all about it until Mum rang me today saying she'd already RSVP'd for us. I thought we could go? That it'd be nice? We won't stay long. Just show our faces.'

I shake my head.

'I'm working the late shift tomorrow night,' I say, 'but you should go. You'll probably beat me home anyway.'

More silence plagues the room.

James grabs a tea towel from the kitchen top and wrings it between his fingers. 'Do you think it's a good idea to work the night shift at the minute, Jen?'

The implication of his question is clear. He doesn't trust me to be in the office alone, and for some reason, it makes me angry. 'Go to your cousin's party, James. It'll look terrible if neither of us go.'

He appears to deliberate, just as his phone rings inside his trouser pocket.

Once he sees who's calling he ends the call, pocketing it once more.

'Who was that?' I ask.

'Mum. I'll call her back later.'

I don't believe him. His phone rings again.

'James . . .'

He sighs and turns it off without removing it from his pocket this time. 'Fine, it's Craig.'

Lancey, I think to myself. 'What does he want? It must be pretty urgent.'

'You don't want to hear it . . .'

'I do.'

James looks irritated.

'He wants my opinion.'

'On what?'

'On whether I think Nick Crewe murdered Phil Walton.'

'Do you?'

James shakes his head. 'I don't think we should talk about this, Jenny.'

'I think we should,' I say back. 'I think it's healthy for me to know what's going on.'

James's eyes water. I tell myself it's just the smoke in the kitchen. 'Do you? You haven't wanted to talk about it at all the past three days. You haven't wanted to talk about anything.'

'Do you think Nick killed Phil?' I reply, ignoring his actual question.

'No, I don't,' he says. 'The murders . . . they're just too different.'

'You think Tony killed Phil, don't you?'

'I . . .'

'James.'

'My gut instinct? Yeah. I think he did.' His face softens. 'Come on, Jenny. He had your Hillside file, and when I got to the scene, I noticed knife marks on the lock of Nick Crewe's door. Intruder marks.'

I frown. 'What does that mean? Intruder marks?'

'It means that it looks like Tony Black broke into Nick Crewe's flat,' James says. 'That he wasn't invited in and, if he was an intruder, that could change things.'

'How?'

His expression turns graver.

'If Nick Crewe is charged for both murders, it means he can plead manslaughter or self-defence in the Gadsmore case. There's a chance he could even get off without any jail time at all because there's not much evidence in the Hillside case either. We have the key, which gives Nick Crewe access to Walton's office and also a DNA link, but there's no weapon. No motive or means or any other evidence that ties him to Hillside that day. The defence could argue the key was planted, and the knife marks won't help disprove that.'

I'm horrified by the thought. 'Nick can't get off, James. He killed Tony . . .'

'Tony Black was a paranoid schizophrenic who cut off his own toe Jen,' James replies. 'I'm sorry but it's true. It won't take much to convince a jury Nick was acting in self-defence.'

I want to believe James is wrong, and he is wrong about something. There is evidence tying Nick to Hillside on the day of Phil's murder. I'd seen it.

'What about Nick's bills or bank statements?' I ask. 'Can't they place him near Hillside on the day Phil died?'

James sighs, adjusting the steak on the grill before turning back to face me. 'No. Nick Crewe lost his bank card two months before he was arrested. Everything he's bought since December has been paid for by his girlfriend.'

I should have known. Heidi showed me that bank statement and Heidi had lied about a lot before ghosting all my calls.

I look at James again. Lost in thought, I hadn't noticed him walk away from me. He's now draining the vegetables through a colander at the sink.

'Tony didn't kill Phil,' I say. 'He was a good man.'

James puts down the colander.

There's a knock at the door.

'I'm not expecting anyone.'

'Neither am I,' I reply, and move to answer it.

Tom is stood on our front porch, squinting in the light of the motion sensor.

I'm surprised to see him and feel awkward, having ignored his earlier call. I can't think of anything to say.

'I'm sorry it's so late,' he says. 'Can I come in?'

'Yes, Tom. Sorry. Of course you can.'

I step back and let him walk past me, closing the door behind us both.

James walks into the hallway from the kitchen his expression reproachful. He must recognise Tom from the police station.

'What are you doing here?' he asks and Tom looks uncomfortable.

'I just came to see Jenny. I was in the area.'

'It's a bad time, I'm afraid. We're about to eat dinner.'

'No, it's fine,' I say, glaring at James. 'I'm not hungry.'

Before James can protest, I grab Tom's hand and steer him into the living room.

'I'm sorry about him. Do you want a drink?'

Tom shakes his head. 'Jenny, I don't want to cause any trouble. I can leave . . .'

'Please don't. I'll be right back.'

I go into the kitchen where James is putting our dinners in the oven and the rest of the crockery into the dishwasher.

'What was that about?' I ask and James frowns.

'You shouldn't have anything to do with those people until this blows over, Jen.'

'Those people?' I ask. 'The crazy people, you mean?'

James looks wounded, like I had just hit him. 'You know that's not what I meant,' he says, and I immediately feel bad.

'I'm sorry. I had no idea Tom was coming over. I can't just kick him out.'

He nods. 'It's fine. I'll let you two talk. Go see Mum and Dad or something.'

'You don't have to . . .'

I stop talking when James grabs my hand. Harder than I'm expecting.

'Don't tell him anything, Jenny. I mean it.'

'I won't.'

James lets go of me and leaves. Shaken, I walk back into the living room to see Tom.

He stares at me guiltily. 'I'm sorry if I got you into trouble.'

'No, I'm glad you came,' I say, and I mean it. 'I need to tell you something.'

8.15 p.m.

I tell Tom more than I intend to and he sits and listens to everything I say, his expression alternating between bewilderment and concern. When I'm done, he leans back on the sofa, looking slightly paler than he did before.

I shake my head. 'But it doesn't make sense for Nick to even have the key. According to Sally, Phil was looking for her missing key for months after Olivia died – and Nick couldn't have taken it that night. Sally said no one else besides the medics entered the basement after we left it.'

'Do you think it's possible Sally misremembered about the key?' he asks, once I tell him what Sally said about no one entering the basement after we left it and Phil searching for the key following that night, making it improbable for Nick to have had the key at all.

'No,' I reply. 'She seemed pretty sure.'

Tom looks troubled. 'Tony didn't kill Phil, Jenny. You know he didn't – and I'm sure Heidi has her reasons for doing what she did.'

I get why he said it. Whatever the reason Tony had my Hillside file and Heidi lied about Nick's bank statement, they had both forgiven me for a lot worse.

Tom and I are quiet for a few minutes. When I feel the grey cloud looming, I look at him to speak.

'I just feel there's something I'm missing,' I say. 'Something that will make all this make sense.'

'Jenny, Nick did this,' Tom says. 'He has to have done.'

'But what if the police can't charge him?' I ask.

'They will. They don't let people like that – a suspect in two murders – go.'

Tom purses his lips. I shrug and lift my knees up to my chin, hoping he's right.

'I'm sorry you got arrested,' I add seconds later, and Tom shakes his head.

'Don't be. I was the one who lied to the police. It was my fault.'

We both know it wasn't, but I appreciate Tom saying it all the same.

'Besides, they dropped all the charges,' he adds. 'My impression is that your husband did me a favour in that department. I wanted to say thanks, but he didn't seem too happy to see me. How much does he know?'

'Not everything,' I say. 'He doesn't know I pushed her.'

'Olivia, you mean?'

I nod and my eyes start blurring.

Tom reaches for my hand and rubs it between his own.

It's an intimate gesture, and I pull my hand away. Perhaps more aggressively than I intended.

'That was my first kiss.'

Tom looks confused. 'Excuse me?'

'When you kissed me at Hillside . . . before everything. That was my first kiss.'

I don't know why I say it. I guess to acknowledge the memory; to remember I was a person before everything happened. One that Tom, a good person felt like kissing.

Tom nods uncomfortably and looks down at his watch while I stare at his scar. It doesn't look so bad any more.

Chapter 33

Before

4 February 2007
9.49 p.m.

I get back to Hillside after visiting Mum in the hospice. It was just as hard as the other times and she's more lifeless now in a lot of ways. She had to be showered this evening and the nurses didn't want me in the room for that, so one of them took me to the family room. I was surprised to see it was more like a family suite, with a bedroom to the side of the TV area.

The nurse pointed to it and said I could stay overnight whenever I wanted, but I said I couldn't and explained why not. She didn't say a lot after that – ran down to get us both cappuccinos, and we watched *Come Dine with Me* in perfect silence – but she did approach me before I left and gifted me a pink heart-shaped crystal; to relieve my grief and suffering. I wanted to throw it at her but I didn't. I managed to nod gratefully and climb into Margaret's car, where she swiftly confiscated the crystal because its edges were too sharp. I was angry when I received the crystal. I was just as angry, when it got taken away.

That's mostly what I feel at the minute. Anger, but more intensely than ever before. My anger feels like a

chain to strangle the world with; one that won't be satis-
fied until I can bring everything crashing to its knees
– but I know my own world will end soon. That will have
to be enough.

Margaret escorts me back into Hillside and, walking
past the reading room, I hear someone call my name. It
doesn't sound like Nick, so I go in and find Tom sitting
at one of the tables, his raised fist waving a newspaper
triumphantly.

'Are you up for it?'

I hesitate. It's been a while since Tom and I last did a
crossword together, but I know I have to act normally. If
my plan is going to work, I need to behave as if nothing
has changed about me.

'Sure.'

I sit down and Tom pushes me the newspaper and a pen.

I look at the clues, but I find them hard to decipher. The
words blur and I'm all too aware of Tom watching.

'We haven't done this for a while,' I say, trying to buy
some time.

Tom blinks harshly. 'I know, I'm sorry. I've been a bit
distracted recently and Sally hasn't been bringing the newspapers in as much.'

I nod and look for more clues but my mind is mush.

After a few more moments of silence, Tom tactfully points
to an empty square. 'Well, four down is Lewinsky. *Infamous
Clinton aide surname.* Eight letters.'

'Of course,' I say, shakily filling it in.

His eyes bore into the side of my head, and I can't escape
the sense that something feels off between Tom and me. I
just can't put my finger on what.

'How old are you, Jenny?'

'Nineteen,' I reply.

He smiles. 'You wouldn't remember this then. You must have been just a kid.'

Normally, the comment wouldn't bother me, but in my anger I seek out something patronising in it.

'How old are you, Tom?'

'Twenty-eight.'

Quiet descends on the room and I twist on my seat, contemplating whether I should feel bad. My question seems to have offended him, as his question had me, but I don't understand why and adrenalin in the form of remorse now courses through my veins.

The quiet continues. Tom flicks the corner of the newspaper with the tip of his thumb and index finger.

'Listen, Jenny. I heard what's happening with your mum. I wanted to let you know how sorry I am.'

I feel embarrassed. Hurt, and my rage returns.

'Who told you?'

'I heard Tony and Sally talking about it in the hallway outside our bedroom,' Tom replies and I sink down against the back of my chair, furious at them both.

'You don't need to be sorry, Tom. It's not your fault.'

'But, are you OK?'

'I'm fine.' I drop the pen from my hand.

Tom nods sympathetically and picks it up to ink in a word. He has to trace over the outline of each letter several times before it shows clearly on the page.

'You know, my mum died when I was younger.'

I stare at him.

'It was a while ago' he adds, slightly blushing. 'I was twelve when it happened. I just wanted you to know that I understand what you're going through. How you feel.'

I gesture to his scar. 'Is that the reason you . . .'

'Maybe.' he says. 'I don't think there was just one.'

I don't know how to reply. I find another clue and reach to take the pen back from Tom.

I'm not really sure what happens next. My fingers brush Tom's and he grabs my hand reassuringly. Soon, it turns into something more serious.

Tom kisses me. Quickly. As if plunging in before he has the chance to talk himself out of it. His lips are thin but his mouth is warm and I don't stop him. I probably should. He's married and a lot older than me; we're in the same room where Nick attacked me and I just got back from seeing my dying mother, but I let him kiss me anyway; an almost dead girl.

I forget Nick's hands and kiss him back.

Tom places his hand at the back of my neck, drawing us closer. My chair drags towards his, making a terrible screeching sound across the linoleum and I pull my mouth away to laugh but Tom follows me insistently, his wedding ring snagging in my hair.

He pulls me onto his lap and I let him. He continues kissing me like he knows this is wrong, but he doesn't stop, his tongue pushing into mine insistently. I wonder which one of us will stop it. I wonder how this all ends.

I don't have to wonder for long. Tom's palm squashes into my nipple. His other hand goes to the top of my jeans and I panic. I climb off his lap and leave the room, relieved that I could. That he'd let me.

Tom doesn't call after me and out in the corridor, my lips stinging red.

I hear yelling. A woman's screams, and I follow the shouts to the lounge where Nick is on the floor and Olivia is kicking him, over and over.

It's a bizarre scene. One my brain struggles to process as people start running past me. I see Margaret pull Olivia back while Ryan scoops Nick off the floor; three red lines clawed down his chin, like a cat had scratched him.

'What's going on?'

Margaret's voice is so loud, all movement comes to a halt. Olivia, in particular, stops thrashing her arms and directs her furious gaze at Margaret.

'He grabbed me. Tried to rape me.'

'Language!' Margaret replies and Nick shakes his head. 'I was just sitting here, and that bitch attacked me. She clawed my chin and started kicking me.'

Olivia lunges at Nick again but Ryan steps in-between them.

'Enough!' Margaret, jerks Olivia back violently by the shoulder.

Olivia winces and I step forward. 'Stop. You're hurting her.'

Olivia looks both surprised and angry to see me, pointing now in my direction. 'Jenny was here. She saw what happened.'

They all turn to look at me. My lips still hurt like someone had pulled them with forceps and my knickers felt damp. I try not to think about that part. What I also don't think about is my friendship with Olivia because I wasn't here. I didn't see what happened and I can't tell on Nick now. He has too much leverage over me.

'I just got here. I didn't see anything at all.' My voice comes out louder than I expected it to, thunderous in its deceit.

Nick smirks. Olivia looks like I've slapped her and yells as Ryan steps away from Nick and helps Margaret to drag her from the lounge. I quickly run ahead of them, not wanting to be left alone with Nick – I know what he's capable of, and that Olivia's story is probably true – thinking about how weird a person I am: self-destructive, and yet so unhappy when things start to implode.

10.47 p.m.

I race back to my room, feeling terrible about what I just did and what I could have done, if circumstances were different. I feel dirty. Like Nick's culpability has crawled under my skin, and I actually regret stopping things with Tom now. Olivia wouldn't be in trouble now, unbelieved.

There's a knock at the door and I see Heidi standing in its frame. Without invitation, she walks in and closes the door behind her.

'Olivia's in the medical centre, in case you were wondering. Quarantine's full so Margaret took her there. Nick's there too.'

The guilt in my stomach thickens but I don't reply.

Heidi raises her eyebrows and begins to wander around the room, eventually stopping at the mirror next to my bed. The one I'd seen her burns in.

'Are you worried?' she asks. 'About Olivia coming back?'

'No.'

'You should be.' Heidi grimaces and looks at the teddy bear on my windowsill. The bear that used to be hers.

'Jenny?'

'What?'

'I know you have Sally's key.' She says it quickly. Quietly. Like a fatal bullet I didn't seen coming.

I clear my throat, trying to keep calm. 'I don't know what you're talking about . . .'

'Don't do it. It won't make anything better.'

The grey cloud swells in my head worse than ever; knowing that after everything I've done, Heidi would try to ruin this for me, just because she could. She doesn't care what happens to me. Saving me has never been one of Heidi's interests.

'Get out.'

'Jenny . . .'

'I said, get out.'

Heidi leaves and, shaken, I take Sally's key from the teddy bear and stuff it into my left shoe, knowing I'll have to act sooner than I'd planned to. That, tomorrow, I'll kill myself.

Chapter 34

After

5 February 2016
3.35 p.m.

Work's harder the second day. I got up late, got to work late, despite being on the late shift. Simon had a field day when I finally rolled in.

'I can't fucking believe it,' he said. 'Fucking millennials,' he added, and two months ago, I would have found that funny. Since then, I've lost my sense of humour. I've lost a lot of things in that time.

I hear Simon's footsteps now, padding across the carpet and turn around to see him place a coffee on my desk. The kind gesture throws me for a loop. The banter I can just about take but, since Tony died, I find it hard to believe I deserve nice people in my life, doing nice things for me.

'Thanks,' I say, pushing the coffee towards my keyboard.

Simon waves his hand dismissively. 'Forget it. All set for the late shift?'

I nod, but not convincingly.

The late shift means running the *Ealing Gazette*'s new website which went live in my absence. Simon and I both did training for it a few months back. Today I can't remember the training.

Simon, however, looks pleased. 'Great. There's meant to be a storm later, so keep an eye on it. Also, look out for any train cancellations and road closures to add to the site, any problems later on . . . don't be shy. Ping me an email. Or just come see me before I leave.' He points towards the corner. 'We're in the same room now, after all.'

I nod and Simon imitates me relaxing his bottom lip and dropping his chin to his chest, his head bobbing like a beach ball in a riptide.

If it's meant to be funny, I don't laugh, and Simon lifts his head. Next, he lifts a shorthand pad from my desk and flops it gently against my temple.

'Come on girl,' he says. 'Pull yourself together.'

I don't say anything. I hear Simon exhale and, finally, he walks back to the opposite corner.

5.43 p.m.

It's just me in the office. Everyone has left – even Simon – and the storm has arrived as he promised, beating uncompromisingly against the single-glazed office windows and jittering the doors.

I don't do much. I keep tabs on all the local road traffic websites for any breaking incidents but there aren't many and I'm glad, not being confident with the online system. Without the distraction of work however, my mind starts to wander and images flash through my head. Inappropriate ones. Tom and I kissing. Nick stabbing Tony. Phil, with blood on the knees of his trousers – and a body bag. Watching it being carried away.

I seldom want a drink but I want one all of a sudden. I'm still taking my meds – I have been since all this began – but I don't know. I'm no longer sure they're working.

My eyes blur and I try to find something to distract myself from it. A crossword would do, but I don't have any newspapers on my desk so I walk over to Simon's, turning towards his old office before remembering what he keeps telling me: that he'd relocated to the main floor.

I get to Simon's new desk and, sure enough, there are newspapers on it. I grab a handful and linger for a few minutes because I've never snooped behind Simon's desk before. It seems easier to do, out here in the open.

I go through Simon's things, and can't help but be disappointed. All I find besides the newspapers is an old Bisto jar full of pens and some old photos, pushed around his desktop screen.

I look through the photos, trying to find Simon's first wife – the one who killed herself – because, in my head, she looks like me. She doesn't, but I do recognise someone in one of the photos. A person who shouldn't be there at all.

It's a light bulb moment. Everything slots into place, and, shaking wildly, I grab the photo and run back to my desk, tossing it on to my table while I root through my bag for my phone. I find it and call Heidi, even though I know she won't answer. She hasn't answered me in days.

'Heidi,' I say, into her voicemail. 'I know who killed Phil. I know everything. Get back to me tonight, or I'm going to the police. I'm serious.'

I hang up and sit on the edge of my desk, too scared to look at the photo again until Heidi calls back.

A few seconds later, a text from her comes through: *Meet me in the storage unit.*

Chapter 35

Before

5 February 2007
8.26 a.m.

I sit with Tony at breakfast. Olivia wasn't in her bed when I woke up but I didn't expect her to be. She must still be in the medical ward, which is good because it gives me more time to plan for later. I got to breakfast early, hoping I'd miss her and I have. I've missed Tom too – and I might be more relieved about his absence than Olivia's. Mercifully, Heidi's not here either.

The key is still in my shoe, Sally's lanyard coiled around my big toe. I know I can't walk around with it indefinitely and that I'll have to sneak to the basement and jump from the landing at some point today, because if Phil or the nurses find the key on me before then, they won't let me stay at Hillside – nor will they release me. They'll move me somewhere else, like they're planning to do with Alicia, and I'd never see Mum again anyway.

'Jenny?'

'Yes?'

My voice comes out hollow. Tony looks concerned.

'We're OK now, aren't we?'

'Of course we are,' I reply more normally, and he smiles.

'Good. Did you hear about Tom?'

I flinch. 'What about him?'

'He's being discharged tomorrow,' Tony replies, and I'm relieved. Maybe I shouldn't be.

Tom leaving can only mean one thing: that Heidi was telling the truth yesterday morning and Nick is going to be moved on to the main ward. If Tom's leaving, from tomorrow, there'll be a spare bed in it.

Tony and I finish breakfast and part ways, him heading to a therapy session with Phil and me heading back to my room, where I plan to wait until Phil has left for the day and I can go down to the basement.

I get to my room, Olivia is here. I try to turn around but she rushes up and slams the door closed behind me.

'Ten o'clock, Jenny. You promised.'

I look at Olivia, her face tear-stained and her hair tangled, and realise now that it was the time she asked me to meet her in the lounge last night but I was kissing Tom. Nick was on the floor, and Olivia was kicking him.

It was ruthless behaviour. To hurt someone and want to keep doing it, but Heidi had warned me Olivia could be cruel. She's merciless when it comes to Nick, in particular, and part of me wants to know why.

Olivia stomps to her bed and sits on it. I follow and sit next to her.

'Olivia?'

'What?' she answers.

'Why does Nick bother you so much?'

Olivia doesn't reply. The thousand-yard stare returns and she tries to get to her feet but I grab her arm before she can, because I can't stand it any more; not knowing the reason behind it.

'Why are you here, Olivia?' I ask. 'Why don't you speak to Karen any more? Did she hurt you?'

Olivia stares at me blankly.

'Karen? No, Karen didn't.'

'Then, why doesn't she visit you?' I think back to what Heidi said. 'How did you end up at Hillside, Olivia? What did you do?'

'Something awful.' Olivia's bottom lip starts to wobble. I eye her nervously.

'What?'

'I killed her cat.'

It's not what I expected her to say. Not at all, but I know she isn't joking and I drop her arm.

'Karen's cat?'

'Yes.' Her confirmation undermines everything I thought I knew about Olivia. I can't help thinking: she's absolutely insane.

'Why would you do that?'

Olivia wipes her nose with the side of her fist and locks eyes with me.

'If I tell you, Jenny, you can't tell anyone else.'

I nod and feel uncomfortable, looking directly at her. The beauty of Olivia's face makes me feel bad about my own, but there's clearly an ugly inside her. A grey cloud, like my own.

9.51 a.m.

Olivia tells me a story about Karen's boyfriend, Malcolm. She tells me he first molested her at thirteen years old and raped her repeatedly following her fifteenth birthday. Aged

260

seventeen Olivia said that she finally plucked up the courage to tell Karen, and when she told Karen what Malcolm had done, Karen didn't believe her. So, she killed Karen's cat.

She wanted to hurt Karen, just as badly.

Olivia doesn't cry telling the story. I do. She wipes away the tears and tells me to stop being stupid.

'That's why, with Nick . . .'

She nods. 'It's triggering for me, Jenny. To be in here with him.'

I squirm uncomfortably but I know I have to tell her. That it's the right thing to do. 'Olivia, Tom is being released tomorrow. I think Nick is moving on to the main ward then.'

I suspect some kind of anguish to appear in Olivia's eyes. All I see is determination.

'I know,' she says. 'That's why we need to try again.'

'What are you talking about?'

'My plan for last night. We'll do it tonight instead.'

'OK,' I reply. My neck spasms from the strain of the duplicity.

11.02 a.m.

Olivia's plan is not what I expect it to be. Her plan is to plant Heidi's magnetic lighters on Nick, proving he smuggles in contraband.

I tell her I'll do it. That it'll be impossible for her to get anywhere near Nick after last night and she agrees. It's a lie, of course, but Olivia doesn't know that and I don't want her anywhere near Nick tonight. Besides, I've thought of a different way to get Nick thrown out of Hillside. A way of taking him down as well.

We talk about Karen some more. I think Olivia feels relieved to have the secret off her chest and relieved that I believe her. It's clear she hadn't told Heidi any of this, and I wonder how Heidi found out about the cat. Is it something Phil would tell her?

'It's not all Karen's fault,' Olivia says now. 'Malcolm was good at twisting things. I was in a bit of trouble at school and he said I threw myself at him, but why would I do that? He's a fucking old man, and . . .'

'And what?'

'I don't like men, Jenny. Not like that.'

Slowly, I nod. There'd been a girl at my old school who liked other girls. She'd been teased mercilessly for it and I never understood, really understood, the so-called reasons why.

The tip of Olivia's nose is red and I touch my finger to it lightly. She laughs. I laugh. She kisses me and I go along with it just like I had with Tom yesterday, because it's nice to feel something other than the grey cloud and my grief. It feels good to kiss Olivia especially. Better than it had kissing Tom.

The door opens. I pull away from Olivia and look towards it.

Sally stood in the doorway, looking shocked but also like she's trying not to be. Olivia wipes her mouth with the back of her hand and, aware of Sally's key still tucked at my sole, I rise from the bed and run away from them both.

11.47 a.m.

I have a few hours to kill before Phil leaves so I decide to go to the medical ward and say goodbye to Alicia. I also want to apologise, for what I did to her weeks ago, because I shouldn't have tried to save her. You shouldn't try to save anyone who was no interest in it.

On my way, I think about Olivia and why I kissed her.

There's no denying I am attracted to Olivia. She's the most beautiful person I've seen up close.

I arrive at the medical ward and open the curtain to Alicia's cubicle. She's behind it like last time with the restraints still attached.

There's a new canvas on the wall behind her: a blue sky with *'Carpe Diem'* written across it in white and I don't think Alicia's dad bought this one because the canvas; I've used one like it before.

I approach her now and free her limbs from their restraints.

'I didn't know you painted.'

I nod towards the canvas. Alicia eyes me sceptically, scratching at the tape beneath her nose and shuffling up the bed.

'Yeah, well it's the first thing I've painted since you got here.'

'You're really good,' I reply, relieved she's talking to me. 'Why'd you stop?'

She sighs. 'They made me, a few weeks into my stay.'

'Why?'

'Because I like to paint fruit.'

'What?'

'I like the shades,' she says. 'How they look in the bowl, whatever, but when I got to Hillside the art staff weren't happy. They wanted me to stop with the fruit and paint doughnuts and fucking hotdogs and I refused because that was stupid. Then . . . they didn't let me paint at all.'

'What made them change their minds?' I ask, confused, and Alicia smiles.

'It's so fucking boring in here, Jenny. I caved in and said I wouldn't paint any more fruit. So, they let me paint this.'

I look at the canvas again, *Carpe Diem*, and feel my brow wrinkle.

'I'm sorry I grabbed you,' I say. 'I shouldn't have done that.'

Weakly, Alicia waves her hand. 'Consider it forgotten.'

I nod and notice that the canvas is the only possession of Alicia's that's not in a suitcase or bag. The rest of her things are packed.

'Have they told you when you're actually moving?' I ask and Alicia shakes her head.

'I think it will be soon. Phil's delayed it as much as he can.'

'Wasn't moving you his idea?'

'Yes,' she says, 'but my dad wasn't happy about it. Me staying here for the time being was a compromise of sorts.'

Alicia's face breaks into another smile, her cheekbones trembling under its weight.

'At least you're painting again,' I say, and she nods.

'At least I am.'

5.02 p.m.

I stay with Alicia for the rest of the afternoon. When Sally comes to change her feeding tube, I find a piece of paper and a pen, scribble 'Nick gave me the key' on it and stuff the paper into my jean pocket, hoping someone will find it after.

It turns five o'clock and I breathe a sigh of relief. Phil must have left his office by now. He must be done for the day, which means my plan is going to work. I'll be able to jump uninterrupted.

Leaving Alicia, I walk the corridors and make it to the door leading to the basement, looking over my shoulder to make sure no one else is around before pulling Sally's key from my shoe. Neither the red or green light is on but I press the key to the lock, and the door opens with a suction sound I hadn't noticed previously.

Undeterred, I walk through it and out on to the landing. It's weird to be here alone, eerily quiet, and I lean my stomach against the banister, studying the fall.

It's important I do. I don't want to end up a paraplegic, so I need to fall hard. Die instantly. Take this attempt more seriously than I'd taken the previous two. I also don't want it to hurt; there's been too much pain already.

I prepare for the jump, my heart racing and stomach swirling as my primal survival instincts kick in. As I'd done before, I overcome them and ready myself to lift up, over the edge.

'Stop.'

Olivia stood a few metres to my right, just in front of the basement door. I have no idea how she got through it. The door should have swung locked behind me.

It's cold out on the landing and I shiver. Olivia does the same.

'What are you doing here?'

'I was looking for you,' she looked shocked. Equally, sickened. 'Tom and Tony are as well . . . Alicia said you were acting strangely.' Her eyes water. 'Jenny, you don't have to do this. Sally isn't going to tell anyone.'

I don't understand what Olivia is saying but I quickly catch on. She thinks this is about our kiss. She thinks that's what I want to kill myself over.

'Are you crazy?' I say. 'That's not what this is about . . .'

'You may want to think about who you're calling crazy, Jenny. I'm not the one preparing to jump to my death.'

The situation is so ridiculous, I smile. Olivia does too but it doesn't reach her eyes, and I watch her feet move closer.

'Stop,' I say warningly. 'Don't come closer.'

Olivia pauses, her arms held out towards me. 'Please, Jenny. Don't do this.'

'Olivia . . .'

'What?'

'How did you open the door?'

She looks confused and throws something towards me. I catch it and see it's one of Heidi's lighters, realising that's what made the suction sound and why the light wasn't red. Someone must have wedged it in the lock before me.

Horrified, I follow Olivia's eyes to Sally's key which I'd left in a careless heap on the other side of the landing.

She points to it now. 'Did Nick give you that? Is that why you didn't back me up yesterday?'

I don't respond.

A tear rolls down Olivia's cheek and she wipes it away with the hem of her shirt, briefly exposing her stomach.

'Don't do this, Jenny.'

'Olivia, I'm sorry . . .'

'If you're sorry, you'll come with me now. You'll forget this.'

I look at her pleadingly. 'You don't have to be here . . .'

'Neither do you, Jenny. You're not a good person if you do this.'

The comment irks me. It'd be a good place in our conversation to jump, but it's hard to build up the nerve with Olivia stood watching.

I need her to go.

'What do you know about being a good person, Olivia? You're a killer. A liar, too.'

Olivia steps back as if I'd hit her, fresh tears pouring down her face. It's not in my nature to say such vicious things but it feels good to say them, like the way a pore feels after pus has been squeezed from it.

I expect Olivia to leave but she doesn't. She steps forward, clearing the distance between us.

'I mean it, Olivia. Don't come closer.'

My words aren't enough. Olivia hesitates but she also shields her body around mine, protecting me from the banister. Worry pounds in my chest as I think of how to get past her, because I need to get past her. I can't fail this time. If I fail this time, they'll never let me back out.

'I'm not going to let this happen, Jenny. It's over.'

I don't know what to do. I refuse to see things from Olivia's point of view and I'm furious she can't see them from mine. She doesn't know about Mum, I guess, and there's no time to tell her, but she's ruining this – and I won't get a second attempt.

I'm so livid I could cry. Who is Olivia to decide whether I die or live? So, I kissed her once? I'd kissed Tom once too. I'm not well at the minute. I'd kiss anyone if they were there.

'You have to move, Jenny.'

'No.'

Her cheeks redden. She grabs for my wrist and I don't think. I push her as hard as I can and she falls. Over the edge. Into the darkness. A few seconds later, I hear a thump.

'Jenny!'

I turn to see Tony and Tom pounding furiously on the basement door, shouting at me to open it. Hurriedly, I drop the lighter, pick up Sally's key and let them in, and we all rush to the edge of the banister and look over at where Olivia just fell.

At first, it seems like everything might be OK. Then, the blood starts pooling.

Chapter 36

After

5 February 2016
6.27 p.m.

I leave the *Ealing Gazette* without any attempt to lock up and head straight to the storage unit. I arrive before Heidi and turn on the light. She appears not long after. Her hair is blonde now. She's wearing a black beanie and jacket but dry, shoulder-length tufts stick out at her collar, like a halo of blonde daggers.

The door shuts behind Heidi with a slam. She shakes rain from her jacket and rolls up her sleeves.

'So, you know?' she asks and I nod.

'What happened? Why?'

'Before I say anything, Jenny, you need to know that it was an accident.'

'An accident?'

'Yes,' she says. 'Tom didn't . . .'

The door bangs loudly into the wall, making us both jump. I think it must be the wind but, to my horror, Tom steps through it. I refuse to look at him and I return my focus to Heidi. 'How could you invite him here?'

She rocks shiftily from foot to foot. 'We all need to talk

about this. Get our story straight. Like we did last time. With Olivia.'

I don't want to look at Heidi any more. I turn to face Tom.

He's stood in front of the door, as if he would like nothing more than to turn around and walk back out of it. I see the temptation. I too would do almost anything to walk away from this, but I need to know the truth about what happened the night Phil died. Otherwise, everything I'd done for the last month – everything it had cost – would all have been for nothing.

'I know it was you, Tom.' My words echo around the unit.

Tom looks pale and aghast. 'How did you find out?'

I pull the photo from Simon's desk out of my handbag and pass it to him. He takes the photo and stares at it, wide-eyed.

'Where did you get this?'

'I found it on Simon's desk,' I say. 'He's your stepfather, isn't he?'

Tom nods and stares at the photo some more.

The photo must be over fifteen years old. Simon's instantly recognisable, he hasn't changed much, but it took me a little while to recognise Tom as the boy stood beside him. He wasn't wearing glasses then but his face was familiar, and what made me certain was his scar. It was just about visible in the photo, Tom turning his face to conceal it.

'How did you . . .' swallow thickly. 'Your mum died when you were twelve, and Simon's first wife, she killed herself.'

Tom nods again. 'You really figured it out from this?'

'There were other things,' I say. 'I knew Sally wasn't lying or mistaken about what happened to the key but, last night,

269

you wanted me to think she might have been.' I clear my throat. Phil also told Sally he was trying to make amends about something before he died, and James told me in passing that from 1991, Phil only saw six patients at a time. That was the year you turned twelve. The same year your mother died.'

Tom bows his head. I feel my shoulders trembles.

'How much does Simon know about this?'

'Nothing,' Tom says. 'He doesn't know anything, Jenny, I promise.'

'But he knows about me? You got me the *Gazette* job?'

Tom shakes his head. 'No. Simon recognised you from Hillside when he first interviewed you, but he wanted to give you a chance. He asked me if I would be OK with it and I said yes. That's all.'

I feel a flicker of relief. Tom returns the photo and I take it.

'You need to tell me everything that happened. From the beginning.'

Neither Tom nor Heidi responds. A silence descends on the unit, a ceasing of the wind and all conversation and I step back so we're in a triangle of sorts. Heidi moves next. She pulls up the patio table to lean against, producing a packet of cigarettes from the confines of her jacket pocket and also a lighter.

'No one minds?'

I shake my head, as does Tom, and she lights up, the glow of the cigarette disproportionately luminous in the feeble light of the unit. While she smokes, I look over at Tom who is now avoiding my gaze, his eyes flickering between my waist and the floor. 'The first part, you already know. Phil emailed me in December and asked me to meet him in his office because he wanted advice about his will. I wasn't lying about that.'

'He emailed you?'

Tom's cheeks flush. 'Yes. Heidi deleted emails between us after. I was lying about him being in Cambridge. I'm sorry.'

'OK,' I say, warily. 'What happened after that?'

'I agreed to help, I borrowed my wife's car and drove to Hillside to meet Phil in his office, just as I told you – but he had lied. When I got to Hillside, Phil didn't want to talk to me about his will. He wanted to talk about something else.'

'Your mother's death?' I ask. 'That's what Phil wanted to make amends about? Your mum was the patient he jailed?'

Tom nods. 'Phil sat me down and explained he had treated Mum as an outpatient – back when he still took them on – but that he'd made a terrible mistake. He pulled her file from one of the cabinets in his office and then showed me a bunch of letters Simon wrote to him years ago.'

'Letters Simon wrote to Phil?' I ask.

'Yes.'

'What did they say?'

'The first letter was Simon begging Phil to take Mum as a Hillside inpatient, because she was getting worse and he knew she was at risk of taking her own life' – Tom's voice shakes – 'and you know what Phil did? He sent a letter back to Simon a few weeks later, telling him not to worry; that Mum wasn't at any immediate risk of harming herself. She overdosed, two weeks later.'

My heart rips at the thought of Simon writing such a letter.

Tom's mouth twinges. 'Phil didn't show me the rest of the letters. He just wanted to let me know he was sorry and that he'd failed Mum when she'd needed him most. That he was human and that everyone makes mistakes. Like you, Jenny, when you pushed Olivia.'

271

My eyes burn. Tom clears his throat nervously.

'Phil went upstairs to get us a drink after that,' he says, 'and I don't know why but I took the rest of the letters. I needed to read them and I wanted to do so alone. When Phil came back, I quickly made my excuses and left. Over the next few weeks I read all the letters. Simon must have agreed to give Phil his correspondence too, as Phil had every single one.

'Phil expressed his sympathies to Simon in the letters but he wouldn't accept blame for my mother's death as he did to me in his office. That made me mad because my life was ruined after she died. I had to move in with my dad and not Simon and, being so young, I blamed myself. I got depressed and cut my face, and then I was sent to Hillside. To the very man who was responsible for everything – not that I knew it at the time.'

'So you murdered Phil in . . . revenge?'

Tom's eyes widen. 'No, but after reading the letters . . . I started to spiral. Mentally. It happened slowly at first but then the spiral took on a mind of its own. Katie was worried sick – and the absolute last thing I wanted was to go back to any kind of institution. So, I emailed Phil a few weeks later and said I was struggling and that I needed to speak to him. He said he understood completely and asked me, again, to meet him at Hillside.'

Tom exhales guiltily. Heidi puts out her cigarette and immediately lights another.

'That was the night he died?' I ask.

'Yes.'

'What happened?'

'I got to Hillside first. It must have been busy that night because there was no one at the sign-in sheet. No one at reception. I wanted to put the letters back in Phil's office before he arrived; I didn't want him to think I'd stolen them. And I could do that because—'

'You had Sally's key,' I say. 'Because you took it from the basement on the night Olivia died?'

'Yes.'

'Why?'

'I thought it was for the best,' Tom replies. 'It didn't even occur to me Phil might be looking for it. I just wanted to get it out of there so there wouldn't be any more questions. I left Hillside the next day and took Sally's key with me.'

I turn to Heidi. 'But you stole the key from Sally originally and exchanged it with Nick? That's why you were so sure I had it, when I wouldn't stand up for Olivia?'

'I did,' she says, blowing smoke in my direction, while Tom sniffs noisily.

'Phil was surprised to see I'd got into the basement without him,' he says, 'he must have known then that I took Sally's key on the night Olivia died, but he didn't mention it. He just looked really concerned and asked me what was wrong. I told him, and he said he was sorry, his apology didn't feel like enough. Mum was still dead and my face was still like this and my relationship with Simon was never the same again because of Phil; Simon started drinking heavily after that. That's what I thought – what I convinced myself was the truth – because I wasn't well, Jenny. I wasn't thinking clearly and I lost control. I stabbed him. I remember doing it but it may as well have been someone else.'

'And the knife?' I ask.

'I'd brought it with me,' Tom replies, 'but only to hurt myself.'

Tom's voice explodes in grief. I wipe my nose hard, the cold of the unit making it run.

It's the truth at last, but it's not nearly as satisfying as I thought it would be. There are still questions I need answers to.

'What happened next?'

Before answering, Tom removes a tissue from his coat pocket and blows his nose.

'I calmed down and thought about what to do. Pragmatically, I knew my fingerprints would be all over Phil's office but I wiped them down as best as I could – and I knew I had an excuse if the police ever found them, because I had visited Phil in December. I couldn't let the police find the letters, though. There was no manageable way of getting my prints off them so I took them back out of the cabinet and then I saw—'

'My file?'

'Yes.'

I stare at Tom, bemused. 'Why did you take it?'

'I knew there was a chance Phil might have written something about what really happened to Olivia inside it. I had to.'

'And did it?'

Tom shakes his head. 'I don't know. I never read it. I wouldn't do that . . .'

'But, you would give my file to Tony?'

'No, Jenny, I did.' Heidi stomps out her second cigarette.

I eye her warily. 'How did you come into this?'

'Tom phoned me after he left Hillside,' she says. 'He knew he didn't have a choice.'

'Why?' I ask, confused.

'Because Heidi saw me take Sally's key from the basement on the night Olivia died,' Tom says. 'She came to see me the next morning, the day I left, to make sure I took it out with me.'

Heidi nods impatiently. 'Tom knew as soon as the police

started asking questions about how the killer got in and out of the basement, I would know it was him. So he looked up my details in Phil's office before leaving and called me.

He told me everything and said he was sorry. I believed him and we decided to cover this up, just like we did last time with Olivia. Tom said he had been careful at the crime scene and we had a good cover story if his DNA was found there. I deleted all the emails between Phil and Tom . . .'

'How?' I ask and Heidi shrugs.

'Phil never had a smartphone,' she says. 'All his emails were on his server which I could easily hack into. I also deleted all the calls between Tom and me that night. Then I emailed the four of us from an anonymous Gmail account.'

I think of the last time I was in the storage unit, when Heidi and I received the fourth email.

'You both did?' I ask. 'You did it together? So that I would think there was no way it could possibly be either one of you?'

'Yes. We did.'

'Why?' I add. 'Why send the emails at all?'

'I knew Phil's murder would unsettle you, Jenny. We needed to make sure you wouldn't breakdown and start blabbing about Olivia. We all lied about that night. We all covered for you. We'd all do jail time if you had a sudden attack of guilty conscience.'

'And Nick?' I ask. 'Why frame him?'

She shrugs. 'Why not? God knows the world would be a better place with him behind bars. All we had to do was get rid of the other evidence. The knife could be traced back to Tom's bank account too easily, so I destroyed it.'

I feel a stab of humiliation, knowing the bank statement Heidi had shown me must have been Tom's. 'And the key?'

'Clean of prints, I knew it would help us frame Nick, so I wiped it, rubbed it in some dirt and planted it in his flat.'

'How?'

'I sent him an email pretending to be the job centre, wanting to meet, and then I picked the lock,' she says. 'It's not hard, once you know how. Then, there was just your file to worry about.'

'Our plan was to destroy that too. Tom and I had been slowly burning pages of it in different areas as a precaution. Then, I thought it would be better to plant some of the pages at Nick's too, as more evidence for the police to find. The clean pages, of course. None that mentioned Olivia.'

'You read my file?'

'I read parts of it,' she says shiftily. 'The problem was that I couldn't risk going back to Gadsmore a second time to actually plant them.'

'Why not?'

'I . . . didn't want to.'

Heidi stammers and I don't push her on it.

'So you called Tony?'

Heidi shakes her head. 'He called me. I gave him my phone number the day you got back from visiting Tom in Cambridge. Once he heard what happened, he wanted to help, so we agreed that he would go to Gadsmore with you, plant your Hillside file at Nick's and then start some kind of fight so the police would come out and find it. It wasn't a great plan but we didn't have time to figure it out perfectly. Once Tom got arrested – we always knew there was a chance of it happening – we were on a clock. We couldn't afford the police looking into Tom too closely.'

'Is that why you emailed me the picture of Sally's key? To hurry me along?'

'Yes. I knew Tony had to plant the file and soon, but he called me that night and said you couldn't get inside Nick's flat. I told him to wait and we would work something else out, but I don't know what happened. Tony must have gone back to Gadsmore instead and tried to plant the file alone. Nick must have caught him, before he could.' Heidi rubs at her eyes. 'Anyway, we should be fine. Tom told me James took your Hillside file from Tony's body and you destroyed the final pages. We . . . we got away with it.'

I want to vomit but instead sink to my knees.

Heidi rolls down her sleeves and, unable to stand, I lean back into a more comfortable sitting position.

'What are you going to do, Jenny?'

'I don't know.'

Heidi's eyes widen. 'I do. You're going to keep quiet about this – just as Tom kept quiet about what really happened to Olivia.'

'No, we can't lie again. I can't—'

'Don't be stupid. We're not throwing any more lives away for this. This all started the night you pushed Olivia. We covered for you then, and it's your turn to repay the favour.'

'That was an accident.'

'And, this wasn't?' She points at Tom. 'Look at him. He's devastated – just you like you were. Let Nick take the fall for this. Think of what he tried to do to you, and to Olivia. Think of all the things he has probably got away with over the last nine years. It's what Tony would have wanted. It's what he died for.'

I can't argue because I know what she's saying is probably true: Tony would have wanted to protect Tom, and Nick absolutely would have hurt Olivia and me if he could have.

'OK,' I say, finally. 'Nick goes down for it. For Tony. For Phil.'

Relief flushes across Tom's face. 'Thank you—'

'I'm not doing it for you. I just want this to be over. All of it. It has to end.'

I get to my feet shakily and then head home, heavy with the knowledge that Tony and Olivia were the only true friends I had at Hillside, and I had killed them both.

Chapter 37

Before

5 February 2007
5.52 p.m.

I stare into the pool of blood forming at Olivia's head. *Is it there? Is this happening?* I know for certain it is once I hear Tony scream and see Tom running down the stairs to reach her. It seems to take him a long time to get there, despite his hurried footsteps. It feels like an eternity when I consider it had taken Olivia merely seconds to fall the same distance.

Tom reaches Olivia, bending down and lifting her hair away from her face, trying to avoid the blood because there's so much of it. He places two fingers at her neck. Phil's office door open, and he and Heidi step out of it. Briefly, I wonder what alerted them to the commotion: Tony's yelling or Olivia hitting the ground.

Phil moves first, pushing Tom out of the way and talking to Olivia, though I can't hear what he's saying from this far up. Tom and Heidi also exchange words but, again, I can't hear them. We all watch Phil shake Olivia gently, but I already know there's no point. There's too much blood – and yet, she can't be dead. People like Olivia don't die. They're not meant to.

I pull forward towards the banister. Tony immediately pulls me back.

'Jenny, stop.'

Tony wraps his arms around me. I struggle and seconds later he relinquishes me, howling in pain. I turn around and see Tony clutching his bad toe – the stump where his toe used to be – and it's my fault. I did this too.

'Tony, I'm sorry.'

I collapse on the ground beside him. He grabs out for my wrist, squeezing around one of my scars too tightly but of course I don't say a word.

Minutes pass. Tony holds my wrist and, sitting up here with him, my brain can almost trick itself into thinking what's going on below us doesn't exist. It's a nirvana that doesn't last for ever. I hear the sound of someone climbing the stairs and Phil appears, blood staining the knees of his trousers.

He looks surprised to see Tony. Not as much to see me and he walks across the landing towards the magnetic lighter I dropped on the floor just minutes ago. That Olivia had thrown to me before that. He picks it up without noticing Sally's key, which sits just a few metres to the left of it.

'Stay here. Both of you.'

Phil runs back down the stairs. Seconds later, his voice echoes up to us and it's clear he's calling an ambulance. I hear him refer to 'an accident'. He doesn't say my name.

Phil stops speaking. Shortly after, several sets of footsteps climb the stairs and Phil, Heidi and Tom all emerge on the landing. Mascara lines streak Heidi's face. Like Phil, Tom has bloodstains on the knees of his jeans and Tony starts crying. The reason for that is obvious. They'd left Olivia all alone.

Phil's still holding the magnetic lighter. I try to find Sally's key with my eyes now, but it seems to have vanished. I don't mention it to anyone. I'm too scared to say anything.

Phil clears his throat. 'You'll have to stay here, the lot of you. The police will have questions – and it's important that we all have the same answers.'

'What do you mean?' Tom asks.

'Heidi came to my office an hour ago,' Phil says calmly. 'She told me of Olivia's plans to harm herself. She told me that Olivia had acquired these magnetic lighters from Nick' – Phil holds the lighter up to all of us – 'and intended to use them to jam the basement door lock open so she could jump to her death. However, Heidi was too late warning me. Unbeknown to anyone, Olivia had already placed one of the lighters inside the lock after I met her this morning.

'The rest of you have been worried about Olivia for weeks. You were all looking for her when you found her here. You all tried to talk her out of it . . . but she jumped anyway.'

Tom and Tony nod. I don't feel myself get to my feet until I'm already standing.

'No,' I say. 'Absolutely not.'

Heidi tuts under her breath. 'Don't be an idiot, Jenny. We need to get Nick out of here and he will be after this. It's too late for Olivia – but she would want this. Olivia would want Nick thrown out of here. You know she would.'

I think of the note in my pocket. How useless it is now.

'No, no one's lying for me,' I add. 'It's my fault. I did this.'

Tony buries his head in his hands. Tom looks distressed. Heidi looks pleadingly at Phil, who steps forward and grabs my arms.

He pulls me to one side and leans to whisper in my ear.

'Jenny, your mother needs you,' he says. 'I don't care what

happened. It's too late for Olivia. You have to be there for her now.'

Tears spring to my eyes. It seems impossible these two things are happening at once but they are. I guess nothing happens inside a vacuum. It also seems impossible that things could get any worse but if I confess to what I did, Mum will die knowing I'm a murderer and I've already put her through so much. There's no way I can do this to her too when the others are willing to give me an out.

Eventually, I also nod. Phil drops my arm and walks down the stairs to be with Olivia, be with her corpse. I sit down next to Tony yet again, horrified by what I've done until the medics come alongside Sally and escort us all out. Everyone, besides Olivia.

Chapter 38

After

5 February 2016
9.21 p.m.

I get home. James is still out at his cousin's birthday, which is good because it means I'm alone and I need to be alone because I can't be trusted around other people and I can't trust them. All I have the capacity for is to hurt or be hurt and the world would be better off without me. Certainly, a few more people would be alive. Tony. Phil. Mum. Olivia.

It's overwhelming, the despair that descends now. The grey cloud, larger than it's ever been, swallowing me whole. It's the illness, I'm sure, but the illness – the grey cloud – is part of me and it has been for too long. There's no distinguishing us from each other. No use, wondering who I could have been without it; there's only the person I am. A fuck-up. A killer. The problem, essentially, is me. And me, I can do something about.

I run to our bedroom en suite and break things, and what I can't break, I ruin. I bend them out of shape and toss them on the ground. Pour them out in front of me and exist in the mess I created.

At some point, I catch my reflection in the en suite mirror and smash that too; pounding my fist into the glass over and over again, until the skin stretched over my knuckles, is raw with tiny cuts, and all I see staring back is a dirty white cabinet and a few chunks of silver, smeared in red.

I'm tired now. I hurt everywhere, but least of all the cuts, which actually make me feel calmer. Calmer than I have in a while because I feel most like myself when I'm bleeding. Life wriggles inside me all the same. The cloud does too and it needs letting out. I pick a chunk of shrapnel from what remains of the mirror and roll up my sleeves.

The scars are how things started in many ways. Fittingly, it's how they should end – and this time, I won't fail. My right hand shakes fiercely but I get it under control enough to dig the mirror shrapnel vertically through the scar on my left wrist, just like Olivia taught me. A Jesus cross. A crucifix.

Olivia was right. The blood oozes out much faster and I quickly switch hands, cutting a line through the other.

EPILOGUE

After

I'm alive. James came home sometime after I lost consciousness that day, kicked the door down and saw the person I had always been; the one I'd kept hidden from him. He took that person to a hospital and the doctors bandaged her up, suggesting she might stay in a different kind of hospital for a while, but she didn't want that and James agreed to take her home. The doctors didn't fight him on it.

That person was me. The bandages around my wrists prove it, but when I get bad like that, it's hard to recognise those actions as my own. It's hard to recognise that person.

I shudder and get out of bed. James is up already but he can't be far. He's taking time off work to look after me and is considering putting in for a transfer and moving us somewhere else – like Sutton is the problem, and the actual problem isn't sleeping beside him. I don't have to go to work at all. I quit the *Gazette*. Simon doesn't understand and wants me to come back but I can't work there, knowing what I now do.

287

I haven't heard from Tom since that day in the storage unit. Nor Heidi. It's a good thing, and I tell myself not to think about them. However, they creep into my consciousness every now and then.

I'm still angry at Tom, although maybe that's unfair. He's no more of a killer than I am and he looks like one even less. That's probably why it took me so long to figure out; why the police had Tom in custody and still let him walk free, because to look at Tom isn't to see the kind of rage required to stab a man seventeen times, but I guess everyone has internal lives we know nothing about. Everyone has some kind of rage inside them, even if they don't have a sickness. Sickness, I think, makes it worse. It makes that kind of rage bubble more quickly to the surface.

I make my way into the en suite, jarring slightly when I see the new bathroom cabinet fitted neatly above the sink. It's sparkling. Good as new – and I have no idea who cleaned up the mess. I only know it wasn't me.

I'm getting better. Slowly. I still think about Tony but I don't wallow in the grey cloud quite as much, though I do lie down a lot, wondering how you get over things when it feels like you're still buried beneath them.

12.23 p.m.

The morning passes slow. James makes an early lunch and we sit on the sofa in the living room, my head resting on his lap. We haven't slept together since I came back from hospital and if he wants to, he doesn't mention it – though he probably doesn't. My scars are bigger this time; ugly, just like my insides.

There's a knock at the door. James gets up to answer it, returning a few seconds later.

From the look on his face, I can tell the knock is for me. 'Who is it?' I ask.

'Ros from the *Gazette*,' he says, with a confused shrug. 'I can tell her to go away . . .'

'No, don't. Let her in.'

It's not Ros. I know that much. Even if she did find out my address, there's no way we're close enough for her to come and visit.

I think I know who it really is, and I only agree to see her because if I don't let her in, she'll find me another way. If I don't let her in, there'll be no escaping her.

James nods and leaves the room. He returns a few seconds later with Heidi in tow, her hair even blonder than it was weeks ago and her face free of make-up. I'm not surprised James didn't recognise her from his Hillside research. I hardly recognised her myself.

She's holding a bouquet of flowers and wearing formal trousers and a navy blouse, both of which don't suit her. She looks nervous. On edge. I guess that's because she doesn't know whether or not I'll tell James who she is really; and the thought makes me smile a little, as she walks forward and hands me the bouquet.

'Jenny,' she says. 'I just wanted to check in. I heard you weren't feeling well.'

Heidi's eyes travel to my wrist and my smile drops, as James looks to me for direction.

'Should I leave you ladies to it?' he asks.

I nod and as soon as he leaves, drop the flowers to the ground.

Heidi tuts and picks them up again. 'You shouldn't do that Jenny. These are expensive.'

Heidi lowers the flowers to the coffee table and sits beside me. Make-up-free, she looks younger, and this close, I can see her eyelashes are blonde too. Blonde, is her natural colouring.

'What are you doing here, Heidi?'

'I'm just checking in. Making sure you're alive.'

'Well, I am. You can go,' I reply and Heidi rolls her eyes.

'Don't be so dramatic. You can talk to me for a few minutes.'

I push myself up the sofa, further away from her. Heidi smooths the front of her trousers with her palms.

'I don't know if your husband told you, but Nick's plea hearing is next week.'

The news surprises me because no, James hadn't told me anything about it. I shrug like it doesn't.

'Is that all you wanted?' I ask and Heidi shakes her head.

'Not at all. I came here to see if you're OK.'

I grimace. 'That's weird. You didn't seem too concerned about my welfare when you and Tom were torturing me for a month.'

'Torturing you?' she asks, looking offended. 'We were protecting you. Everything we did—'

'Destroyed me. Everything you did killed Tony.'

My anger returns in waves. So does the grey cloud and I know it was a mistake, to let her in.

Heidi smooths her hair behind her ears.

'No, Jenny,' she says. 'Everything we did kept you out of jail. The only reason Tony got involved in this is because he knew the investigation was getting to you and the only reason I agreed to help Tom was to protect all of us. Who knows what he would have told the police if they'd caught him for real.'

I know what she's suggesting. That, if caught, Tom may have told the police what really happened to Olivia.

'Tom wouldn't do that . . .' I begin but trail off once I see Heidi's eyebrows lift.

'See?' she asks. 'Now who's defending him?'

She's right. She always is. She's always one step ahead of me and I'm always one step behind her.

I lean back on the sofa and turn my head.

'Well, if that's everything . . .'

Heidi sighs. 'It's not. I didn't come here to fight with you, Jenny.'

'Then why did you come here?'

'I came because I'm leaving,' she says. 'I'm moving away, and I wanted to say goodbye. Tell you to look after yourself, or whatever is appropriate to say in these situations.'

Reluctantly, I turn back to face her. Her eyes move across my bandages again and I tuck my hands underneath me.

'Where are you going?' I ask and she shrugs.

'I'm not sure yet. Amsterdam? Paris? Doesn't matter. Just away.'

Heidi's eyes water. It's unmistakable and would smudge her usual make-up, had she been wearing it.

Awkwardly, I stare at her. 'Can I ask you a question? Can you answer it honestly?'

She nods. 'I can try.'

'On the night Olivia died, did you put the lighter in the basement door?'

'Yes,' Heidi replies. 'It didn't work, did it? The lighter jammed; but all it did was keep the door open.'

'And you told Sally I had her key that morning? She didn't believe you, so you tried to tell Phil? That's what you told him in his office?'

'Yes.'

'Why?'

'Because I didn't want you to die, Jenny. Is that so hard to believe?'

'Kind of,' I reply and Heidi smiles.

'Fair enough. Can you answer a question for me?'

I eye her warily. 'I'll try.'

'Did Olivia ever tell you why she killed her aunt's cat?'

I nod and Heidi's smile turns to a grimace. 'I shouldn't be surprised Olivia told you and not me. She always liked you better.'

My skin prickles, but I tell myself it's paranoia. Heidi can't know what happened between Olivia and me in the hours before she died. Only Sally knows about that.

I notice women now and again. On the street. At work. Certain women catch my eye and sometimes I catch theirs, but I could never go there. It was men I hunted down after Hillside, after Olivia. Men, whose bodies were harder and skulls less fragile. James was one of them.

'I went to see Ella before this,' Heidi says now and I blink at her.

'Tony's wife?'

'Yes. Tony was my friend too.'

'How is she?'

'She's handling it. The baby's cute. Smiley. Looks just like Tony.'

Heidi's eyes water again. Roughly, she wipes them with the sleeve of her navy blouse.

'I'm sorry, Jenny. For everything. It wasn't cool that we didn't tell you sooner. I don't know why we didn't. Everything just got bigger than I thought it was going to be, and Tony . . . I didn't . . . it wasn't supposed to end like that.'

I don't respond. I don't know how to.

Heidi exhales wearily and stands up, smoothing the front of her trousers.

'I meant what I said before,' she says, nodding to my wrists. 'Take care of yourself. I'll come back, if you don't.'

Heidi leaves. I wait for the front door to slam and sit back on the sofa, trying not to think about her. Trying not to think about them all.

2.43 p.m.

I'm still on the sofa. James has gone out food shopping, which is the first time he's trusted me enough to leave me alone for more than five minutes.

There's a knock at the door. Persistent knocking which is different from Heidi's and also Tom's. I get up and answer it.

It's Alicia's dad, wearing the same outfit I saw him in last and carrying something under his arm. I'm shocked. Also, a little embarrassed because the last time I'd seen him, I was running out of his house.

'Mr Davies,' I say. 'How are you?'

His eyes linger over my bandaged arms, like Heidi's had done.

'I'm well, thank you. Do you have a few minutes?'

I hesitate. Then, open the door wider. 'Yes. Please, come in.'

Mr Davies follows me into the living room. He settles on the sofa where I'd just been sitting and lowers the large, rectangular object he's holding so it rests between his legs.

'Can I offer you a drink, Mr Davies?'

He smiles. 'No, thank you. Please, call me Roger.'

I nod and sit a few feet away from him. His gaze lingers on my bandaged arms.

'When did that happen?'

'A few weeks ago.'

Normally, I would be more guarded but I don't feel the need with Mr Davies. He knows death and darkness, just as well as me.

He winces. 'It looks painful.'

'It doesn't hurt too much,' I reply and he nods abashedly.

'I hope you don't mind my being here. When you left my house that day, so abruptly like that, I asked the big lad for your details. I only meant to ask for your phone number but he ended up giving me your address, so I thought I'd make the trip.'

Every mention of Tony is a stab to my heart. Mr Davies also looks pained.

'I saw in the paper that he died . . . The same man who murdered Dr Walton, I believe?'

'Yes. It was.'

'Nice man. Awful shame,' he adds, and I murmur in agreement.

We watch the television for a bit. It's on mute but the picture still runs and in my peripheral vision, I feel Mr Davies watching me, his eyes are on my bandages yet again.

'I'll never understand it,' he says. 'All you girls. Educated. Smart. Independent. Everything to live for and everything going for you and yet none of you seem to think it.'

His comment rubs me the wrong way.

My wrists itch and I know I have to get rid of him.

'Is there something you wanted, Roger?' I ask tiredly.

He nodds. 'Yes. I wanted to give you this.'

Mr Davies pushes the item that was sitting between his knees towards me. I pull it the rest of the distance, so that it's now sitting between mine.

'What is it?'

'Open it.'

I do as he instructs and reveal a canvas from underneath the wrapping, *Carpe Diem* written at its centre. I recognise it. It's the painting that had been hanging at Alicia's bedside, the last time I saw her.

Mr Davies clears his throat.

'Phillip Walton sent that to me after Alicia passed away,' he says. 'I thought you might like to have it.'

'Roger, I don't think I can . . .'

'Please, I want you to have it. Alicia . . . her disease . . . she didn't have many friends in the end, but you were her friend, Jenny. The only one I can think of now.'

Mr Davies takes a tissue from his pocket and blows his nose. It's my understanding that I can't refuse him, even if I want to and I pull the canvas closer to me.

'Thank you. I've seen this before actually. I told Alicia I liked it.'

Mr Davies smiles. 'Well, then. She'd be happy I gave it to you.'

We small-talk for a little while longer, and Mr Davies finally leaves.

Afterwards, I walk back into the living room, feeling stronger than I have in weeks. Surprised, a visit from Mr Davies, of all people, was the kind of catharsis I needed.

I pick up Alicia's *Carpe Diem* canvas and think about her. Everything she could have achieved, had her life gone a little differently, everything Olivia could have, if she hadn't come on to the landing that night, or I had followed her off it.

Next, I think about what Mr Davies said about me remembering Alicia. I'd have to be alive to do it, and my stomach shakes in protest; the grey cloud so deeply ingrained that it rejects the idea all this would stop. That I won't try again, and, next time, succeed. Maybe I can do it: stay alive and I think I have within me the capacity for change. It would have seemed unfathomable before, that I would know a lot of dead girls and not be one of them. That the day hadn't seized me yet.

Helpful Resources UK

Author's note: Approximately 1 in 4 people in the UK will experience a mental health problem every year (mind.org. uk). Below are some UK-based charities and organisations which anyone who is struggling can contact, if they so wish (all information accurate at time of writing).

Suicide, suicidal thoughts/idealisation or attempted suicide

Samaritans, www.samaritans.org, 116 123

Mental health issues or conditions such as depression, schizophrenia, personality disorders, PTSD, anxiety or self-harm

Mind, mind.org.uk, 0300 123 3393

Samaritans, www.samaritans.org, 116 123

Eating disorders

Beat, beateatingdisorders.org.uk, Helpline: 0808 801 0677, Youthline: 0808 801 0711, Studentline: 0808 801 0811

Rape, sexual assault or other forms of sexual violence

Rape Crisis England and Wales, rapecrisis.org.uk, 0808 802 9999

Bereavement

Cruse Bereavement Care, cruse.org.uk, 0808 808 1677, email: helpline@cruse.org.uk

Acknowledgements

Cracked was born in August 2015 and I've written in several places along the wild road to publication. One such place was my aunt Sue Considine's house, and I would like to thank her and my uncle Mickey for having me during those intermittent months. I'd also like to thank my cousin Michael Considine for vacating his room. A huge chunk of the first draft was written at that desk.

To my first full draft readers, Jess Lee and Lauren Dolan, thank you both! It was such a thrill to talk about the book as if it actually existed at that stage and both of your insights were invaluable. Also thanks to Tracy Baines, who was with me right at the beginning of this journey. I'm sorry for not returning your books but I still have them so please get in touch!

To Anna Davis and Rufus Purdy of the Curtis Brown Creative Writing Course team, endless gratitude. It was only after being afforded a scholarship place on the 3-month novel writing course that I began to think seriously about being a writer and thanks to Anna, for steering me in the right direction and believing there was something in this book worth not giving up on. Thank you also to my course tutor Louise Wener and to HW Fisher for funding my place.

To my CBC course mates, what a ride! I was sick with nerves before the first session but everyone was so lovely and it was so much fun. I loved all of your books (still do) and thanks to Rachael Blok, Ella Berman, Ailsa Caine, Claire McVey and Keir Livock for reading my material after the course ended.

To my best friend Alicia Gonzáles Betancourt, I adore you. Your unwavering encouragement and voice notes really kept me in the game and you teach me so much about being a good dude. I'm sorry for missing your messages while edits were going on but girl, I'm flying out to see you ASAFP.

To my agent Rebecca Ritchie, one of the nicest people I have ever met and my first real champion in publishing. Thank you for taking me on, answering all my questions and alieving my concerns. I am so excited to work together more.

To my editor Eve Hall, thank you for pushing me to mould a much better manuscript than the one you graciously took on and for conceiving a title I truly love. 'Cracked' would not be what it is without you. (Thank you also for prising the manuscript from my cold, clawed grasp near end times. I'm like a dog with a bone, I know this).

To the Hodder & Stoughton team and every single person who worked on this book in some capacity; my publicist Jenny Platt, marketer Melanie Price, copy editor Morag Lyall and Sorcha Rose, so many thanks.

To my twin sister Katherine McCreesh, who read Chapter One of *Cracked* approximately 100 times and refused to read any further. Thanks for the many walks, talks, pub and Chiquito trips that constituted my several confidence crises while writing this book. To my other siblings Niall McCreesh and Ellen Grummell, thank you for pushing me through every draft by querying whether this book actually existed (here it is; at last).

To my father Kevan McCreesh, thank you for your financial support. Thanks also for giving me a roof over my head when I needed one and for offering to walk around London handing out business cards with the *Cracked* cover on them.

To my mother Geraldine McCreesh, whose empathy knew no bounds and who left us far too soon. Books can't teach you everything and you taught me what it was to truly put myself inside the mind of another person. There was no better teacher than you.

To every person struggling with the issues presented in this book, you're not alone. Reach out to someone. And finally, to every poor or ill or sad writer who thinks they're too lacking or stupid or uneducated to keep going; I see you. I am you. You got this.